LIFETIMES

CHRIS COPPEL

CRANTHORPE
—— MILLNER ——

First published by Cranthorpe Millner Publishers (2022)

ISBN 978-1-80378-077-1 (Paperback)

www.cranthorpemillner.com

Cranthorpe Millner Publishers

CHAPTER 1

1978

Sylvie Lucére stepped from the train at the Villefranche station. She was one of the few people who actually enjoyed their commute to and from work. Riding the local train along the stunning coastline of the Côte D'Azur, she felt privileged to be able to commute between the pristine seaside town of Menten and her own picturesque village.

Sylvie walked down the hill and into Villefranche's tiny central square. She was about to enter her terraced home when Madame Gillette beckoned from her front doorway, five houses down.

"Qu'est-ce qui se passe avec tous les animaux sur votre toit?".

Sylvie had no idea why the nosy woman was asking if she knew about the animals on her roof. She stepped back to get a better view and was shocked at what she saw. Her neighbour had been right to ask why there were so many rodents and lizards slithering across the top of her little house.

She made a mental note to call the landlord the following morning, then thanked Mme Gillette and entered her home. Sylvie had something far more pressing to worry about than some silly creatures that had obviously become disoriented in the fierce, summer heat.

Even though it was a scorching day, it didn't matter to Sylvie. There was a glorious little beach only five minutes away and she planned to be on it as fast as she could.

Though normally on the shy side, Sylvie had recently bought her first bikini from the MonoPrix in Nice and couldn't think of a better time to try it out. She knew that she didn't look like the models she'd seen in Vogue and Elle, but then again, who did? She felt that she had a more athletic body than the emaciated women who graced the magazine covers and thought that a two-piece was the perfect way to give herself a more feminine appearance.

Sylvie ran upstairs to her bedroom and removed the dark-green swimsuit from the armoire. She took off her work cloths and threw them on the bed. Usually, she would have taken the time to fold and hang them carefully, but she wanted to get to the beach as soon as possible.

It wasn't just the sun, sand and sea that Sylvie was anxious to enjoy. The last two times she'd been there, she'd seen Anton Driére swimming out in the bay. Sylvie had always had a secret crush on the young fisherman, but recently, ever since seeing him walk out of the Mediterranean looking like a bronzed god, she couldn't seem to get him out of her mind. She told herself that her new infatuation had nothing to do with her impulsive bikini purchase, but she could hardly lie to herself and get away with it.

Naked, she stepped in front of her new mirror; the one that had been mysteriously left on her doorstep a few days earlier, and examined her body. Sylvie wasn't vain. She was just trying to work out if she was suitable competition for the other girls her age on the Villefranche beach, many of whom had been trying to get Anton's eye for most of the summer.

As she clinically studied herself, the surface of the mirror shimmered. Only for a millisecond, but it was enough for Sylvie to have noticed. She stepped closer and touched the glass. Before she could even comprehend that her finger had passed beyond the reflective surface, two wizened arms reached out from within the mirror and grabbed her. Sylvie tried to struggle but it was like being held by a vice.

She was about to scream when a face emerged through the mirror. It was like no face she'd ever seen and looked almost mummified. The blackened skin was stretched so tightly across the facial bones that it had become almost transparent. What made it even creepier was that its eyes were closed.

"Come with me," the thing said in a raspy whisper. "It's time for me to feed."

Its yellow eyes snapped open, and Sylvie immediately went rigid. It was as if she were suddenly frozen solid and could feel herself rising off the ground. The ancient mouth formed into a twisted smile as Sylvie began gliding towards the mirror. She felt as if the scream that had built up inside

3

her was about to explode when everything went dark.

Sylvie couldn't feel any part of her body, nor could she see anything in the utter blackness, but she could hear. At first, she wasn't sure what the sound was, but then she knew.

It was the sound of someone suckling.

CHAPTER 2

Present day

Craig Edmonds assumed that Ahote turning up at his house had something to do with the news report he just seen on TV about the missing girls in Australia. Unfortunately, that was not why he was there. Instead, he had news of Beyath. The witch had apparently killed again.

Once the two were settled outside on the front deck, Ahote explained the situation to Craig.

"A few days ago, InDim noticed an anomaly in the timeline of one surviving member of Beyath's familial blood line," Ahote explained. "A young French woman who had the misfortune to have been a distant cousin of the witch, ceased to exist from 1978 on, even though the dimensional shroud data shows that she should still be alive and living in La Napoule, in the South of France.

"It appears that Beyath's death in 2021, had no effect on her existence prior to that point. Experts had hoped that with her being an interdimensional entity, surviving on a plane where the past, the future and the present basically all exist simultaneously, killing her in 2021 would have erased her entirely from her time-space continuum.

"They were wrong," Ahote stressed. "Not only did Beyath still exist within her dimension, but her need to feed the light appears to have accelerated. The old schedule of feeding once every twenty-five years could no longer be counted upon. Beyath was now feeding at random times. According to her case file, time-log, she has fed twice since being killed within your home. The latest event was in 1978 in a small town in Southern France. The problem with her taking her blood relations from past years rather than at a predictable time in the future, is that with each person she kills, their direct descendants cease to have ever existed."

Steeler, the family's golden retriever, wandered onto the deck and laid his head on Craig's lap.

"I thought you were here about the missing girls in Australia," Craig said.

"I am aware of that incident, but don't believe that they will have need of our particular skill. That entity left behind a very specific electromagnetic signature and a team has already located the dimensional breach. A group has gone through the rift to seek out the creature. What is needed from us is to again try to stop Beyath."

"I can't believe it," Craig said. "This will be the third time I have had to kill her."

"Maybe this time you will get it right," Ahote replied.

Craig was about to defend his actions when he saw the brief hint of a smile cross the other man's lips.

"Really? Now you develop a sense of humour?"

Ahote shrugged.

"Do I have to go back to your little shack?"

"You don't have to. That was only to make you feel more comfortable the first time. I can start the time-walk anywhere; however, considering that your family is standing inside your home and is, at this moment, staring at us through the sliding door, it might look a little strange for us to simply disappear."

"Give me half an hour and I'll meet you there," Craig said. "I need to tell Jenny what's going on."

"Can you find your way?" Ahote asked.

"It's not as if there's anything else out there on Old Mesa Road," Craig pointed out.

*

Once Ahote had driven off in his vintage Jeep Cherokee, Craig left the children watching old reruns of the ubiquitous *SpongeBob SquarePants* and snuck Jenny away so he could talk to her in private.

"I'm not going to want to hear this, am I?" she asked, her arms tightly crossed. "Was Ahote here about that thing we saw on TV? Was it about those poor girls that disappeared in Australia?"

"I thought the same thing, but that's not why he was here."

Jenny saw the look of fear and hatred momentarily break through her husband's normally calm expression.

"Oh, shit," she whispered. "It's Beyath again, isn't it?"

Craig nodded. "It seems we didn't kill her after all," he replied.

"But I saw her die," Jenny insisted. "That mirror cut her in half."

"That's true. It did, but only in that specific moment in time."

"Here we go," Jenny said, rolling her eyes. "You're going to tell me how time-space relativity within her dimension changes everything we take for granted."

Craig looked at his wife with a mix of shock and pride.

"You've actually been listening to what I've been telling you." He grinned.

"It's hard not to when you've been babbling on about time travel and alternate dimensions ever since you and Ahote first teamed up."

"We teamed up to save you, if you recall."

"And I am still, and will always be, unspeakably grateful; but just occasionally, it would be nice if we could talk about the things we used to, before witches and time travel seemed to become the only topic you are interested in."

"Until I can sleep through the night without seeing her moving you towards that portal, the topic is bound to be pretty damn close to the surface."

"Fair point," Jenny said as she leaned in and gave him a peck on the cheek.

"Beyath has started killing other members of her bloodline again," Craig explained. "This time she seems to be feeding on a different schedule. A woman disappeared in

France in 1978 and was a direct descendant of hers."

"Why is that so important, now?"

"Because the people at International Dimensions who track this stuff, monitor variables with our timeline that show any past or present disappearances that relate to Beyath's family tree. When we killed her, she had only been feeding every twenty-five years in chronological order."

"I remember," Jenny said.

"This is the first instance of her going backwards in time in order to feed her light," Craig advised. "In her prior timeline, the woman in France grew old, had a family of her own and was still alive up until a week ago. Then, suddenly, all traces of her vanished from 1978 on."

"That does sound as if she was taken," Jenny said, wrapping her arms around herself to ward off the creepy sensation that was starting to build inside her.

"It's hard to believe that Beyath came so close to taking you," Craig said.

"She didn't just try, did she? She took me right here in this house."

"Only in one timeline," he reminded her. "And we corrected that one."

"I know. I saw you do it."

"The weird thing is that Beyath has always fed at twenty-five-year intervals," Craig said. "We know she took your aunt … or at least tried to, in 1996 and your great uncle vanished in '71."

"And then she came for me in 2021," Jenny said in little more than a whisper.

"She's been very consistent, yet suddenly, for no apparent reason, she's taken another blood relative in 1978. Why would she go back?"

"I don't know, and as much as I hate to ask the obvious, but how can you be certain that this woman was taken by Beyath? Couldn't she have just as easily disappeared on her own or though some event that has nothing to do with time travel and alternate dimensions?"

"Well, first, there's the fact that she is a distant relative of yours and is a direct descendant of Beyath's, then there's this …"

Craig took his phone out his pocket and opened a text that had been sent to both Ahote and Craig while they'd been talking on the front deck. It was a scan from the *Nice-Matin* newspaper from July 1978. It was an article about the disappearance of Sylvie Lucére from her house in the tiny Mediterranean village of Villefranche. Craig scrolled to the photo that accompanied the article. It showed a small bedroom that had obviously been ransacked.

"So?" Jenny said. "Just because someone tore up the place doesn't mean that …"

Craig enlarged the photo so that one particular wall was clearly visible. Reaching almost from floor to ceiling was a heavily carved wooden frame. Craig saw the colour drain from his wife's face. He scrolled down showing the floor in front of the frame. On it was a mound of silvery shards. Jenny knew exactly what she was looking at.

They were pieces of a broken mirror.

"How long will you be gone?" Jenny asked.

"As far as you are concerned, I should be back in about an hour."

"Don't be such an ass," Jenny replied. "How long will you be back in time?"

"Between getting to France, killing Beyath then returning, I don't know; might be as long as a week."

"What if something goes wrong?" she asked, trying hard to keep her emotions in check.

"Nothing will," he promised her, despite knowing full well that if something did go wrong in 1978, he might well cease to exist in any timeline.

*

As Craig drove along 89, he tried to keep his mind off what lay ahead and instead reflected on what was happening to their local town. Like deer running in every direction to avoid a fire, residents of the crowded cities on the east and west coast were buying up homes and vacant lots in and around small towns in order to have a place to ride out the pandemic and the growing social unrest.

From the Vermillion Cliffs area, all the way into Kanab, construction was booming. Skeletal wood framing could be seen dotting the hillsides, making life miserable for the residents who'd built there decades earlier so they could enjoy the solitude and unspoilt surroundings.

Craig hung a left onto 89A and drove out of Kanab until he reached Old Mesa Road. Though washed away eleven years earlier, he knew that once he reached the ten-foot-deep flood channel, the road would miraculously have returned. Such was life when working with Ahote and his ability to time-walk.

He remembered the first time when he'd thought the old man to be delusionary. It wasn't until Ahote had driven him through the town itself and seen that he had indeed travelled back twenty-five years, that he took the man seriously. Had Ahote not shown him such indisputable proof, Craig would never have accepted Ahote's explanation that what he was doing was not time travel. It was the ancient tribal ability to revisit a moment in one's own timeline. Thankfully, that same ability permitted a second person to accompany the host during the walk.

Craig saw the iconic Messy Rock off to the left just as the time fog (Craig's term, not Ahote's) appeared, obscuring almost all visibility. Just as he had done after Jenny had been taken, he continued driving forward onto a stretch of dirt road that he knew with his rational mind, had been almost surgically erased eleven years earlier after a hundred-year monsoonal storm dropped two years of rain in less than an hour.

A few miles later all battery-powered technology ceased to function which included his Kane County police vehicle. Craig knew that meant that he had reached the perimeter of Ahote's time field. He left the SUV and walked through the thickening fog until it suddenly cleared, and he could see the tired looking, single-room cabin.

Ahote was standing at the door looking at his watch.

"What kept you?" he asked.

"Jenny needed some extra reassurance," Craig explained.

Ahote nodded his acceptance.

"Besides, time's fluid, remember?" Craig grinned.

"Time is relative. You seem to be the one who gives it fluidity." Ahote said as he gestured for Craig to enter his home.

CHAPTER 3

"Will we get the usual help from your contacts in the UK?" Craig asked.

"We will be going back to 1978," Ahote reminded him. "I didn't have any support back then. In fact, International Dimension won't formally exist until 1994."

Craig looked concerned.

"Don't worry. Even with all the extra manpower, you and I are the only ones that made a difference against Beyath. We will just have to do away with any of the finesse and find some more basic way to kill her."

"If you recall, Steeler played a major role in killing Beyath the last time," Craig reminded Ahote.

"As you can't bring your dog with you, we will have to somehow defeat her without canine intervention," Ahote said with just a trace of sarcasm.

"How the hell are we going to do that?" Craig asked. "She's able to put me in a trance the second she appears."

"This time I'm going to be in the room with you."

"I thought you told me that she won't appear if she

senses that others are there."

"We have to assume that Beyath knows perfectly well that there will be people who will travel back to 1978 to try and stop her," Ahote explained. "We tipped our hand in 1996. She will almost certainly be expecting us this time. I plan on making it even easier for her by standing in plain view in front of the mirror. That will doubtless entice her to come after me. When she emerges from the portal, you will kill her and this time, we will ensure that no part of her returns to her dimension, dead or alive."

"You think that will work?" Craig asked.

"I think it's the only option we have."

"But why would she come through the portal at all if someone is standing there waiting for her?" Craig asked.

"To kill me, of course. Beyath almost certainly knows by now who I am, and that I am at least partially responsible for the last two attempts on her life. Seeing me standing there, unarmed, would be way too tempting a target for her to ignore."

"I agree. But what's to stop her killing you the instant she sees you?"

"Nothing," Ahote stated. "That's why your timing has to be perfect. The one thing that's in our favour is that Beyath must take human form before she enters our dimension. You will need to get at least a few rounds into her at the exact moment that she emerges and becomes human."

"Human?" Craig said.

"She may be four hundred years old and has spent her life in an alternate realm, but from the moment she steps foot in our world, she is human. Ancient … but human."

"It doesn't sound to me as if you've left much of a margin for error. One slip on my part and she'll take you."

"Tell me, when you were a sniper with the Marine Corp, did you have any margin for error?"

"Point taken," Craig replied, nodding.

"We'll have plenty of time during the trip there to discuss the details more fully. If I may suggest, we should probably get started."

"May I ask one question before you go into your trance thingy?"

"Trance thingy?" Ahote said, shaking his head. "Like the ancient tribal shaman of old, I am able, through the power of my mind, to walk myself back in time and you label it as a trance thingy?"

"What would you call it?" Craig asked.

"Certainly not that," he replied. "What was your question?"

"If we don't have any support from the UK team, what do we do about travel, money and a place to stay?"

"That, for a change, is a good question," Ahote replied. "Because I know that I am called upon to travel back before a time when my support network could help. I have funds and credit cards available for use in any specific decade. As for the flight, I walked back earlier and booked us on Pan Am from Los Angeles to London, and then London to Nice on BEA."

"Wow," Craig responded. "You really have to stay on top of this time travel stuff."

Ahote glared at him.

"I know it's not technically time travel, but it kind of is!"

"Please stay silent while I ignore that last statement and focus my mind," Ahote announced.

"Of course." Craig nodded. "How long will it take?"

Even before Ahote could answer, Craig noticed that his friend had shed over forty years. He was now a man in his late thirties even though his eyes still showed the weight of his lifetime of experiences.

"It's done."

"How come the last time when you took us back to 1996, you had to get yourself into an almost meditative state?"

"This time, I did that before you arrived. While we've been talking, we've gone back forty-four years."

Craig shivered. "That's so weird. That's before I was even born."

Craig noticed some boxes by his chair that hadn't been there a moment before.

"Open them," Ahote said. "I had to guess on your size, but I think I got close."

"Got close to what?"

"I bought you some clothes for the journey."

"What's wrong with what I'm wearing?" Craig asked.

"Nothing ... in 2022," Ahote replied. "But we are going back to 1978. People used to dress up for air travel back then."

"You've got to be kidding," Craig said as he began opening the boxes. You're not expecting me to wear this are you?"

17

"I am if you hope to blend in."

"Are you going to be wearing something like this?" Craig asked.

"I am a Native American. I will dress as I always have."

"Right," Craig replied, doubting his friend as he pulled a dark blue blazer out of a Bullocks clothing box.

"That will go well with the khaki chinos in the other box," Ahote said, grinning.

"When do we leave?" Craig asked as he looked disapprovingly at his new clothes.

"Our flight leaves tomorrow at six o'clock from LAX." Ahote replied.

"What time is our flight from St George?"

"We won't be flying from St George. This time we will drive."

"Drive? That'll take over eight hours." Craig said.

"Correct. Let's get your things packed so we can get started," he said pointing to a bright blue Samsonite suitcase.

"Don't change the subject," Craig stated. "Why can't we fly like last time?"

"Those jets don't fly from St George in 1978." Ahote responded.

"What do they fly? It's still gotta be easier than driving the whole way."

"SkyWest is a new airline in 1978. They've only been in operation for five years."

"So what?"

"They only fly small, six seat aircraft. It's not safe."

"If they're flying them, they must be safe," Craig insisted.

Ahote stared at him. "It's bad luck to fly in their planes," Ahote said.

"I forgot," Craig said, nodding. "You hate flying."

"Yes, I do, but that's not the problem."

"Then what is?"

"They fly something called a Navaho Chieftain."

"So what?"

"I'm not going to be taken into the sky by a Navaho Chieftain," Ahote stated stubbornly. "We are driving."

Craig desperately wanted to delve deeper into this new wrinkle in Ahote's usually stable outlook but could tell that the other man had no intention of discussing the matter any further.

"When do we leave?" Craig asked.

"I thought we'd leave now and spend the night in Las Vegas. That way we can break the journey in half."

"But it's getting close to ten at night," Craig advised.

"Actually, it's only just past two in the afternoon. I chose to walk us back a little earlier so we could travel in daylight."

"Great, but Las Vegas?" Craig said, unable to mask his dislike for the sprawling mass of neon and concrete.

"We are talking about Las Vegas in midsummer of 1978. I think you'll be surprised at how uncrowded it is."

"Great, so instead of millions of tourists we only have to worry about the mob."

"I somehow doubt they will find either of us of much interest."

"Okay," Craig said, shrugging. "Maybe I can at least win a

jackpot."

"I thought you didn't gamble."

"I don't," Craig replied. "I was trying to be funny."

"Try harder," Ahote replied, straight faced.

"You are such a killjoy sometimes."

Ahote smiled.

After providing Craig with a passport and some cash, they carried their matching Samsonite suitcases outside.

"Where's your jeep?" Craig asked.

"Not yet built," Ahote reminded him.

"So how are we going to drive to L.A.?"

Ahote walked out of sight behind his tiny home. Moments later a powerful sounding engine roared to life. Craig was about to investigate when a white, convertible, Cadillac Eldorado pulled around to the front of the shack. Ahote sat within the bright red interior grinning up at him.

"I felt that if we had to endure a road trip, we should at least do so in style."

Craig slowly walked around the car.

"It's immaculate. A classic like this has got to be worth a fortune."

"It's actually only two years old and its current blue book value is just above $8000."

"You mean it's value back in 1978."

"I mean it's value today, in 1978."

"You love messing with my head over this time travel stuff, don't you?" Craig asked.

"Actually ..." Ahote started to say.

"Don't say it. I know, It's not time travel."

Ahote nodded.

Craig threw the two cases into the voluminous back footwell then climbed in next to Ahote.

"Oh, man. These seats are comfortable," he said as he sat back against the burgundy leather.

Ahote raised his eyebrows then put the car in gear. Leaving a plume of dirt in their wake, the massive vehicle sped along the unpaved road. Despite the speed and the car's easy-ride suspension, which was causing the vehicle to porpoise along the rutted road, Ahote managed to insert an 8-track tape cartridge into a player mounted under the dash.

"What the hell is that thing?" Craig asked just as the sound of Fleetwood Mac filled the car with *Second-hand News* the opening track from their *Rumours* album.

"Wow," Craig said, shouting over the extreme volume. "I haven't heard this in years."

"How strange," Ahote said, grinning. "It only came out a few months ago."

Craig gave the other man a quick stink-eye, then had a thought.

"As we're not exactly in a rush, could you swing through town? I'd love to see what Kanab looked like back then ... I mean now."

"My pleasure," Ahote replied.

The first thing Craig noticed was how small Kanab was. Whereas in 2022 the sprawl, if you could call it that, started almost as far out as the small airport. In 1978 there was no sign of there being a town until a few hundred feet before the junction of 89 and 89A. Strangely, there were still an inordinate number of service stations. Gone were all the modern chain hotels, instead, the main street was littered with creepy looking motels that could have doubled for the infamous Bates Motel in Alfred Hitchcock's *Psycho*.

"Seen enough?" Ahote asked.

"It's so small," Craig replied. "They don't even have a supermarket."

"There are only about a thousand permanent residents in 1978. Honey's and Glazier's markets won't be built until the 80s."

Craig sighed. "I've seen enough."

CHAPTER 4

The road from Fredonia to St George in 1978 was nothing like its modern counterpart. It was narrow and not particularly well paved. Thankfully, the Caddy cruised along at a comfortable 70mph without transferring any of the rough road to its passengers.

As they drove through St George, Craig stared out the window in complete awe. The city that he knew was a big box metropolis built to within a few feet of the 15 freeway. Not in 1978. The south side of the freeway was hardly developed at all with only an occasional home or small apartment building. The north side was mostly residential and looked to be a far more peaceful place to live than in 2022.

As they entered the Virgin River Gorge, the iconic swath that had been blasted through solid mountain to give the freeway access to and from the west, it was almost completely devoid of vehicles. That gave Ahote the chance to really open up the big Caddy.

"Hard to believe that at one point, we would have had to

detour through Santa Clara and come down the 91," Ahote commented.

Craig had no response. All he could do was look out at the soaring cliffs with an entirely new respect. Because they had the convertible top down, he was able to recline his seat and stare up at where the mountain range had recently been blasted away. Because the scars were so fresh, unlike in 2022, he could still make out the massive, cleaved areas that would, over time, soften and blend in with the rest of scenery.

Once they passed through the depressingly insignificant town of Mesquite, they encountered no other signs of civilization for over an hour until they began the decent into Las Vegas.

Craig knew the skyline well and was stunned by the difference forty years had made. The most noticeable thing was how clear the air appeared to be. He could see right across the city to the where the 15 climbed west towards Los Angeles. Modern Vegas was filled with towering hotels and condo blocks. The city he was looking at had a few tall hotels like the old Dunes and Tower 1 of the Flamingo, but most of the other classic hotels were far more modest than their modern-day counterparts.

Ahote drove onto the strip and pulled in at the Sands Hotel where he'd booked them into adjoining rooms in the garden annex. Craig only had time to drop his suitcase on the floor when Ahote knocked on his door.

"Come on," he called out. "Let's hit the slots."

Craig was stunned by his friend's enthusiasm considering

that Ahote was normally so calm and reserved. As they walked towards the main casino, he was chattering like an excited child.

"For some reason, I didn't imagine you to be that interested in games of chance," Craig mentioned. "Don't tell me you've changed your rule about betting on results you already know?"

"Of course not." Ahote replied adamantly. "That would be very dangerous for the timeline. I just enjoy the nickel slots. Even if I play all night, the worst thing that could happen would be that I'd lose twenty dollars. Don't forget, the slot machines in 1978 are still mechanical and very basic. You just put a nickel in and pull the lever. For some reason, I find it oddly relaxing."

"I'll just watch if you don't mind. Part of my alcohol and drug rehabilitation is to avoid all addictive triggers; gambling being number three on the list."

"Understood," Ahote said as he opened the tinted glass door that led into the casino.

The first thing that hit them was a wave of cold air. Because of the dryness of the heat (Vegas humidity didn't start until the 1990s) they hadn't noticed how hot it was outside. Stepping into 72 degrees felt like they were walking into an industrial freezer.

Craig watched Ahote feed one particular slot machine for over an hour. It wasn't until he was up by ten dollars, that he collected the pile of nickels from the chrome-plated dispensing tray and announced that he was done.

"Better now?" Craig asked.

"Much. Now let's eat."

Craig had hoped that they would find a place that did serious steaks or burgers, but Ahote made a B-line for the Sand's all-you-could-eat buffet. Craig was about to suggest they find something a little less like a cattle feeding station when he saw the price. According to the giant standee at the hostess desk, it was $4.99 for as much as you could consume. He decided that he couldn't pass up the chance to see what five bucks could buy back in 1978.

They were seated next to a fake waterfall that, while attractive, kept both their bladders active throughout the meal. They'd only been seated for less than a minute when Ahote got up, and with a glint in his eye, headed for the end of the buffet line.

Craig smiled and followed him. The first twenty feet or so was nothing but appetisers. Everything from a simple slice of melon to massive shrimp cocktails in frosty, stainless-steel cups. The next fifty feet was for the entrees. Roast beef, ham and turkey were all on offer in the carvery section. Beyond that were stews, pastas, salads and an omelette bar. There was even a sea food section with lobster tails and Alaskan king crab legs.

It became an unspoken competition as to which of them could pile their plate the highest. Craig was embarrassed at their display of untethered gluttony but couldn't seem to stop adding more food.

"We can keep coming back for more, if we want," Ahote whispered as if it was a little-known secret.

They ate until their bellies swelled against their

garments. During a lull before they attacked the dessert section, Ahote turned to Craig with a look of concern.

"What we are about to do will not be as simple as what we managed to achieve in the UK. Beyath is certain to be aware that we will intersect our timelines at some point. She knows that that's the only way we can get to her."

"I've been thinking. What if we just follow her into her dimension?" Craig offered. "We could go right through the mirror before she knows what hit her."

"Beyath's dimension is not like those that humans have visited. Once in her realm, she no longer exists on a physical level as we know it. Because of her powers, she can roam freely in a subatomic environment. She is like a free-floating, sentient vapor. If we tried to pass through the portal, we would almost certainly disintegrate."

"That's not a nice option," Craig commented.

Ahote shrugged. "I'm just stating a fact."

"I understand why we can't go into her dimension, but doesn't she have to spend time in a ... what did you call it ... a transition space? You described it as a halfway point where she begins the transformation into human form."

Ahote nodded.

"Can we travel into that ... whatever it is?"

Ahote stared at him for a few seconds.

"I don't know. Let's hope we don't have to find out," he replied before looking back to the buffet spread. "I thought I saw chocolate cake."

CHAPTER 5

Once they retired to their rooms, Craig lay on his king-size bed and used a remote control the size of a Stephen King novel to turn on a TV the size of a Fiat 500. The set only got a few channels and he settled for watching *One Day at A Time* with Valerie Bertinelli.

Craig was asleep within ten minutes. He only woke up when his room was filled with the sound of the National Anthem followed by deafening static. He'd had no idea that the affiliate stations used to cease broadcasting every night at midnight.

The next morning, they grabbed a quick breakfast in the hotel coffee shop. Ahote had suggested the breakfast buffet, but Craig was pretty sure that he was still digesting a few items from the night before, so wanted to eat light before the second half of the road trip.

There's wasn't much to see between Vegas and the Cajon Pass back in 1978. Even the sprawling city of Barstow was little more than a small town where people could top up on gas and cheap food before making the climb between the

San Bernardino and the San Gabriel Mountains.

Once over the pass, they took the 10 freeway all the way into Los Angeles, then the 405 south to the Century Blvd Exit and LA Airport. As they entered the one-way system, Craig was shocked to see how different LAX looked. Without the Tom Bradley terminal and the modern control tower, the place looked almost calm compared to the manic feel of its 2022 version.

They had hours to wait, so after checking in, they cruised the duty free and gift stores. Back then, they were very basic and uninspiring. Airport departure areas had yet to take on the appeal of shopping malls and food courts.

Their flight left on time. Even though Ahote was having to foot the bill, they were seated in the first-class section. Craig was looking forward to the fully reclining bed/seats and personal entertainment console he'd experienced during their time-walk to 1996. He had no idea that such amenities didn't exist in 1978 and only came into being a decade or so later.

Craig was wondering how they were supposed to watch a movie without a seat-back monitor when a projection screen unfurled from above the forward bulkhead. The lights then dimmed and the one and only movie was projected from the back of the cabin. It was *The World's Greatest Lover* starring Gene Wilder. Dinner was surprisingly good and after watching the film, which they both enjoyed, they fell asleep until they were woken up in time for a quick breakfast prior to landing.

Once on the ground, they had time to change terminals

to catch the 2:47pm flight to Nice. They were flying with BEA on a Hawker Siddeley Trident and Craig was fascinated by its odd design. It had three engines at the back, one of which was mounted at the base of the vertical stabilizer.

The flight was quick and uneventful though Craig was a little alarmed at the excessively steep take-off and the constant noise of the engines. What really scared him was the landing. The Trident seemed to be about to set down in the Mediterranean Sea until thankfully, at the last possible moment, a spit of land appeared under them, and the jet softly landed on time.

They took a taxi directly into Nice, and after driving a few hundred yards along the Promenade des Anglaise, pulled up in front of the Hotel Negresco. They separated for a few hours to shower and get their heads together before Ahote gently knocked on Craig's door.

"We have to make one stop before dinner," Ahote announced.

He led Craig on a walk along the seafront until they reached the port. They then made their way inland to the Rue Lascaris where Ahote searched out a specific address. Number 982 was a shabby building on the shabby end of the street. A tanned man, with a jagged scar running up the left side of his face was leaning in the doorway. Something about his defensive posture and the size of the knife he was using to clean his fingernails spoke volumes as to the legitimacy of whatever went on inside.

The man gave Ahote the once-over and was about to say something when Ahote passed him a note. The man read it, looked surprised then opened the front door.

"*Tout en haut!*" the man said.

Ahote held his hand out, palm up in the universal gesture for 'I don't understand.'

The man pointed upwards and said, in broken English, "Up top."

Craig and Ahote climbed up four floors on the narrow staircase. Judging from the sounds and smells that were filtering from behind closed doors, prostitution and hashish consumption seemed to be the main commodities within the building.

As they reached the top landing, a thin man with stringy black hair stepped up to Ahote and gave him a very professional frisking. He then turned to Craig. Despite all his training and a deep desire to lay the guy out, Craig raised his arms and let the man have at it.

Once searched, the man opened the only visible door and stepped aside to let them both enter.

"You must be the man who calls himself Ahote," Claude Fressier said as he stepped out from behind a glass topped desk. He was a big man, but Craig could tell from his ease of motion that he could be fast if the need arose. His skin was tanned a dark brown and his blond hair was slicked straight back.

"Mister Fressier, I assume," Ahote said, holding out his hand.

"How was your trip?" Claude asked, shaking it. His accent was French coupled with something Germanic.

"Good. This is my partner and your client," Ahote said,

gesturing towards Craig.

Craig gave him a puzzled look.

Claude studied him and smiled. "You still look like a Marine. That confidence and poise never goes away."

The two men shook hands.

"As I explained on the phone, new guns are almost impossible to find in France. *Les flics* seem able to keep those under some degree of control. The best I could do is a Smith and Wesson."

Craig suddenly caught on to the point of this strange meeting.

"May I see it?" Craig asked.

"Of course." Claude reached into a side drawer and produced an old, stained, oilskin gun cloth held together with rubber bands.

He tossed it over to Craig who caught it one-handed.

He slipped off the bands and carefully unwrapped the weapon. He was not impressed by what he saw. The gun was old, even in 1978.

"It's a model 39. It was a good gun when it was first made in 1950," Craig said with a tinge of sarcasm.

"I think you'll find that that one was made in the late sixties, but I agree with you that it's probably not all that you were hoping for."

"I'll make do, so long as it fires and doesn't explode in my hand."

"It won't. We test fire all weapons before passing them on to our clientele. That one there was slightly modified for you only yesterday." Claude reached back into the drawer and threw over a six-inch-long rectangular box.

"I can guess what this is," Craig said, smiling as he opened the top flap and shook out a newly milled sound suppressor.

"Ahote suggested that you may need a silencer. We had that one manufactured especially for you."

Craig checked it out and was pleased with the quality of the work.

"It's a wet can," he commented. "What's in the baffles, water or gel?"

Claude gave him a questioning look. "I don't know what gel is, but we use water. The suppression is by far the best, but of course, there is one drawback."

Craig nodded. "Water drips after use. I've seen that in action."

"Are you satisfied?" Ahote asked.

"Looks good to me," Craig replied.

Ahote produced five, hundred-dollar bills and handed them to Claude. He in return, reached under his desk and produced a worn backpack which he handed to him.

"I've included a box of ammunition, a belt clip and a shoulder harness. It's more discreet than carrying a handgun though the streets of Nice."

"Good point," Ahote replied.

"Also," Claude added. "I would suggest that you dispose of the weapon as soon as you have used it. I believe your intension is for one single use?"

"That's right," Craig replied. "Do you have any suggestions as to where we should dispose of it?"

Claude smiled. "I have always been particularly fond of the Mediterranean."

CHAPTER 6

Ahote led Craig back to the port then down a warren of side streets within the old town. They emerged in the Place Rossetti where he made a beeline to one specific restaurant.

"Just exactly how many times have you been here?" Craig asked.

"In this era, never. But I've been a few times with Connor as a sort of a reward after a couple of successful missions."

"It's a shame we can't use him on this one," Craig commented.

"Too complicated. In his timeline, he isn't even aware of Beyath and his future involvement with International Dimensions."

"Then why didn't you bring him back instead of me?" Craig asked.

"If you recall, Connor promised his wife that he would stop time-walking. I have respected that wish."

"That brings up a question I've been dying to ask. When we came to the UK the first time, Connor mentioned time-walking with you on a couple of missions. Weren't the two of you ever worried about running into your younger selves?"

"No," Ahote replied.

"So, what about the whole time-paradox issue?" Craig asked.

Ahote laughed. "You mean the nonsense that if you meet yourself in the past, it will cause some sort of time rift? I have no idea when or where that bogus theory started, but there's not a shred of truth to it. The fact is, at least with time-walking, it's physically impossible to meet up with your younger self. It would be like trying to push two magnets together. The natural order of things just won't let it happen."

"How do you know?" Craig asked. "Did you ever try to do it?"

Ahote looked mildly embarrassed.

"Just once when I was still learning to time-walk. Despite the elders telling me not to, I sought myself out and found that no matter how hard I tried to approach the younger me, I could never get nearer than about twenty feet without suddenly being unable to move. Anyway, that's enough on that subject. Can we please have a quiet dinner without any talk of time-walking, vengeful witches or time-space relativity?"

"What else can we possibly discuss?" Craig said with a smile.

"Sports," Ahote replied as they reached the entrance to Le Poissonnerie.

They were seated next to leaded windows that looked

onto the square and Nice's historic cathedral. Ahote tried to convince Craig to try some typically French offerings such as escargot and steak tartare (snails and raw hamburger with raw egg), but Craig ordered a good old-fashioned steak with fries.

The food was good, and the conversation was steered away from all taboo subjects. Craig had thought that Ahote was being facetious when he'd suggested sports, but it turned out the man was seriously into US and UK football, or soccer as Craig knew it. He seemed to know every conceivable statistic of every major team for the past couple of decades.

"When do you have time to learn all that stuff?" Craig asked.

"You've answered your own question. Time! Don't forget that I can go back and watch a game at any point in my timeline."

"Are you saying that you were at every single NFL and UK Premier League game in the last twenty years."

"Not all of them. Just the interesting ones."

"How could you possibly have had enough time to do that?"

"Don't forget that while I walk, my current timeline doesn't progress at all. Theoretically, I could visit every sporting match, ever, and not use up any of my current life span."

Craig had a million more questions, but Ahote reminded him that they had strayed into the time-walking topic and wasn't going to discuss it at that point. Instead, Ahote ordered a Tarte Tatin with Crème Chantilly.

After the meal, the two walked slowly back to their hotel along the Promenade des Anglaise. They remained silent, both deep in thought about what the next day would bring. It was past nine o'clock and the shoreline was dotted with lights for as far as they could see. The dark, mirror-like reflection of the still, Mediterranean water reflected their illumination, giving the coast a ghostly halo.

*

Craig met Ahote in the lavish, baroque style dining room for an early breakfast. Both men were tense.

"I wish we had more of a plan," Craig said in a lowered voice.

"There is no way to plan ahead for an eventuality that is utterly unknown. We just have to hope that I am as tempting a target as I think I am, and that you will be as good a shot as you were in Hambleden."

"I had a rifle I was familiar with and was able to practice. This time I have a questionable weapon, no practice, plus, my expertise was never with a handgun," Craig reminded him.

"That's reassuring coming from a deputy sheriff," Ahote said between bites of his cheese omelette.

"We don't even know if Beyath is here yet."

Ahote slid a folded copy of that day's *Nice-Matin* across the table to Craig.

"I don't speak French," Craig said.

"You don't need to. Look at the front page."

Craig unfolded the paper and saw the picture of a crumbled bus at the bottom of a ravine.

"That happened last night on the Grande Corniche, only a few miles from where Beyath is waiting. As always, the consequence of her arrival has taken many lives."

After breakfast and a brief return to their respective rooms, the two walked inland until they came to the city's train station. Ahote bought two return tickets to Villefranche at which point the pair made their way to Quai 11. After a short wait, they boarded the local commuter train that ran up and down the Cote D'Azur.

The trip was short, less that fifteen minutes, but it may as well have been an eternity, such was the change in scenery. They departed the somewhat tired station in the city's centre and initially passed through some not particularly scenic suburbs. Then, without warning, they emerged above the glistening bay of Villefranche sur Mer. Moments later the train stopped at the town's tiny station.

It was basically a narrow platform on either side of the track, with a minuscule ticket kiosk and two benches. It didn't matter. People didn't come for the station. They came for the town itself.

Nestled on the west side of the bay, the medieval village was indescribably quaint and serene as its mirror-like reflection rested atop the still waters of the Med. Ahote had time-walked the streets a few days earlier in the 1978 timeline, so knew the exact location of the terraced house.

The narrow, cobblestone streets were too small for

vehicles and sloped steeply up the side of the hill. Craig had never been anywhere so authentically ancient in his life. Though he'd been in the Venetian and Paris hotels in Las Vegas where they tried to emulate the beauty of European architecture, when faced with the real thing, Craig realised just how tacky the faux reproductions really were.

Ahote led the way up an alley that was barely wide enough to permit Craig to walk without scraping his shoulders. They emerged in a tiny, village square with a church on one side and a row of ancient looking doors that were deeply set into faded pink plastering.

Number 27 was not just recognisable by the number above the door. The steeply canted roof was the big give-away. Nestled around its narrow chimney were countless creatures that most certainly shouldn't have been there. Mice, rats and large Mediterranean lizards were congregated on the ochre-coloured roof tiles. There was one small ventilation hole just visible below the roof, but judging by the animals that were hanging out of it, the attic was already full.

There was a small gathering of local residents who were staring up at the bizarre sight, wondering what had caused such an unusual infestation. They were blissfully unaware that during Beyath's transitioning period from a molecular vapour to human form, creatures of the night were drawn to the location of the tauntingly seductive force that lay inside.

"What time does Sylvie return?" Craig asked.

"She catches the five-fifteen train every day from

Menton to Villefranche. We have plenty of time."

"Are you absolutely certain that Beyath has completed her transition?"

"She will only complete the transition once she passes through the portal, but if you are asking whether she is ready for that final stage, then the answer is yes," Ahote advised.

"This might be a dumb question, but how do you intend to get inside the house with these people watching?"

"They will be gone in a few minutes," he assured Craig.

They stood just out of sight in the alley and waited. A few minutes later a young gendarme walked into the square and approached the gathering. There were a few moments of raised voices and hand gesturing, at which point the nosy neighbours disbanded and left the square. The policeman removed an instamatic camera from his black satchel and took a couple of pictures of the goings on atop the roof, then he too exited the village square.

"It's so creepy that you know stuff like that," Craig commented.

"I only know it because I time-walked here on three occasions before you arrived at my home."

"That doesn't make it any less weird," Craig said with a smile. "You still haven't answered how we're going to get inside the house?"

"I plan on using a mental curse on the lock," Ahote replied.

"Seriously?"

"No, of course not," Ahote said, shaking his head. "You

really are gullible sometimes. One of the endearing aspects of a small village like this one in 1978 is that the locals never lock their doors. We're just going to walk right in."

"We're just going to walk right in," Craig mimicked the other man adding a whining quality to his voice.

"Very mature," Ahote commented. "Are you ready?"

"If I say no, can I go home?" Craig replied.

"No," Ahote replied.

"Then, lead the way."

Ahote and Craig walked confidently across the square and stepped into number 27. Craig was stunned at how small the place was on the inside. There was a tiny living room, a minuscule kitchen and a basic bathroom at the back. Ahote led the way up stone stairs to the building's only bedroom. Both men had to duck slightly so as not to hit the low ceiling with their heads. The room was simply furnished. There was a single bed, a side table which looked to be an antique, a chest of drawers and an armoire in one corner.

Ahote gestured for Craig to go immediately to the glass door that opened onto the balcony. Thankfully, the door was immediately to the left, so he didn't have to pass in front of the portal, thus making himself visible to Beyath. Even though he was only able to see the mirror from an oblique angle, he could see that it was identical to the one he and his family had received on that fateful night.

Craig stepped outside and was happy to see that, because the balcony was at the back of the house, it was shielded from view in almost every direction. He positioned himself to the side of the of the glass door so that he couldn't be seen from inside but still had a view of the mirror. He removed the backpack and withdrew the silenced pistol.

Inside, Ahote waited until Craig gave him a thumbs up then, after a few silent words of self-encouragement, he stepped in front of the portal.

"Beyath," he called out. "I know that you are here. I also believe that you know who I am, and what it is that I do."

Ahote took a couple of steps back so that he wasn't close enough to the mirror so the witch could simply reach out and grab him. He stood next to the armoire and waited for Beyath to walk through the portal. Ahote knew that he didn't have to say anything else. She had almost certainly heard his words and would make her appearance momentarily.

Craig only had a side view of the mirror. When Ahote backed away he could no longer see him, but that didn't bother him in the least. He didn't need to see Ahote. He only needed to see Beyath.

Ahote kept his eyes rivetted on the mirror's surface, waiting until he could see the first ripple in the reflection. He was so completely fixated on the portal that he didn't notice the armoire door slowly open by itself.

A full-length mirror was mounted to the back of it.

Ahote didn't see the wizened arms emerge from the reflective surface. Beyath managed to stretch her entire top half into the room before Ahote sensed that something was wrong. He spun around and for a brief second was face to face with Beyath's skull-like head. Before he could even react, Beyath grabbed him, and with inhuman strength pulled him inside the mirror.

Before Craig even knew that there was a problem, his vision blurred, and he felt as if he was being dragged backwards at hypersonic speed through a sieve.

CHAPTER 7

2022 (fractured timeline 1)

Craig sat on the deck behind the house nursing a cold beer. It was a warm day for April, even in the high desert, but he didn't even notice. He'd been crying again. It had been three months since he'd come home from the Sheriff's office to find his wife gone and his two children sitting on the sofa, both catatonic.

After the investigators finally cleared him of any malfeasance, he'd been allowed to go back to work, but with Jenny gone and Sally and Tim being cared for by his mother-in-law, Helena, he was completely alone. Even Steeler, their devoted Golden Retriever, was being housed by Julie, his adoptive mother until such time as Craig felt that he could get himself back into some sort of a normal routine.

The problem was that nobody could come up with any rational cause for Jenny's disappearance. After investigators had interviewed the people who'd spoken to Jenny on that fateful afternoon, they were able to discern that she had still been in the house communicating with her customers right up until three o'clock. As Craig had been on a call-out with another deputy from two thirty until he headed home at the end of his shift, there was no way to place him at the crime scene with sufficient time to have made her vanish before calling the police.

Craig had managed to keep his old PTSD demons at bay for the first few days, but when social services 'suggested' that his children stay with relatives, it had ripped the bandages right off his psychological wounds. Even though he'd taken to knocking back the occasional beer, he had so far managed to keep the spectre of his old, pre-Jenny binge-drinking at bay.

The last two days had been especially hard. He'd driven to Sedona and spent the weekend with his mother-in law and his children. Thankfully, she and Craig had always got on well, and Helena had never for a second doubted his innocence. Even when the investigators started applying heavy pressure on Craig, she'd stood by him. Helena knew the statistics on missing wives and guilty husbands, but she also knew how much the two loved each other.

Visiting with his children was one of the hardest things he'd ever had to do. Though their catatonic state had improved slightly, the doctors feared that a full recovery was unlikely. The problem was that they couldn't find the cause of their condition.

When Craig had come home and found the pair sitting on the sofa, their eyes glazed and their mouths hanging open, he'd had no idea just how bad a shape the kids were in.

Because of a lack of any physical symptoms, doctors felt that they were suffering from some sort of mental breakdown. As neither child could speak, it was impossible to find out just exactly what had caused their young minds to rupture.

Craig and Helena had sat at the dining table with Tim and Sally and tried to carry on a natural conversation. Both children had regained some mobility, but still couldn't walk by themselves or control their bodily functions. Thankfully, both were eager to eat and drink, so the feeding tubes were no longer needed.

As she did every day, Helena opened her laptop and found a group of pictures that represented one period in either their lives, Jenny's life or all of them together. On one particular evening, Helena's slide show focussed on the barbeque she and Wally had thrown many years earlier for Jenny and her latest boyfriend, Craig.

Craig didn't need to see photographs to be reminded of that day. He could remember it as if it was yesterday. Though not blessed with a particularly exceptional memory recall, Craig could bring back every single memorable moment he'd spent with Jenny, and there were many of those.

*

Craig had picked up Jenny from her apartment in the sleepy, seaside-town of Leucadia, in Southern California. She was wearing bright yellow shorts, a coral-coloured tank top and a white floppy sunhat. It was mid-summer, and she was as tanned as her blond complexion would allow. After tossing her overnight bag onto the back shelf of Craig's Karman Ghia, she jumped in and gave him a quick kiss.

"How are you feeling?" she asked.

"Scared to death," he replied.

"More than you were during your time in Iraq and Afghanistan?"

"It's a different type of fear," he said.

"My parents are hardly that scary." Jenny grinned.

"Not to you maybe, but to me, it's way worse."

Craig put the car in gear and pulled onto the coast road then turned inland a few blocks later. Once on the 5 freeway, they drove to the outskirts of San Diego and got onto the 8 heading east. It was a long drive to Phoenix among scenery that was monotonously uninspiring. There are parts of the southern deserts that are breath-taking, but the part that hugs California's border with Mexico is bland, and what there is to see has been scorched to a uniform, lifeless monochrome.

They pulled in for gas and a burger at Gila Bend, then after stopping off for a quick visit with Julie, Craig's adoptive mother, they swung north.

Two and a half hours later they saw Bell Rock off to the right.

"Wow," Craig said, stunned.

"That's just the beginning. It just keeps getting better and better."

Craig had never been to Sedona, and though Jenny had shown him countless photos, they didn't do justice to the colour and majesty of the rust-red terrain.

Jenny told him to turn left onto 89A then to turn right onto Mountain Shadows Drive. The street was entirely residential and, judging by the look of the properties, was obviously an expensive neighbourhood.

Jenny's home, or at least where she used to live, was a few hundred yard up the road on the left-hand side. It was a single-story Adobe style ranch house. It was painted a dark umber to blend into the land and surrounding hills. A stamped concrete driveway formed a semi-circle leading up to the front door.

As if by some strange parental telepathy, her mom, dad and grandmother emerged before Craig had even applied the handbrake. Both parents gave their daughter some serious hugging before focussing their attention on the interloper. The man that was vying to take their place. The man who had almost certainly deflowered their sweet virginal child.

Wally's handshake had been a bone-crusher as his cold blue eyes never left Craig for a second.

"So, this is the famous Marine we've heard so much about," Wally stated. "I was a navy man myself."

"Nothing wrong with squids, sir," Craig replied. "Somebody's got to drive us to and from the action."

Wally simply stared at the younger man. The three women held their breath waiting for Wally's reaction to the slight.

To everyone's astonishment, Wally suddenly laughed and draped an arm over Craig's shoulder. "Once a jarhead, always a jarhead," he said, smiling.

"Oorah, sir. Oorah!"

"Let's get you both inside and get some beers flowing," Wally said as he stepped back into the house.

Craig glanced over at Jenny with a concerned look. He had presumed that she would have told her parents about his battle with PTSD and alcohol and that he had been on the waggon for over six months.

"She told me," Helena said a few moments later as she shook his offered hand. "I thought it best for Wally to get to know you first before having his impression of you coloured by something that you have under control."

"Thank you, ma'am."

"Let's not be having any of that ma'aming around this house. You can call me Helena like everyone else, and this is my mother, Margaret. She demanded to be here to meet you."

"I feel like I'm under a microscope," Craig muttered.

"You are," Margaret said as a smile crossed her sun-wrinkled face.

"Don't mind her," Helena said. "She has a way of making everyone feel uncomfortable at first. Even at her age, she can still make a person as self-conscious as can be, and don't get me started with mom and that old shotgun she keeps in her closet. Between her and Wally, any visit from a potential boyfriend has always been an emotional gauntlet. Just be yourself and you'll be fine.

"Thank you," Craig replied. "I'm embarrassed to ask, but what do I call your husband?"

"Until he says otherwise, I'd suggest 'sir'."

Wally barbequed steaks while Helena put together a southwestern salad replete with homemade, crispy, corn strips. When Craig declined the offer of a beer, Wally looked him straight in the eye and barked, "Why the hell not, son?"

Craig barked right back at him, "Recovering alcoholic, sir."

"Got it under control?" the man asked.

"Completely, sir."

Wally studied him a moment longer.

"There's soda and juice in the fridge. Help yourself."

They sat on what appeared to be their own private bluff and looked back down the canyon towards Oak Creek Canyon as they drank and talked. Jenny seemed to gravitate to her father, and both were discussing the classes she'd taken and what her next plans were going to be. Meanwhile, Margaret kept glancing over at him with open curiosity. Craig, sensing her stares, smiled back at her.

"So, what are your plans, Craig?" Margaret asked. "Jenny tells us that you'll be getting a discharge soon."

"End of the year, ma'am ... I mean Margaret," Craig nodded. "Not completely sure what I'm going to do, other than make a life for Jenny and me."

"A good life, I hope."

"That's the plan, Margaret," Craig replied, smiling.

"I think we can drop the Margaret. It makes me sound a thousand years old. Call me Maggie," she said, her emerald-coloured eyes studying him.

"Yes, ma'am ... I mean, Maggie."

"You must have some idea of what you want to do with your life?" Maggie asked.

"I always imagined staying in the military. Being a Marine was supposed to be my career."

"You could hardly remain a sniper for the rest of your life," she observed.

"To be honest, I never gave much thought to what I'd do beyond that," Craig admitted. "I guess if I had to pick some other job, I'd probably go for being an MP or something like that."

"How about the non-military equivalent?" Maggie asked.

"I'm starting to get a strong feeling that you are leading up to something," Craig replied.

Maggie laughed.

"That's very perceptive of you. Wally and I were discussing your situation before you arrived today and he suggested we put you in touch with a friend of ours in St. George, Utah. He's the sheriff there and could almost certainly point you in the right direction if you wanted to go that route."

"What? Me, be a sheriff?"

"Why not? It'd basically be the same thing as an MP, but you'd get to settle in one location and make a home for your family."

"In Utah?" Craig exclaimed. "Neither of us are Mormon."

"A third of the population of Utah isn't Mormon. It's a beautiful state to live in and ..."

Maggie didn't finish her thought.

"And what?" Craig asked.

"Nothing," she said. "It wasn't important."

"Please ... finish what you were going to say," Craig probed.

"I was going to say that Utah is a semi-dry state so that might just be an extra bit of help with ... you know."

"You can say drinking. It's not exactly a secret."

"What are you two gossiping about?" Jenny said as she approached the pair. "I hope my grandmother hasn't been trying to run your life for you?" she asked.

"Actually, she has, but I'm kinda glad she did. She came up with an interesting idea."

"If it involves us moving into this house, it's never going to happen."

Maggie shook her head and tsked her granddaughter. "As if I would do something like that."

"No," Craig replied. "Maggie here suggested that I consider working for the sheriff's department in Utah."

Jenny didn't look the least bit surprised.

"Uncle Milt could help him with the application and training," Jenny observed.

"Would that be Uncle Milt in St George?" Craig asked, teasing them both.

*

As it happened, Milt had been very helpful and had suggested that he attend the training courses at Dixie College in St George, which was as far south as you could get in the state.

Craig and Jenny had decided that it was best if she stay with her folks while he was undergoing the twenty-four weeks of training. Despite the distance, Craig saw a lot of Helena, Wally and even Maggie each weekend during his time at the police academy annex.

At his graduation, his adoptive mother Julie, Wally, Helena, Maggie and Jenny all sat together and hooted and hollered when his name was called to step up and collect his certificate.

CHAPTER 8

Craig was about to open another beer when he heard powerful engines pass overhead. He looked up and saw a good-sized private jet soar over the house. It was low in the sky, and Craig assumed that it was intending to land in Kanab.

It was a big plane for such a small airport, but ever since they lengthened the runway the previous year, it wasn't unheard of to have something that size touch down in their neck of the woods. Craig wondered what business the occupants could possibly have in Kanab.

It never dawned on him for a second that the sole passenger was there for him.

By the time the rental jeep turned onto Johnson Canyon Road, Craig had downed another couple of beers and was enjoying the buzz. It was the only way he could keep the thoughts of Jenny and the kids out of his head, at least for a little while.

Craig watched the red jeep turn up his dirt drive and wondered what the hell the occupants could want with him.

He got shakily to his feet and walked around the house to the forecourt.

Craig stood watching as a man in his late fifties or early sixties stepped out of the jeep. Despite his age, the man looked tough. If he had to guess, Craig felt he was ex-military, maybe even special forces. His grey hair was cut short to his scalp and his blue eyes were cold and piercing.

The man walked towards him as a smile appeared on his rugged face.

"My name's Connor," the man said in a strong Northern Ireland accent. "And you won't initially understand what I'm about to tell you, but we are friends."

*

Connor didn't mince words. He explained how, in an alternate timeline a man called Ahote, together with Craig, had travelled back to 1996 and journeyed to the UK in order to kill Beyath before she could take Jenny. Even though the witch had somehow survived and still tried to take his wife, Craig and Ahote had saved Jenny and succeeded in killing Beyath. Or at least they thought they had.

Connor further explained that Craig and Ahote had learned that the witch had killed a young woman in 1978 and that they had time-walked back to try and destroy her once and for all. Somehow, Beyath knew what they were planning and was able to take Ahote into her dimension, almost certainly so that she could feast on his lifeforce.

"The moment Ahote ceased to exist, so did his timeline

from 1978 onwards," Connor explained. "You therefore never had the chance to save your wife and children from Beyath because Ahote wasn't there to explain what was to happen and help you battle the threat."

Connor also explained how, in the original timeline, Ahote had been helping the group known as International Dimensions for over thirty-five years. During that time, he had helped save countless lives. Because Ahote ceased to exist from 1978 on, every person whose life Ahote had saved, perished instead.

Craig at first thought that the man was completely insane. It wasn't until Connor used his cell phone to face time with Edward Jenkins, the ex-Prime Minister of the UK, that he started to believe him. Jenkins confirmed what Connor had said and explained that together, they had to find a way of travelling back in time so that Ahote could be saved.

Once Connor disconnected the video call, Craig said nothing. All he could do was stare at the other man.

"We need your help," Connor stated.

"Fuck that," Craig replied. "I need a beer."

He started to get up but Connor, with frightening ease, pushed him back onto the bench.

"We don't have time for you to have another meltdown," Connor's Northern Irish accent sounded even more prominent when angry. "You need to get your shite together and help us save those people, which, let's not forget, includes your wife and children."

"My children are alive," Craig corrected.

"They may be alive, but they're certainly not living," Connor shot back. "If we can stop Ahote from being taken in 1978, they will be able to be children again, instead of walking zombies.

"Don't you fucking call my children zombies," Craig screamed, as he tried to lunge across the table.

Connor pushed him away as if he was swatting a fly.

Craig looked as if he was going to try again, when Connor said, "This is your only chance to bring them all back. Do you really want to blow that opportunity?"

"How do I know that anything you've been saying is real?" Craig asked.

Connor again produced his phone and played a video. In it, Craig, an older Native American man, Connor, Jenny and both of Craig's children were sitting out on the deck, eating and laughing."

"I don't remember that day at all."

"That's because it never happened in this timeline," Connor replied. "Look at the timestamp."

Craig reached over and spread his fingers on the screen so he could zoom in on the date in the top right-hand corner. He felt an icy chill rise up across his back.

"This says it was two weeks ago," Craig stated, confused.

"It was, but in the original timeline before Beyath erased Ahote in 1978. As you can see, your family is alive and well. I would image that you would like to bring back that timeline and see them all again, alive and healthy."

"Who's the Indian guy," Craig asked.

"That's Ahote. That's the man Beyath took from us."

'Okay," Craig said, sighing. "You've got my attention. How the hell do we set things straight?

"Together, we are going to try and convince the only living person who's physically capable of time-walking to help us change the past."

"Who's that?"

"Ahote's son," Connor replied.

"If this guy Ahote has a son that can do the same time travel trick, what's the big deal? In fact, if you have him, what do you need me for?"

"There's a slight problem. His son left the reservation when he was a teenager and never time-walked again."

"Why is that a problem?" Craig asked. "Is this time-walking thing something you have to practice?"

"The problem is that he shunned his tribe and all their beliefs and ceremonies after Ahote abandoned him."

"That was a shitty thing to do," Craig commented.

"He didn't really abandon him. In this timeline, Ahote was taken by Beyath in 1978, leaving behind a grieving wife and angry son."

"Wait a minute," Craig said, holding up his palm. "If nobody knows anything about this Ahote guy since 1978, how come you seem to know everything about him. Including what he supposedly did in the alternate timeline?"

Connor grinned.

"What?" Craig asked, frustrated.

"You're finally starting to ask the right questions. International Dimensions can document every timeline on which it had an impact. They are able to track timeline and event anomalies, including those that occurred prior to the creation of the operation."

"How is that even possible if everything gets rewritten each time a change is made in the past?" Craig asked.

"Everything is recorded and automatically uplinked to the shroud which is ..."

"You mean cloud, don't you?" Craig corrected him.

"No, I mean shroud. It's made up of a series of supercomputers that have been placed within alternate dimensions so that anything that's uploaded can't be affected by a timeline variance in our dimension."

"Now you're just making shit up," Craig said, stunned.

"Monitoring teams across the globe have constant access to the shroud. Their job is to track timeline changes that were either caused by our actions or that impact our future actions. It was data from the shroud that first alerted us to Beyath going back in time to take the young French woman in 1978. Now of course, we know that the whole thing was a trap. She didn't need the woman. She just wanted to destroy Ahote."

"In that case, why didn't she take me as well?" Craig asked, trying to get his head around what the Irishman was telling him.

"She didn't need to. By taking Ahote, she basically destroyed your life. Beyath doesn't just feed off the light of her bloodline, she also feeds off misery and pain. You see Craig, keeping you alive yet distraught, gives her enormous pleasure."

"But how can she even know of my pain. It's not like

we're connected," Craig said, then immediately paled. "Are we?"

"No. You have no direct connection with Beyath; however, it would not surprise me if she didn't check in on you, so to speak, just to taste a quick drop of your misery."

"I thought she could only come through that special carved mirror like the one we received?"

"That is her preference; however, if she chooses to do so, she can emerge from any reflective object," Connor explained. "She does, however, require a full-sized mirror if she is to take someone back into her realm."

"It's been months," Craig said. "I don't think I've seen her."

"Then count yourself lucky."

*

After packing an overnight bag, Craig climbed into the rental jeep next to Connor. Fifteen minutes later they boarded the waiting aircraft. It was the first time Craig had ever been in a private jet and was astonished at the luxury of the interior.

"Do you always travel like this?" Craig asked.

"Only when someone else is paying," Connor replied. "Make yourself comfortable. As soon as you're settled, we can take off."

Once both were seated in the oversized seats, Connor pressed a button on his armrest console.

"We're ready back here," he announced.

A few seconds later the jet began to taxi towards the

runway. Kanab being a small town with few exciting distractions, word had spread about the big jet, and a small crowd had gathered by the perimeter fence to watch the Gulfstream take off.

Once they reached the far end of the runway, the jet did a 180 then without any hesitation began to accelerate. Craig had no idea how fast a private jet could get airborne. There was none of the slow acceleration and lumbering down the runway which was the norm for a commercial plane. The Gulfstream reached take-off speed within seconds then took off at a forty-five-degree angle.

The flight east took just under four hours. Craig had only been to DC once before but had only ever landed at Andrews airbase so had missed seeing the Capital from the air. The Gulfstream flew an approach pattern that gave them an uninterrupted view of DC from the port side of the aircraft.

Despite the city's dysfunctional reputation, from the air it was breath-taking.

They landed then taxied to the executive terminal at Dulles International Airport. A Lincoln town car was waiting for them on the tarmac. Connor entered an address into the onboard GPS system and within a few seconds, was given the route to follow.

After passing through the toll booths that were situated so that everyone leaving the airport had to pay for the honour of doing so, they turned onto 66, heading east. Forty minutes later they crossed over the Potomac then turned onto Rock Creek Parkway. Within seconds, they drove under the Kennedy Center overhang before passing the infamous

Watergate complex on their right.

They stayed on Rock Creek Parkway until they reached Connecticut Avenue. Connor followed the GPS commands through a residential area before reaching Porter Street, NW. Number 79 was a red-brick, Tudor-themed house on a substantial lot.

Connor pulled the car up to the curb.

"What time was he expecting us?" Craig asked.

"He's not expecting us at all," Connor replied.

"Don't you think it would have been a good idea to forewarn the poor guy?"

"And give him a chance to avoid us? No, I don't think so."

"How do you know he's even here?" Craig asked. "He could be on vacation or away on business."

"He's not though. He's been home for the past forty-eight minutes."

"How the hell do you know that?"

Connor held up his cell phone. On the screen was a map of DC and in the top left corner a red dot was pulsating gently.

"That's not possible," Craig stated.

"Sure, it is. They've got an app for everything nowadays." Connor winked and he reached for his door handle.

CHAPTER 9

Craig had seen photos of Ahote so had a vague idea what his son might look like. When the door swung open, all preconceived notions were swept away as Craig came face to face with Jack Winston.

The man was in his mid-sixties, was roughly the same height as Craig but had twice the girth. Craig estimated that he must have weighed in at 400 pounds at the very least, and none it appeared to be muscle. He couldn't have looked less like his father if he'd tried. Which, Craig realised might just be intentional.

The man swept a few strands of grey, thinning hair back off his face then looked at each of the visitors in an almost bored, uncaring way.

"Yeah?" he said in a raspy voice. "Whadoyawan?"

"I'm sorry to bother you Mr Winston, but we need to talk to you about your father," Connor advised.

"I don't have a father," the other man replied and began to close the door.

"If you'll just give us a few minutes to explain, I guarantee that you will be glad you did," Connor said.

"If this is some scam, or he's kicked off and left me his debts, I swear I'll ..."

"It's none of those things," Connor said. "I give you my word."

"Perhaps if we could come in," Craig suggested in his best deputy sheriff voice, "we can tell you why we're here without the neighbours hearing."

With obvious reluctance, the man stepped aside to let the two enter his house.

The inside looked to have once been comfortable, nicely decorated and expensively furnished. Though all those trappings were still in evidence, the place didn't look as if had been cleaned in many months. A thin layer of dust lay upon all surfaces. Clothes were strewn across furniture and scrunched up wads of paper were scattered throughout the parts Craig and Connor could see.

Apart from the general mess, there was a distinct odour of domestic neglect, interwoven with the sickly smell of rotting food.

"Sorry about the mess," Winston said as he held out his hand. "You wouldn't know it, but this place was a show home. When I originally bought it, it had been sitting abandoned for almost twenty years. I restored it from the ground up."

After glancing around the unkempt interior, Connor and Craig introduced themselves then stood waiting, awkwardly. It took a moment for Jack to take the hint.

"Sorry. Let's go into the dining room. It's a little tidier."

"Don't you have someone to clean house for you?" Connor asked.

"I did, up until two and a half months ago," Jack replied.

"What happened?" Craig asked.

"She walked out and filed for divorce," Jack replied as he led the pair into what might once have been an elegant dining room in the days when it had been kept clean. Unlike the other rooms, this one looked as if it hadn't been touched in years.

"Cynthia didn't believe in formal dining rooms," Jack told them. "She preferred to eat in front of the TV."

He swatted dust off a couple of dining chairs and gestured for Craig and Connor to be seated.

"So, what's this all about?" Jack asked, still standing.

"I think you may want to sit down," Craig suggested. "This takes some explaining."

"I'm fine where I am," he insisted.

As Connor started to explain the different timelines for his father, Jack went pale and ultimately sat on one of the dining room chairs without even bothering to dust off the seat. By the time Connor reached the part about Beyath taking Ahote back in 1978 and thus changing his entire timeline, Jack was looking sweaty and discombobulated.

"Why should I believe you?" Jack said in little more than a whisper.

"Isn't it easier than believing that your loving father abandoned you back in 1978 and has never once made any effort to get in touch?"

"It happens," Jack replied.

"Remember when I told you that International Dimensions keeps a record of all related personnel and activities of every timeline?"

Jack nodded.

"Everyone who works with International Dimensions has a photo or video record kept on file of one defining moment within each timeline."

Connor removed his cell phone, scrolled to one specific file then pressed play before holding it out for Jack to see.

Jack half-heartedly watched the screen, not expecting to see anything even remotely impactful.

Instead, he saw Ahote with his arms around a younger Jack at some sort of formal dinner event.

Jack couldn't breathe. It wasn't just seeing the image of his father hugging him and applauding. It was what was on the plaque attached to the podium just behind the two of them.

NATIONAL COUNCIL OF AMERICAN INDIANS
GENERAL MEETING 2004

"That was the day you were nominated as president of the council," Connor explained. "Your father was very proud of you."

"But that never happened," Jack said weakly.

"Do you see that woman standing off to the right, smiling and clapping?"

"Yes. Why?"

"That's your wife, Winona."

"I've had three wives and they've all left me. I don't know who the hell she is, but she wasn't one of them."

"That's because this image is from the original timeline. The one in which your father Ahote never left you or your mother. A version where you grew up confident, secure and proud of your heritage. You dedicated yourself to helping your people. In addition, you married well and had three beautiful children."

Jack stared at the looping video and started to cry.

"Why the hell are you showing me this?" he said between snuffles. "Maybe that was how it once was, but it's not how things turned out, is it? When my dad ran out on us, I left the reservation and changed my name. I made a lot of money as a lobbyist here in DC and have had a pretty good life."

"Have you?" Connor asked. "All three of your wives were campaign volunteers that you seduced at work, and all three of them walked out on you. Not one of the marriages lasted more than three years. You drink too much, you're grotesquely overweight, your health is so far in the danger zone that one good bout of the common cold would probably kill you. You are an emotional wreck who has spent his life unconsciously seeking approval from the father who abandoned him. Is that really what you would call a good life?"

"That's a bit rough," Craig commented.

"I have to be rough. Jack here, or Nahele as he was originally named, has to understand the importance of what I'm telling him."

"Why?" Jack asked.

"Because, between us, we're going to make sure that the timeline you are looking at on that phone is the only timeline that ever survives."

"How is that even possible?"

"It's possible because of you Jack. You are the one remaining person who is physically capable of time-walking on this earth."

"I haven't time-walked in over forty years."

"It's not something you forget." Connor stated. "You may be a little rusty, but I have no doubt that you could still take one of us back if you wanted to."

"And do what, for God's sake?"

"Together, we have to stop your father from ever being taken."

Jack's mouth sagged open as he stared at the phone screen. He then lowered his head onto the dusty table and began weeping.

Craig looked over at Connor with an expression of alarm.

"He'll be fine," Connor mouthed silently.

Craig took a deep breath and looked back at the emotional wreck of a man.

"At least I hope he will," Connor whispered.

CHAPTER 10

It wasn't an easy thing to get Jack ready for time-walking. Though mainly an inherited trait, the ability to step back into one's own timeline does come with a few caveats. One of them is that the walker cannot be under the influence of any mind-altering substances otherwise their concentration will likely never be focussed enough to open the walking portal.

Jack, it turned out, was a functioning alcoholic, consumed Clonazepam like it was candy, was on Effexor for depression and somehow still managed to smoke enough California Kush to put him into a nightly sleep-coma.

After making a few phone calls, a full-time nurse moved into the house and a private doctor came by once a day to make sure that Jack wasn't in any real distress, other than the obvious withdrawal issues.

Connor and Craig rented an Airbnb condo on Connecticut Avenue and took turns sitting vigil with the man. By the tenth day, Jack was over the initial hump and was actually hungry for something other than pizza.

By the end of the second week, his pallor had returned

to something akin to normal, and he'd even managed a walk around the block. Something he admitted he hadn't done in years. Though the doctor continued to monitor his progress, there was no longer any need for a live-in nurse.

On the fifteenth day, Jack tried his first time-walk in over four decades. It took almost an hour of deep concentration and he only went back a few minutes, but the fact was, he was still able to do it.

Over the next few days, he practiced the hardest part of the ritual, going back to a specific moment in his timeline. While Ahote could seemingly walk back to a specific time from wherever he was, Jack could only go back to the exact place his younger self had been at that memory moment. This initially proved complicated as the time-walk envelope would not allow him to ever encounter his past self and would thus, boomerang him back to present day. Connor assumed this was some artifact related to Jack's poor health and mental stability.

After countless walks, and with his time-accuracy down to being within a twelve-hour window, Jack finally worked out how his father was able to walk back to the moment of the memory but vector away from the actual location where it took place.

That was probably the biggest breakthrough of the entire process.

After a time-walk back to his teens, Jack returned and asked, "What if I just stay in the past and do a better job of living my life?"

"It doesn't work that way," Connor replied.

"How do you know?"

"Your father explained it to me. Don't forget, your time in the past is temporally fragile. A disturbance to your time bubble will always bring you right back to present day."

"Damn," he said, obviously disappointed at having to return to his current life.

The next day, Connor began time-walking with Jack. After twenty-four hours of successful trials, Connor announced that it was time for him to go back to 1978 with Jack so that he could make every possible advanced arrangement, so that when Craig walked back, everything he would need would already be in place.

In their timeline, Jack and Connor travelled all the way to 1978, travelled to France and stayed for over a week. During that same period, Craig only just had enough time to run to the nearest Starbucks and buy coffees for the three of them. By the time he returned, the walkers were back.

"That was amazing," Jack stated. "I just spent a week on the French Riviera without any adult supervision."

"You were by yourself?" Craig asked, surprised.

"I had things to do that didn't require a horny teenager holding me back," Connor explained.

"Did you accomplish everything you needed to do?" Craig asked.

"I did. I'll write everything down for you so that you know where to go and when."

"Can I ask one stupid question?" Jack inquired. "Why can't you do the mission? I don't understand why Craig needs to go at all. Nothing personal Craig. It's just that

Connor and I already have a routine going."

"Simple," Connor answered. "Beyath already knows Craig which makes him the perfect lure to bring her through the portal."

"So, now I'm just bait?" Craig said shaking his head.

"Not at all," Connor replied, smiling. "You were always destined to be bait."

*

Craig spent the next couple of days practicing time-walks with Jack until both felt comfortable. Then, after a light dinner and an early night, Craig and Jack sat alone in the house on Porter Street as the man who was once called Nahele, eased himself into a state of deep concentration.

"It's done," the younger version of the man announced in a higher pitched voice. Without the years of hard living and heavy eating, Craig could see the resemblance to the photos he'd seen of Ahote. Jack had long black hair and the same strong, sharp-edged face. He stood up and Jack's oversized clothing slipped off him and gathered on the floor. He grabbed the 1978 clothes that were folded next to him and quickly put them on.

"You ready?" Jack asked.

"I guess so," Craig sighed. "This is all very new to me."

"According to Connor, it's not knew to you at all. In fact, you've made the trip to France once before."

"And look how well that turned out," Craig replied.

"This time it will be successful," Jack said,

enthusiastically. He then caught sight of his discarded pile of fat-man clothes on the floor. "It has to be."

*

The taxi ride to Dulles Airport was surreal, at least to Craig. The fact that they were driving though a 1978 version of Washington DC was like a National Geographic documentary come to life. The city looked cleaner back then. There was also much less traffic, and what there was, was a pleasure to observe. Just about every car on the street would end up being a classic in 2022, yet here they were just going about their business as city workhorses.

The drive to Dulles took a third less time and felt more like a sojourn into the countryside. Without all the developments that had sprouted up between the city and the airport, there was nothing but green fields and unspoiled woods.

Because they were starting on the east coast, Connor had booked them (on his previous time-walk) on an Air France flight to Nice with a quick plane change at Paris' Charles De Gaulle Airport.

Craig felt as if he was in a trance. Everywhere he looked he saw some aspect of the earlier era that made him smile. Even the coin-operated TV sets in the airport departure lounge were almost comically retro.

The flight to Paris took just under seven hours, and with the connection, they were in Nice two hours after that. Craig felt utter terror as the twin-engine Caravelle looked as if it was about to do a water landing before the Nice airport runway appeared at the last possible moment.

After checking into a cheap hotel near the Gare Du Ville (they did not have the fiscal resources that Ahote had for himself in every time period), Craig followed Connor's written directions to a run-down building near the port. They ended up on the top floor, talking to a gangster by the name of Claude who had a gun ready for Craig to take with him.

It was a semi-automatic Beretta Puma that had seen a lot of wear. Claude insisted that it was perfectly capable of doing what was needed. Craig asked about a silencer and was told that they couldn't find one that would fit that particular weapon.

"My friend made arrangements for a newer model handgun with a noise suppressor," Craig stated.

"This is all I have," Claude said with a shrug as he started to reach for the weapon. "If you don't want it …"

"Okay," Craig said, holding his hands up in mock surrender. "We'll take it. I just hope it doesn't blow up in my hand."

"If it does, remember, no refunds."

CHAPTER 11

With Craig having no personal memory of having been to France, they were at a loss where to eat. Though modern-day Nice is littered with every possible US fast-food franchise restaurant you could imagine, back then, nothing looked familiar. It wasn't until they reached the port and saw a neon sign with the word 'PIZZA' emblazed in flickering blue light that Jack commented that pizza had been all he'd eaten most nights on the last trip with Connor.

Even though the place didn't seem to have the range of toppings that Craig was used to, he settled for a mushroom and onion pizza while Jack went for the basic cheese and tomato option. The only beer on draft was French so Craig ordered *un verre a 500ml* for himself and a Coke for Jack.

"Should you be drinking?" Jack asked.

"It's my life."

"Fair point. I just thought that after your breakdown when you were still on active duty ..."

"That was a long time ago," Craig replied. "And who told you about that?"

"I had a lot of time with Connor on the last time-walk. Your situation may have come up."

"Look," Craig said defensively. "A few months ago, I lost my wife and my children. I think I'm entitled to a little break from this new reality."

"Just so long as you have it under control," Jack said, before biting off a wedge of greasy pizza.

"If you're worried about tomorrow, I'll be fine. Beyond that ... let's face it, if I fail, I'll be dead. If I succeed, my life goes back to the way it was. My family will be back, and I will be at peace with the world."

"What if you fail, yet survive?" Jack asked.

"Then I will probably stay here in 1978 and drink myself to death."

"So long as you have a plan," Jack answered with raised eyebrows.

*

Craig's drinking was not under control. Despite Jack's continued suggestions for him to temper his thirst, Craig drank six of the giant glasses of lager. Jack had to practically prop him up during the walk back to their hotel.

Jack got him as far as his room then left Craig to his own devices. He knew he should probably stay with him, but deep down, Craig's lack of self-restraint disgusted him. The irony was not lost on him that in his own timeline, in present-day DC, he drank and smoked himself to sleep most nights.

He rationalised that this situation was different. Craig was the only person on the planet who could bring back his father. Jack couldn't understand how the man couldn't lay off the sauce for one night, especially considering what he would have to face the next day.

Though oblivious to the young man's disappointment and anger, Craig ended up paying the price. After passing out, fully dressed on top of the threadbare bedcover, he awoke hours later, shivering uncontrollably. He ended up spending the rest of the night in a foetal position trying to stop his entire body from shaking.

Craig at first thought that he was having some sort of physical reaction to the beer when it dawned on him that, though the booze hadn't helped the situation, what he was experiencing was a full-blown return of his PTSD.

If Jenny had been around, she would be administering one of his 'special' pills which he hadn't needed since the original breakdown in Iraq. The problem was that Jenny no longer existed in the current timeline and it had never entered Craig's mind to pack them himself.

It wasn't just the physical manifestations of the disorder that were taking hold of him. Craig was experiencing a full-blown panic attack. The thought of him going head-to-head with Beyath in less than six hours filled him with raw, gut-wrenching terror.

By the time Craig met Jack for breakfast in the basement dining room, he was as white as a sheet and his nerves were shot. Craig tried to hide his physical and mental condition from the younger version of Jack.

"Great," Jack said, shaking his head. "What the fuck's wrong with you?" he seethed in a low whisper. "You don't look like you could successfully fight off a puppy, let alone a sixteenth-century witch."

"I'll be fine," Craig lied. "Just let me get my shit together and we'll head out."

Jack didn't look remotely inclined to believe that the ex-Marine was going to be anywhere close to battle-ready if he gave him forty-eight hours to recover, and they only had two.

The plan was to get to the townhouse in Villefranche as soon as Sylvie Lucére left for work, hoping that Beyath wouldn't be expecting anyone to be there that early in the day.

"Is this something to do with this mission?" Jack asked as he pushed a copy of that day's Nice Matin newspaper across the table. On the front page was a picture of what was left of a tour bus that had plunged down a cliff. As neither could read a word of French, Craig had to take the photo at face value.

"Connor said that this sort of occurrence was a sign that Beyath was close to completing her transition. Apparently, when she is preparing to become human, the residual negative energy impacts local events, resulting in some sort of tragedy."

"How do you know this is that tragedy?" Jack asked.

"Didn't Connor show you this when you were here with him?"

"Not a chance. He told me the moment that we arrived

that I was to have nothing to do with the mission other than to provide the time-walk."

"Did he say why?" Craig asked.

"Something about, if I became involved in any way, he couldn't guarantee that Beyath wouldn't find a time and place in my timeline, to kill me in order to guarantee that I could never help you guys."

"That's heavy," Craig observed.

"You think!"

*

They caught the local commuter train from Nice station then sat silently until it arrived at Villefranche only fifteen minutes later. They hardly paid any attention to the beauty that surrounded them as they made their way to the village square.

"I think I should come in with you," Jack insisted. "You have no idea what you're going to run into, and I would certainly be more help inside that out."

"You are too valuable," Craig replied bluntly. "If something happens to you, we're all fucked. Please just do as I say and make sure that nobody else tries to get in the house, especially your father and me!"

"I thought that that you two didn't go into the house until much later today?"

"No one knows how much Beyath's messing around with timelines can affect historic records, even those of International Dimensions. It's unlikely that they will show up this morning, but if they do, you'll need to somehow keep them away without ever getting close to them."

"Why?" Jack asked. "Wouldn't it be better to have more backup?"

"Theoretically yes, but I can never get close to myself, remember?"

"God, this relativity stuff is hard to follow," the teen replied.

Craig ignored him. He was feeling like shit and didn't need some kid to screw up the mission. He was having enough trouble keeping the chills and shakes under control without having to worry about Ahote's son.

They reached the picturesque square and at Craig's signal, Jack walked away from him so he could set up his observation post a little farther down the row of terraced houses. Craig stepped up to number 27 and hoped that Connor was right about Sylvie never locking her door. He'd planned to nonchalantly walk inside as if he was a close friend, but before he could even grasp the door handle, a burly French woman came bounding out of number 31, five houses along to the right, and began peppering him with unintelligible French.

"*Mais, que faite vous, la*?" she shouted, wanting to know what Craig was up to.

He felt his heart sink, knowing that the woman was obviously going to make things inordinately difficult for him. Then, as smoothly as if he'd done it all his life, Jack stepped out of the shadows, took the woman gently by the waist and pirouetted her back the other way, steering her back through her own front door.

Craig had no idea what the kid planned on doing next, but there was no question that he had just saved the day. He stepped quickly into the tiny house and closed the front door. Craig stood in the minuscule entry hall and listened for any sounds that shouldn't be present. The only thing he could hear was his own raspy breathing and his racing pulse throbbing in his head.

Craig climbed the stairs, two at a time. Once on the landing, he peered to the left and was able to see most of the small bedroom. The portal was hanging on the wall, exactly as Connor had said it would be. Craig unslung the backpack and retrieved the old Beretta. He double checked the magazine, tapped it against his thigh then reinserted it into the bottom of the gun.

Craig racked the slide to chamber a round, then with every fibre of his being screaming at him to run the other way, he stepped into the room.

CHAPTER 12

1968

Maggie pulled up in front of the small, two-bedroom house she lived in with Allen, her husband of only eleven months. She eased out of her 1962 Chevy Nova and waddled up to the front door. The car was nothing much to look at, but it got her from A to B. Even though it was only eight years old, it already had over 120,000 miles on it. That was the problem with living way out in Cave Creek, Arizona. No matter where you needed to go, it seemed to involve at least a twenty-five-mile trek in each direction.

For some reason she felt excited to be home, not because of any sense of comfort or security, but rather that she couldn't wait to look at the mirror again.

*

The mirror had been the cause of some real consternation within the house for the last few days. When it had been dropped off in the middle of the night, Maggie Frost didn't want anything to do with it. Allen on the other hand saw no problem accepting the surprise gift and bringing it into their home.

It hadn't seemed to matter how many times Maggie told her husband that taking in a 'gift' without knowing where it came from, was bad luck, Allen hadn't seemed to care. The man didn't have a superstitious bone in his body and as Maggie was unable to offer even the slightest clue as to the origin of the superstition, he had completely ignored her pleas to leave it outside where the creepy delivery truck had dumped it.

Allen had to ask a neighbour to help him inside with the crate as Maggie refused to be party to bringing 'the monstrosity' into the house. It had taken him the better part of the morning to unpack the thing. Once done, he had leant it against their living room wall and stood back admiring it.

"Look at the carving. This could actually be worth some money," Allen had said.

Maggie couldn't see what Allen was getting so excited about. Yes, the carving was kinda special, if you liked rodents at play, but the damn thing hadn't even been in good shape. Parts of the frame were chipped, and the mirror had lost some backing in places, plus it had a crack in the top, left-hand corner.

It hadn't been until the next day when Maggie had gotten home after spending the day window shopping in Phoenix with her best friend Suzie Chambers, that she had started to feel differently about it.

When she had walked back into the house, it was gone four o'clock and as she had passed the mirror, she immediately spotted the difference. Her sweet husband had obviously spent the time she was gone cleaning and repairing it. He'd done a fine job, too. Gone were the chips, the bad backing and even the crack.

Maggie had no idea how he'd done it, but she had been glad he'd spent the time to fix it up. For some reason she no longer felt creeped out about it anymore. In fact, she had insisted that it be placed in their bedroom.

Neither had been able to get much sleep on Sunday night as there seemed to be something crawling around in their attic. As they didn't own a ladder and there was no other way of getting up there, they had decided to leave it till the next morning when Maggie could call the rental agency to get someone to check it out.

The agent had promised to get someone over as soon as they could, which Maggie knew was code for never. They were still waiting to have the cold tap in the bathroom unstuck as well as a ton of other little niggles that needed seeing to. Maggie hadn't really cared. If the sound of critters treating your home like some sort of a thoroughfare got on your hackles, then you should probably not be living in the desert in the first place.

Maggie had turned on their archaic TV that only seemed to get two stations and had been surprised when the local news had interrupted her morning chat shows with a live report about a Greyhound bus crash on the road to Sedona. It had somehow left the road only a few miles from Cave

Creek and had rolled into a ravine before sunrise, that morning. There was no accurate number of dead yet, but the newscaster had said it was expected to run into the teens.

Maggie had switched the set off and sat by the dining area so she could look out at the parched scrub grass that was meant to be their back yard.

Something had caught her eye.

The house was an L shape, so, if she craned her neck against the sliding door, she was able to see the part where the master bedroom jutted out. At first Maggie hadn't been able to identify what had initially caught her attention, then in the shadowy area between the gutter drainpipe and the cracked stucco wall, she had seen something moving.

It had taken her a moment to work out what it was as its shape and size didn't seem to make sense. Once her brain had unscrambled the optics, she had wished she hadn't looked so hard.

At least a dozen tarantulas had been crawling up the side of the house. Usually, when she saw them wandering around the desert, they were relatively slow and didn't look that menacing. These guys seemed to be battling each other to see who could climb up the wall the fastest.

Despite the obvious creep factor, Maggie hadn't been that worried. Unlike the smaller spiders that seemed to be able to find a way into the house through openings the size of pin head, the tarantulas were so big that they'd be hard pressed to find any way into the main part of the house.

She'd learned early on that there was little point in

worrying about desert creepy crawlies, as her mom had called them. This was their home long before she and Allen ever moved in. Maggie felt that everything that got built in the desert was temporary. The desert belonged to the critters. If anything, mankind only had a short lease agreement on the land before it returned to its heat baked, natural state.

*

Maggie balanced the brown paper shopping bag in one hand while she opened the sun-faded front door with the other. As she stepped inside, she felt the satisfying waft of chilled air from the swamp cooler. They couldn't afford to rent a place with actual air-conditioning, but on most days, the evaporating cooler seemed to do the trick so long as humidity was low.

Allen was adamant that 1968 was going to be their year. Their first child would be born, and he would finally get his long-awaited promotion at the small art gallery in Scottsdale where he sold overpriced Hopi artwork. The other hope was that they could move closer to town and hopefully find a place with central air.

Maggie put the groceries away, chugged some water right from the pitcher in the fridge, then walked into their bedroom and took off her oversized T-shirt. Her folks kept insisting that she buy proper pregnancy clothing, but they were on a tight enough budget as things were. Maggie found out that if she went up a size in T-shirts every few weeks then transitioned to the larger men's sizes during the later months, she'd be saving a small fortune.

Just the act of getting the sweat-soaked shirt (the car air-conditioning was acting up) over her head left her momentarily breathless. Once she'd recovered from the exertion, she stood in front of the new mirror and checked out her baby bump.

There was no doubt that the little girl inside her was gonna outgrow her current home in the next few months. Maggie's belly was getting pretty damn big and Helena (the name she'd decided on if it was a girl) was starting to become increasingly active.

The point of 'no humility', as Maggie called it, had been passed the previous week. One minute, she had been able, albeit with a little effort, to see her toes while standing, then suddenly, she couldn't. Allen had laughed himself silly but, for some reason, it had depressed the hell out of Maggie for a couple of days.

Maggie watched her reflection as she rubbed her swollen belly and smiled at the lunacy of the situation. Maggie had been a good Methodist, raised in all the right ways, less than half a mile from the Unity Methodist Church in Page, Arizona.

Maggie's life had pretty much been ordained for her from the start. Even as a young girl, she knew she would marry Jacob Peterson as soon as she reached eighteen. It wasn't as if she felt any real love or even desire towards him, but he was going to be a good, steady provider and besides, traditions were to be followed.

That was the way.

Then the strangest thing happened. A family moved into the old Clarkson house down the road. When news reached her home that they weren't even practicing Christians, they became the object of great fascination within the tightly-knit neighbourhood.

Maggie had been as nosy as everyone else, then, as her family drove to church one Sunday, she saw their new neighbour's son out front, mowing the lawn. While her parents shook their heads and opined at how wrong it was for a boy to be working, half-naked on the Lord's Day, Maggie's only thoughts were on the young man's perfect physique and gorgeous dark hair.

When, just shy of three months later, she and the boy she came to know as Allen, snuck of to Las Vegas and eloped, you'd have thought Maggie had run off with the devil himself judging by the reaction of her family and friends. The fact that Allen Frost, at only twenty, had already earned a Batchelors degree in Fine Art and had a job waiting for him in Scottsdale didn't register with her parents one little bit.

Maggie often wondered whether, if she'd made more of an effort to stay close with her family, they would be living somewhere better than the poorly maintained rental in the middle of nowhere.

While staring at her reflection in the mirror, Maggie rubbed a little baby oil onto her swollen tummy. She found the repetitive motion both calming and strangely pleasurable. She felt a tingling sensation begin to grow between her legs and suddenly realised that she was aroused.

Amused by the unexpected reaction to the oil and the physical contact, Maggie at first didn't notice the change in the mirror. The surface started to shimmer, sending ripples radiating out from one central part.

Strangely, once she noticed it, Maggie wasn't in the least bit frightened. She just wasn't that easy a person to scare. If anything. The molten look of the reflective surface fascinated her.

Then the skeletal hand appeared.

That did scare her.

It scared her a lot.

CHAPTER 13

1978

Craig hadn't known what to expect, but his first reaction was that everything looked surprisingly normal within the tiny French home. Even knowing what was to happen later that day didn't take away from the fact that it was a typical looking bedroom belonging to a single young woman.

An antique chest of drawers was off to one side against a rough painted wall. Three of the four drawers were open and had bits of clothing hanging from within as if all were trying to escape their forced confinement.

The top of the chest was covered with assorted makeup, nail polishes, a bowl of fun but cheap-looking jewellery and a disorganised pile of hair bands and clips.

Next to it was the mirror. It looked a lot different from the old *Nice-Matin* photo that he'd been texted back in Utah. Then again, that image had shown the mirror part to have been obliterated. The one he was looking at was pristine. There was something about it that spoke of another time, yet it looked as if it could have been made only days or maybe weeks earlier.

Craig was reticent to step in front of the thing. As no one living could tell tale of what occurs when Beyath appears, he didn't want to give her too easy of a target.

Craig edged his way between the chest of drawers and the left side of the mirror. The carved wood of the frame was pressing into his left arm as he tried to avoid any part of himself being in front of the looking glass.

Craig closed his eyes and tried to get his breathing under control. It didn't help much. Finally, with one last deep breath, he stepped in front of the mirror, the Beretta pointed right at its centre. His plan, if you could call it that, was to tempt the witch to come through her portal, then put as many rounds into her as he could before she could retreat or put him into some sort of a trance.

"I'm right here, you bitch!" he shouted. "Come and get me."

Nothing happened.

"What's the problem? Not strong enough yet? I thought you were supposed to be this unbeatable force of evil. If that's the case, come out here and show me."

The surface of the mirror rippled.

Craig's grip on the gun increased.

A raspy voice filled the tiny room.

"You don't yet know the pain I am about to cause you," Beyath's voice hissed.

Craig was about to reply when the entire room began to shimmer. Milliseconds later, he felt his body being pulled by some unearthly force as it was dragged into infinite blackness.

CHAPTER 14
2022 (fractured timeline 2)

Craig stared at himself in the cracked bathroom mirror and hated what he saw. He couldn't believe that the tough young Marine that he used to be had turned into the haggard looking wreck that was staring back at him.

Apart from the bleary, red-rimmed eyes and the sheen of oily, flop sweat which all stemmed from the leftover booze in his system, he didn't look like a well man.

Craig pulled down the baggy skin under his right eye and was alarmed at the colour inside his bottom lid. Craig was pretty sure that that shade of yellow wasn't a good sign.

The sound of a door slamming somewhere down the communal hallway caused him to jump. Then again, just about everything elicited that response. Craig looked at his watch and wondered, as he did most days, if it was too early to buy himself a quart of cheap tequila so he could keep his nerves in check.

He decided that seven-thirty was an acceptable time. The

fact that he hadn't attempted to eat breakfast yet, didn't faze him in the least. Craig walked into the only other room in the studio apartment and plopped himself down on the fold-away bed; the one that he hadn't folded away in over five years. Why would he? It wasn't as if he was expecting company.

The only person who had ever bothered to come see him was his adoptive mother Julie, but she seemed less willing to make the drive from Arizona with each passing year. She used to bring his monthly allowance herself as sort of a happy routine, at least for her.

To Craig, it had just felt like an intrusion.

After one particularly bad visit when she'd threatened to have him forcibly admitted to rehab for one last try, his vocal reaction had been so volatile as to have actually scared her. Julie then set up an automatic transfer from her bank and the visits decreased to about once every six months. Craig didn't care. He told her on many occasion that he didn't even need her money and that the Marine Corp disability pension was plenty enough for his needs.

That was a lie and despite all the rhetoric, he was secretly glad that Julie's money kept appearing in his account at Bank of America. He didn't know what would happen if she ever did cut him off completely. As it was, the combined funds were only just enough to keep a roof … well, a ceiling anyway, over his head, some food in his belly (on the rare occasions when he bothered to eat) and most importantly, his medicinal bottle (or two) of tequila.

Craig didn't even like tequila, but for some reason it

seemed to hit his bloodstream quicker than anything else, so it became his drink of choice. When his PTSD had become bad enough that the Marine Corp eased him out of active duty, Craig found that he actually felt better without any of the meds. Though they worked up to a point, he always felt lethargic and mentally dim.

Tequila made him feel strangely content even if the mornings were kind of rough. Craig found that even that drawback could be overcome simply by starting on the Mexican happy juice a little bit earlier in the day.

Craig's only attempt at moderation was to stay away from the far more economically viable, jumbo bottles at the supermarket. Even in his booze-soaked state, he knew that if he drank as much as he felt he craved, he could easily finish off one of Save-Aid's half-gallon, generic tequilas in one day. While it no doubt would soften the edges of his verve-wracked existence, the vomiting and malaise of the following day wouldn't be worth the short-term benefits.

There was also the subconscious awareness of what those half gallon bottles had already done to his life. When Craig's father had given up any pretence of being able to support his family, he'd turned to the big half-gallon jugs of wine. Those oversized bottles were indelibly linked somewhere deep in his memory banks to the horrific end that had befallen his parents at the hand of jug alcohol, depression and a snub-nose Ruger 38.

Craig slipped on his well-worn pair of jeans and a questionably clean promotional shirt for a now-defunct cable TV provider that he'd found at a local thrift store. He laced up his dollar store sneakers then went through his normal, at least for him, routine before stepping out into the big unfriendly world.

Craig lowered his head, resting his brow against the door and took a couple of extra-deep breaths while repeating the same mantra six times in a row.

"There is nothing to fear outside this room. The fear only exists in your head. Ignore the thoughts and you are safe."

After the sixth repetition, he unlocked three bolts and stepped out into the dimly lit hallway. As he made his way to the stairs (even one hundred repetitions of the mantra couldn't get him to give the rickety elevator a try), he kept his eyes focussed on his feet. The stairway was poorly lit and smelled of urine, stale cabbage and had a back odour of bleach. Craig made it to the front door of the building and stepped out into bright sunshine.

He'd broken his sunglasses months earlier and had to shield his eyes with his hands. He again reminded himself to buy a new pair before he seriously damaged his retinas. California sun will with do that.

Craig walked out of his building on the corner of South Bonnie Brae and 5th Street and made his way to the Save-Aid on 6th. The biggest obstacle of his day was getting across the busy street. There were lights, but at some point, a few months earlier, Craig had started having agonising leg and feet cramps at night that caused him pain throughout the next day.

Even though he was only in his early forties, his self-destructive lifestyle and limp, a result of the nightly cramping, reduced his walking speed by half. If he caught the pedestrian light just as it went green, he knew he had exactly fifteen seconds to get across the four-lane road. That was if he didn't encounter any other issue along the way such as tripping, which he was doing more and more often, or worse, running into another Save-Aid customers swerving along the street with their daily haul of cheap booze.

Craig managed the crossing without incident and walked the two blocks to the discount pharmacy. He stepped into the overly airconditioned store and while trying to shield his eyes from the impossible neon brightness, made his way to the liquor aisle. He passed two enormous display trees filled with cheap sunglasses, but by that time had completely forgotten (again) that he needed a pair.

As he did every day, Craig perused the Tequila section with the look of a man trying to find the right wine to pair with shellfish. For some reason, Craig loved to read the labels on the premium brands. They always seemed to describe a far better experience than he was used to. After reading one particular label that promised an unspoiled Agave field in the lee of a volcanic valley, Craig saw the price. Shaking his head, he reached for a bottle that had a plain white label with the word Tequila on it; nothing else. The name was promise enough.

Craig didn't care what bullshit they printed on labels. He knew what he was buying.

Half a day's relief from the chills, the nausea, the fear and worst of all, his own memories. The nastiest one was about the girl outside the fruit stand in Bagdad. He could still see her young brown face in his scope and thought that she looked pretty. Usually, the people in his sights had brown eyes, but hers were emerald, green. She seemed to be looking back at him, but Craig knew there was no way she could see him under his camouflaged netting on a rooftop over 800 yards away.

The young woman's face suddenly hardened as she raised her cell to dial in the number of the arming device that was strapped to a hidden IAD somewhere along the roadside. Before she could even press the first number, Craig's spotter gave the kill order.

The girl was dead exactly one second later. Her head momentarily distorted from the pressure caused by the shell entering between her green eyes then the back half of her skull exploded outwards in a spray of blood, bone and grey matter. Amazingly, she somehow remained standing for a couple of seconds before dropping like a sack of flour.

That was the memory that seemed to creep up on Craig the most, usually when he least expected it. It was as if a movie started playing in his head no matter where he was or what he was going.

The tequila helped that a lot. Craig found that as long as he kept his blood heavily diluted with the cheap spirit, the horrific, mental re-runs seemed to stay locked in the film vault. It was only on the days when for some reason he couldn't get his tequila fix, that things went to shit.

Craig approached the row of check-out counters of which only one was in use. Standing next to the checker was a fit looking man in his late fifties or early sixties. His grey hair was cut short, and his physique told of some serious training and stamina. The man was holding out his iPhone, showing the employee a photo.

Craig was too far away to hear what was being said, but when the checker nodded enthusiastically and pointed directly at Craig, every nerve ending went on high alert. He didn't believe that anyone was specifically looking for him, considering his life was disconnected from just about all strands of society. But when the older man's eyes locked with his, Craig knew that he was the target.

With uncontrolled PTSD fuelled by cheap tequila, paranoia was never far from the surface. Seeing the man step towards him was justification enough, even if unwarranted, to drop the plastic bottle and run.

Thankfully, the store had a side entrance that led to the parking lot. Craig managed to outrun his pursuer, despite his limp. Just as he reached the sliding glass door, he heard the man shout his name.

While that should have calmed the situation, it only escalated it with Craig. Before the shouting, he'd been holding on to the possibility that he was being mistaken for someone else. Once he heard his name, that ray of hope dissolved instantly.

Craig ran across the small lot and down an alley that smelled of rotting food and motor oil. He stepped behind a rusty dumpster and held his breath. He expected to hear footsteps approaching fast but didn't hear anything except the sound of rats devouring something only a few inches from his face within the metal receptacle.

He stayed where he was for almost half an hour before taking a quick peek down the alley. There was no sign of the man. Craig walked in the opposite direction from the pharmacy and backtracked his way to his apartment building. He'd never needed his morning drink as badly as he did at that moment but realised that his own safety had to take priority over his self-medicating.

He approached his building from the opposite direction than was his norm and was relieved to see that there was nobody waiting for him outside. Just as he started to relax, he heard a vehicle speeding up behind him. Craig tried to spin around, but his sore leg wouldn't take the torque and basically gave out. Craig fell to the ground only ten feet from the cracked steps that led up to the entrance of his apartment block.

In one last desperate attempt to get away from whomever was after him, Craig tried to drag himself across the sidewalk. He heard a car door opening and saw the grey-haired man running towards him. He knelt next to him and in a bizarre show of emotion, patted Craig's shoulder as a tear rolled down his cheek.

"Craig," the man said in a distinct Northern Irish accent. "You don't know me, but I swear to you that we are friends."

Craig tried to move away from the man. It was obvious that the stranger was insane or was some sort of lunatic. Craig's mind was definitely not working on all cylinders, but he knew that he'd never before laid eyes on him.

"My name is Lyle Connor," the man said. "You are Craig Edmonds. You were a Marine sniper. What you are currently living is not the life you were destined for. In your original timeline you have a beautiful wife, two adorable children and a golden retriever by the name of Steeler. You don't drink and your PTSD is almost completely under control. You live in Utah where you are the Deputy Sheriff of Kane County. I am here so that we can get you back to when and where you are supposed to be."

Craig didn't believe a word the crazy man was saying, yet his words hit him hard.

He started to cry, and what was worse was that he didn't seem to be able to stop.

Connor nodded his understanding of the other man's emotion and gently helped his friend to his feet.

CHAPTER 15

Connor sat Craig on the front steps of his building then retrieved a plain, brown paper bag from the passenger seat of his rented Lincoln. Once he'd helped Craig up to his apartment, he handed the bag to him. In it was a bottle of Heradura Gold.

Craig looked at the premium brand tequila as if he was seeing a mirage. Even back when he was still a Marine, he never drank the good stuff. Cuervo was about as up-market as he ever got. For some reason, he couldn't bring himself to open the bottle he was clutching. It was as if it would disappear if he tried to actually drink it.

Connor gently retrieved a semi-clean glass from the utility kitchen tucked at the opposite of the room. Though it was little more than a microwave and a single hotplate, it served all Craig's needs.

He gently pried the bottle away from Craig and twisted the top. He half-filled the glass and handed it back to him. Craig looked at it as if he wasn't sure what to do next. Connor helped lift the glass to his mouth. Once he tasted the familiar liquid, he downed it in one.

"Smooth," he said with a weak smile. "Very smooth."

"Glad you like it," Connor said as he placed the bottle aside. "You can have some more after we have a little talk. What I have to tell you is not going to be easy for you to comprehend. I'd like to ask you to not have any more to drink until I've finished what I need to say. I need your brain to be working while I talk to you. Is that acceptable?"

Craig looked longingly over at the bottle.

"What I have to say will only take about half an hour. Then you can drink all you want. Is that a deal?"

Craig looked to Connor, then to the bottle, then back to Connor.

He finally nodded.

*

It actually took close to an hour for Connor to finish what he had to explain to Craig, mainly because the other man kept interrupting and having Connor repeat what he'd just said.

Once the saga was complete, Craig just sat there looking perplexed.

"You must think I'm stupid or something," Craig said as he shook his head from side to side.

Connor produced his iPhone and played a short video that had been prepared especially for that moment. It showed Craig's graduation from the St George police training facility in St. George, Utah. In another, Jenny and his two children ran up to him and hugged him so hard he toppled onto a soft grassy knoll. In a third video, Craig was barbequing ribs and burgers as friends and family celebrated his fortieth birthday in the backyard of their bright yellow house ten miles outside Kanab, Utah.

"That can't be real," Craig said through choked sobs.

"I give you my word, that it is real. That's the life you were supposed to live until Beyath fucked up your entire timeline."

It took Craig almost two minutes before he could say anything.

'Okay," he said, his voice shaky and weak. "Let's say I believe the whole evil witch thing and how I was once able to kill her with help of this Ahone guy,"

"Ahote," Connor corrected him.

"Whatever. I still don't get what happened to put me here … like this. I mean how the hell did I go from being that," Craig pointed towards the iPhone, "to … to what I am now?"

"I don't blame you for having trouble with that part of your story. Did you understand the part about Ahote being taken by the witch, and that you went back with his son, Jack, to stop that from happening?"

"Kind of," Craig replied.

"Good. What happened was that Beyath …"

"That's the witch, right?"

"That's the witch," Connor confirmed patiently. "Beyath was able to go back still further and take Margaret before she could give birth to your future mother-in-law, Helena."

Craig nodded slowly despite all the names meaning

nothing to him.

"Keep going," he muttered.

"Stay with it," Connor said, reassuringly. "You're almost there."

"I hope so, cause this shit is starting to hurt my head."

"Not surprising, but if you can come to grips with the next part, I think you'll start to understand the whole concept."

Craig again nodded.

"With Margaret and the unborn Helena gone, your wife, Jenny, never existed, so there was nobody to save you back when you were twenty-two and starting to go off the rails. When you met Jenny in San Diego, she saw more in you than the guy who was slowly drinking himself to death. Motivated by her love for you, you found a reason to get help. Together, you and Jenny fought your demons, one by one until, with the right counselling and medication, you were able to make a good life for yourself and your family. In this timeline, with Jenny never having existed, there was nobody to give you the one thing you really needed."

"What was that?" Craig asked.

"Love," Connor replied.

"That makes me sound like some sort of a pussy," Craig observed.

"No, it doesn't. Having the strength to face the darkness inside showed almost superhuman strength. What you're doing now, slowly killing yourself, that makes you a pussy."

"Whoa!" Craig exclaimed. "That was low. I thought you were on my side?"

"I am. That's why I'm here. I want you to find that

strength again and join me in finding a way to go back far enough to destroy Beyath once and for all."

"What will that do?" Craig asked.

"If my people are correct, that should reset the timeline back to where it should have been from that point forward. You will have your family back, Ahote will be alive and well and all the entities that he helped destroy, will go back to being dead."

"And you're telling me that I'm the only one who can do all that?"

"'Fraid so," Connor replied with a shrug.

Craig sat staring at his lap for what to Connor, seemed like an eternity.

"What do I have to do?"

Connor smiled.

"You have to become the Marine you once were."

Craig looked over at the bottle.

"Not overnight," Connor added. "I have a team waiting for you back at Camp Pendleton."

"Oh shit, I can't go through bootcamp again," Craig said, cringing.

"This will make bootcamp look like a party weekend in Hawaii."

"You're not selling it very well," Craig mumbled.

"I wouldn't do that to you. At this point, I believe that honesty is the only reassurance I can give you. You are a certifiable alcoholic, your PTSD is running rampant, your health is for shite, and whatever skills you had, have been lost at the bottom of a thousand bottles."

"You make it sound like a bad thing," Craig said weakly, trying to be funny.

"We need you healthy, sober, in control of your emotions and able to wage a one-man war on one of the most supernaturally evil forces the world has ever known."

"Is that all?" Craig replied in an attempt at flippancy.

"Actually no. There's a whole other side to what you have to learn."

"On top of the list you just gave, how hard can that be?" he asked.

"You tell me," Connor replied. "As part of your training, you are going to have to learn how to time-walk."

"Wait a minute," Craig got unsteadily to his feet. "Why the fuck do I have to time-walk. I thought Ahote's kid was the time-walker?"

"He is, but you are going to have to go back to a time when he was only a small child. There's no way he can travel back to a specific memory moment."

"Just exactly how far back do I have to go?" Craig asked.

"1968," Connor replied solemnly. "You need to be there when Beyath takes Margaret and her unborn child ... your future wife's mother."

"I get the importance of that date, but even if I could time-walk, which I can't, 1968 is twelve years before I was even born."

"You're absolutely correct," Connor replied.

"So?"

"The folks at International Dimensions have come up with a possible solution."

"I get the feeling that I'm not going to want to hear this," Craig sighed.

"Actually, It's kind of interesting. Ahote's father is still alive."

"So?"

"He was the person who first instructed Ahote on how to time-walk. No one knows his age and he is pretty frail, but he's willing to work with us."

"Work with us, doing what?" Craig shot back.

"Finding a way for you to time-walk within his memory."

"Fuck this bullshit!" Craig stated as he stepped around Connor and grabbed the bottle. He didn't even bother with the glass. Craig just upended the Heradura Gold and swigged down a quarter of the contents.

"Better now?" Connor asked.

"Getting there," Craig replied with a slight slur.

"Don't you want to hear more about how you are going to time-walk back to 1968?"

"Nope," Craig announced as he took another swig from the bottle.

"Make the most of that. Tomorrow, you start detox," Connor advised.

Craig laughed then noticed that Connor was looking deadly serious.

"You're joking right?"

"Do I look like I'm joking?"

Craig stumbled to the door and yanked it open with the intent of getting away from the crazy Irishman. Two uniformed Marines stood blocking the exit.

"As I said," Connor sighed, "make the most of it."

CHAPTER 16

As if to prove to Connor that he still had some control over his life, Craig chugged the rest of the tequila straight from the bottle. He then smiled defiantly at the other man before dashing to the bathroom to bring up the tequila and what little food he'd eaten the previous day.

When Craig returned to the main room of his depressing hovel, he tried to give Connor and the two Marines the finger but had lost the ability to coordinate such a complex hand movement. He looked down at his hand as if wondering what had gone wrong, then slowly draped himself onto his bed where he proceeded to lose consciousness.

*

The drive down to Camp Pendleton took just over an hour and a half. Craig missed the entire thing as he was out cold, sitting upright between the two burly Marines within a grey, unmarked SUV.

As they approached the base, the driver turned off the 5 freeway, taking Las Pulgas Canyon Road to avoid using any of the main entry point to Camp Pendleton. Once they reached Basilone Road, they turned right and drove through the base until they arrived at C-Street.

The Marines hoisted Craig's inert form out of the back of the GMC and carried him into a non-descript white building. It was obvious that they were expected. A couple of orderlies helped move Craig inside, at which point, without any words, they nodded at Connor then left the building.

Connor stayed at Craig's side as he was wheeled down a long white corridor. At the end, they turned right and walked between a pair of unmarked swing doors.

Three men were waiting. All were dressed in scrubs and carried themselves with an air of seniority. One man stepped forward and shook Connor's hand. He was tanned, fit and sported only a small amount of grey at the temples. There was something about his dark eyes that announced that he wasn't to be fucked with.

"I'm Doctor Gainer. I assume this is the person we've been hearing so much about?"

"It is indeed," Connor replied.

"Did you tranquilize him?" Gainer asked.

"I did not. He did that to himself."

"What with?"

"Tequila," Connor stated.

"Make?"

"Heradura Gold," he replied, wondering why he'd been asked that question.

"Good. At least we don't have to deal with gut rot on top of everything else," Gainer said. "Right, leave him with us. We'll need seventy-two hours to get him to a point where we can start treatment. Before then, the poor guy will be completely out of it as he detoxes. You're welcome to hang around if you want, but it isn't going to be pretty. Judging by his pallor and his muscle loss, I'd say he's been drinking himself down the rabbit hole for a couple of decades at least."

"That's about right," Connor agreed."

"I checked out his record. It appears he started trying to drink away his PTSD while still active, right here in Pendleton. You'd have thought that we would have taken better care of our boys back then.

Connor didn't know what to say and chose to shrug. It was probably the best political response he could make.

"I've got to round up a few other people that are going to be needed during his training," Connor advised. "Do you feel that after seventy-two hours he will be able to understand what's being said to him?"

"I haven't been told what your debrief will involve, so that question is not one I can answer. If you are asking whether he will be able to understand basic sentences, then yes. Seventy-two hours will be enough time, though you won't be able to start any real training for at least a few weeks after that. You'll have to wait until he's on the right meds for the PTSD."

"Understood," Connor responded. "Will he at least remember me from today?"

"I doubt it. The booze will have frazzled his short-term memory."

"Just so long as he still has some of his Marine training in him," Connor said.

"I've got to say that, judging by the state of the guy, I'm not sure what it is that's expected of him. If you're hoping to get the same Marine back that existed when he was a sniper, I doubt that's ever going to happen. He drank to get rid of the memories and the pain, and in doing so, almost certainly screwed up a lot of the circuitry in his head. We're talking about wiring that can't be fixed."

"I understand that, but if we can at least get back half the man he used to be, that will hopefully be enough for what we need."

"I can't imagine what sort of operation would be satisfied with that sort of prognosis."

"Trust me, Doctor. You really can't imagine it at all."

As Connor was being driven away from the treatment centre, he felt guilty leaving his friend behind. Especially knowing what Craig was about to go through. Then again, if the treatment was successful, Craig would be given the chance of changing his entire life back to one where the demons and the pain are under control.

The SUV drove to the Camp Pendleton Airfield and deposited Connor next to a waiting, unmarked, Leer jet. The moment he climbed on board, the plane started to taxi and was cleared for immediate take off and vectored to Luke Airforce Base on the outskirts of Phoenix, Arizona.

For the next three days, Craig went through hell. He was strapped to a hospital bed and was transfused with a recovery cocktail of fluids, acamprosate and diazepam. The first twelve hours weren't that bad as he suffered through nausea, sweating and a growing headache. Halfway through the second day, the withdrawal symptoms started to kick in despite the closely monitored medications.

It started with tremors in his extremities then spread to his entire body which began to spasm. It was at that point that Craig began feeling an all-encompassing sense of anxiety. Even with the meds, he felt as if he wanted to jump out of his own skin. As if that wasn't enough, he began to hallucinate. At first it wasn't that bad. Craig heard music. It seemed far away and if he focussed hard on it. It sounded like some sort of a Dixieland melody.

Then things worsened.

Objects within the room started to change shape. The TV monitor that was suspended from the wall, became a looming head, its screen; a gaping, teeth-filled mouth. The plain white curtains transformed into the wings of a giant insect.

Nurses and doctors stopped by frequently and offered optimistic words, even though Craig never understood anything that was said until halfway through the third day.

By then, he was drained of all strength and was scared to close his eyes and sleep for fear of the nightmares that were waiting for him when he dozed off. Almost every dream put him back in Iraq. They all involved those that he'd shot. In the nightmares, they didn't die, at least not all the way. Each seemed to somehow be able to track him back to the base and attack when he was least expecting it.

One of the worst ones concerned a young teenage boy who reached for his cell phone as a convoy approached. He couldn't have been more that fourteen or fifteen and Craig's shot had been on target as always. A third eye appeared in the middle of his forehead as the bullet pierced his skull. The metal jacketed round ruptured and expanded, blowing out the back of the kid's head, leaving a hole the size of a cheeseburger.

The boy dropped before his finger ever reached the phone dial pad. In the dream, Craig packed up his gear and made it back to Bagram in time for lunch. Later as he was sitting in the rec tent watching one of the *Lethal Weapon* movies, he sensed something approaching from behind him. He turned and saw the boy he had just killed a few hours earlier. His head was distorted with the right side being at least a third bigger than the left. There was little blood coming out of the entry wound, but the damage at the back was causing blood and gore to pour out onto the floor.

Craig tried to get to his feet, but they kept slipping on the coconut matting. He glanced down and saw that it was covered in blood. The boy grabbed Craig by the neck and lifted him off the ground.

Even though the tent was packed with Marines, nobody seemed to notice what was going on with Craig. He managed to call for help, but all the troops were glued to the old movie.

The boy brought Craig's face close to his and for a brief second, Craig could actually see through the entry wound to the giant exit hole beyond.

Craig tried to shake himself free but couldn't as the boy's grip was like a vice. The worst part was when the boy started to smile. Instead of a mouth it was the top of a bottle. Craig suddenly realised that the boy planned to force him through the tiny hole. The boy's symmetrical mouth closed over Craig's nose, and he could feel himself being drawn into the glass-like aperture. Craig felt his flesh and bones being crushed as he was sucked deeper and deeper into the bottle.

Thankfully, Craig woke up, but even though he knew that none of it had been real, he could still feel the sides of the polished glass and it grated against his ruptured face.

*

On the morning of the fourth day, a man he hadn't seen before walked into his room and sat next to the bed. Craig had become so used to doctors and nurses stopping by to check on him, that he assumed this new guy was part of their team.

"I've got to tell you," the man spoke with a strong Northern Irish accent. "You look like complete shite."

Craig tried to hold his head up but couldn't manage it.

"You may not remember me," the man said. "But we have worked together a couple of times and I feel that we even became friends."

117

"I don't remember you at all," Craig managed to say through dry, chapped lips.

"There's a good reason for that. Are you ready to hear it?"

"What's your name?" Craig asked.

"Connor. Lyle Connor."

CHAPTER 17

It took three more days before Connor was cleared to start his debrief. Prior to that, Craig may have been able to listen and even respond, but the doctors assured Connor that the patient wasn't yet capable of retaining much of anything.

After a nurse removed Craig's restraints, Connor sat by the side of his bed and told him everything he'd explained in Los Angeles. Connor had hoped that his friend would have remembered at least some of their earlier conversation before bringing him to Pendleton, but it was clear that none of that data had taken root.

From his reaction, it was obvious that Craig recalled nothing and because there was no alcohol in his system to dull the impact, the words hit him hard. When Connor showed him the videos of him in the original timeline with Jenny and their children, Craig started to convulse.

Nurses and doctors appeared almost immediately. He was given an injection and the seizure began to abate.

Doctor Gainer stepped into the room and gestured for Connor to join him in the hallway.

"I know that getting this man back on his feet is a high priority, but if it's rushed, he could easily end up with brain damage which, I assume, would negate his value to whatever you people have planned."

"I was only trying to give him an overview of what had happened to him."

"I know that I can't be privy to the details of what you and he are doing here, but it's obviously complicated and too much for him to assimilate at this point. Is there a way to give it to him in smaller pieces? Bring him along more slowly?"

"Not really," Connor replied. "I can't tell you what this is about, but suffice it to say that people are dying every day because of a mission that was never fully completed."

"And my patient is the only one who can complete it?"

"He is."

"He's not in good shape," Gainer reminded him. "I understand the urgency ... at least I understand that there is an urgency, but if we overtax his brain and nervous system too early in the treatment, you could lose your last hope forever."

"How long do you think it will take to get him to a point where he can function well enough to be of use to us?"

"As I don't know what his use is, that's a hard question to answer," Gainer replied. "But judging by the additional security and secrecy that have been implemented on the base, I have to assume that whatever he needs to do won't exactly be a walk in the park."

"It won't," Connor said.

Gainer looked at the other man as he came to a difficult decision.

"Normally, with anyone suffering from severe PTSD, I would first recommend intense counselling before turning to serotonin inhibitors such as SSRIs or SNRIs. That slow but proactive response to the condition usually helps those that can be helped."

"What about the ones that don't have the luxury of a slow treatment?" Connor asked.

"Then it's a case of starting treatment as soon as possible before ..."

"Before what?"

"Before the patient starts self-medicating and most likely causing themselves even more harm. In mister Edmonds' case, he started using alcohol almost at the onset of the symptoms, refused treatment and has been slowly trying to kill the pain ever since. I don't know if we can bring back the man you need. There's no question that there has already been some brain damage. How severe? We won't know for a while."

"How long does your recommended treatment take?"

"Anywhere from six months to ..."

"That's not good enough," Connor interrupted. "We need him yesterday."

"I am under orders to do whatever it takes to get him on his feet, but I have to again warn you, if we move too fast, we might just break him. If we can somehow expedite the treatment and get him back on his feet, I can't help feeling that whatever you people have planned for him, will most certainly result in catastrophic damage. He could well have a complete psychiatric episode and be left unable to help you or himself."

"Doctor Gainer," Connor sighed. "Let me be blunt. We don't care about his longevity. If he successfully completes the mission, none of this will matter."

"That's pretty cold," Gainer replied. "I swore an oath to ensure that I would give my patients the best care I possibly can. Knowingly sacrificing one of them for some secret military gain is abhorrent."

"I can't argue that point without breaching national security protocols of at least two countries. Please believe me when I say that if you get that man on his feet, and he succeeds in his mission, you will never regret your actions for one second."

Connor wished he could have added that the doctor wouldn't regret his actions because, if Craig succeeded, the entire timeline would revert back to the original destiny meaning the doctor would never even meet Craig, let alone treat him for PTSD and alcoholism.

"I will start him initially on an SSRI and will get him up to a high dose over the next two weeks. That should at least mask the PTSD anxiety. The alcohol addiction, at least chemically, is out of his system already, but the effects and the cravings will remain for a long time. I will also expedite his psychological counselling so that it can begin at the same time as the SSRI reaches full dosage. You should be able to begin the training, soon after that. That means that for the next two weeks, mister Edmonds will be left in peace while we do what we can to put some of the pieces back together. Is that a deal?"

"Do I have a choice?" Connor asked.

"Not if you don't want him to stroke out and end up in a vegetative state."

Connor considered the doctors words.

"It's a deal, but in two weeks, he's mine no matter what condition he's in."

"How the hell do you sleep at night?" Gainer asked.

"I don't."

*

Two weeks later, Craig was released from the 'clinic' and moved into a residential house on the outskirts of the base. Connor gave Craig the master bedroom while he settled for one of the guest rooms. Like most base accommodation, the house was furnished with an eye to functionality rather than décor.

Prior to moving in, a temporary three-metre fence was erected to keep any neighbours from being able to see what was going on within the property. Connor felt that was overkill as the house was the only building on a street that branched off De Luz Road and dead-ended against an untamed hillside.

Since being weaned off benzodiazepines as his system was introduced to an ever-increasing dose of venlafaxine, Craig had started to feel less like jumping out of his own skin. The anxiety was still there, but he was starting to be able to control the attacks, at least some of the time.

Even though all traces of alcohol were out of Craig's body and the symptoms of the initial detox had subsided, his cravings for a drink were as strong as ever.

With only a few days before Craig started what Connor referred to as bootcamp 2.0, the hardest thing for Craig to handle was the boredom. He wasn't allowed to leave the house without Connor, and only then if it was to hike back into the surrounding hills.

The house had no TV or Wifi connection. One ethernet line was wired to Connor's bedroom and that space was kept under lock and key, even when Connor was in it. The idea was to ensure that Craig couldn't watch or hear anything that could remind him of death, violence, war or even conflict.

Gentle Native American flute music wafted through the 1950s prefab. Every day, a petite Taiwanese woman named Tia Lash came by and led Craig into the beginning stages of mindful meditation.

At first, Craig had resisted having never in his life believed in anything as 'dumb' as spiritual awakening. Despite his balking at the very notion of meditation, Tia Lash had already managed to lead him into a meditative state by the second day. When the young Asian announced that she was going to use acupuncture as an aid to help Craig relax more fully, he at first refused to let her anywhere near him with her selection of needles. It was only after Connor agreed to be a guinea pig, and let Tia insert a dozen of them into his neck and scalp, that Craig finally let her go to work on him.

Craig had just finished a thirty-minute meditation and acupuncture treatment when there was a knock on the door. Connor opened it and stood aside as Julie Maddow stepped into the house.

Craig hadn't spoken to his adoptive mother in months. He'd been too far down the rabbit hole to bother with anyone who wasn't there to provide either alcohol, or occasionally, food.

The last time Julie had seen Craig, he'd looked bad, but nothing like the gaunt shell of the man that she saw in front of her. Even though she wasn't Craig's birth mother, she'd raised him after his parents died when he was only five. She tried not to show the shock she was feeling but couldn't stop her brown eyes from misting up.

Craig tried to get to his feet, but Tia forced him back onto the yoga mat so she could remove the final few needles.

"Does that hurt?" Julie asked.

"Not if she does it right," Craig replied.

Tia flicked one of the needles.

"Ouch!" Craig cried as he glared up at Tia. He immediately saw her scowling expression.

"Which of course she always does," he added, resulting in a brief smile and nod from her.

Once the needles were removed, Craig got to his feet and gave Julie a huge hug. Before she could say anything, Craig started to cry.

"Jesus," he said, shaking his head. "I'm sorry. My emotions are all fucked up."

"Ditto," Julie said, as she wiped a tear from her eyes.

Connor and Tia discretely left the two alone so they could talk privately.

"Can I get you anything?" Craig asked. "I should warn you, the choice is fruit juice, herbal tea or water."

"I'm fine," Julie said, drying her eyes on a sleeve. "I'll have something later when I bring my stuff in from the car."

"You're staying?" Craig asked, surprised.

"They didn't tell you?"

"You'd be amazed how little they tell me. They're treating me like some sort of fragile flower. They're scared that the least thing will cause me to wilt away and die."

"You look as if you came close," Julie commented.

"So they tell me."

Craig gestured to the dining area, and both sat on vinyl, floral-patterned chairs.

"What exactly did they tell you?" Craig asked.

"Connor came to see me when you'd first been brought here to Pendleton. He told me that your PTSD had gotten worse and that he'd made arrangement for you to get specialised treatment on the base."

"What else did he say?"

"That you are needed for some sort of a mission and that it was very high priority as well as being top secret."

"And that was it?" Craig asked.

"He asked if I was willing to stay here with you during your training," Julie added. "He never told me what exactly you were training for."

Craig got to his feet and walked down a short hallway to Connor's room then knocked loudly on the closed door. He heard a deadbolt being withdrawn just before the door opened.

"What am I allowed to tell her?" Craig asked expecting to be told that he had to keep his mother in the dark.

"Everything," Connor answered. "She's been vetted and knows not to say anything about what we're doing here."

"Isn't that a little risky?" Craig asked.

"She's staying until the training is complete. Shortly after that, the mission will begin, at which point either none of this will have happened, or we will be so royally screwed that what she knows will be the least of our problems."

"I don't want her hurt any more than is necessary. I've already put her though enough pain."

"That's easy then," Connor said, smiling, "don't fuck it up."

Connor closed the door in Craig's face.

CHAPTER 18

Craig explained why he was there and what was expected of him. He told Julie how, in the original timeline, he lived in Utah with his wife Jenny and their two children, Sally and Tim.

"I'm a grandmother?" Julie whispered as a tear rolled down her cheek. "Is any of this possible? It sounds like something out of a science fiction movie."

"I'm as shocked as you are," Craig explained. "I have no memory of any of it because, if what Connor is saying is true, I never lived that life. Whereas, in this one, I'm just some dipshit soldier that couldn't live with what he'd done during the war, in the original one, I have the perfect family and even save all their lives."

"But which one is real?" Julie asked, confused.

"They both are," Connor said as he stepped into the room. "I don't make a habit of listening to other people's conversations, but I wanted to make certain that Craig here got the facts straight. What we do when fighting interdimensional incursions is beyond the understanding of most people. When you add in time-walking, it's almost too complex for anyone to get their head around."

"It's certainly too much for me," Julie said. "Is it true that you want Craig to go back in time again?"

"Yes."

"And he is going to be the one doing this … time-walking?"

Connor nodded.

"And you know how to do this?" Julie asked Craig.

"God no. Apparently I have, or did have, some sort of predisposition to basic time-walking back when I was a grunt, but if I did, I sure as hell am not aware of it."

"Is Craig expected to go back in time and fight this witch person by himself?" Julie asked.

"No. We both will," Connor stated.

"We?" Craig said, surprised.

"Who else did you think was going to go back with you?" Connor said, smiling.

"But you …" Craig started to say.

"I'm what?"

"You're old," Craig finished the thought.

"I don't think you're in any position to point fingers, do you?" Connor replied. "And just so we're clear on everything, I may have a few extra years on you, but I'm as fit as I was when I was on active duty."

"I thought you still were on active duty," Craig volleyed back.

"Different employer," Connor grinned.

"Well now that you've completely muddied the water,

129

can I speak with my mother in private?"

"You only had to ask," Connor said as he headed back to his room.

*

Craig spent the next week reconnecting with Julie while perfecting his meditation skills and adapting to life without tequila. Each day, he felt the anxiety fractionally diminish. It was always there in the background, but at least it no longer felt as if he was possessed by it.

After a weekend spent hiking with his mother and barbequing steaks for the three of them, Craig was ready for the next phase of his rehabilitation. He was still terrified of what was in store, but at least he felt that his mental state was up for the challenge.

At eight o'clock Sunday night, Craig was collected by two Marines in camo fatigues. He was driven to an empty barrack building which would be his home for the next four weeks.

The moment he walked into the long, rectangular building, the memories of when he'd first joined up after 9/11 came flooding back. Even though it was a different barracks, the rows of metal bunk beds and adjoining footlockers looked identical.

The smell was the first thing that hit him. It was a mix of shoe polish, disinfectant and sweat. Even though he had the building to himself, he chose the same bed as he had all those years ago.

He couldn't believe that he was back in bootcamp, albeit an abridged version. They didn't have the option of putting him through a full thirteen weeks of hell, but then again, they weren't trying to mould a young man into a killing machine. Their goal was to get Craig fit enough, and trained enough, to handle one single mission.

The one and only concession to his age and mental state was that Craig was permitted to return to the house at weekends so he could spend time with his mother and Connor. The hope was that by doing so, the training wouldn't break his sprit as was the underlying intention of the regulation, full-length, bootcamp. It was the tried and tested method of taking rebellious teenage drive and spirit and redirecting it into subservient responsibility mixed with a healthy dose of Marine Corp pride.

One of the biggest differences in Craig's bootcamp experience was the lack of a screaming staff sergeant. While normally the perfect cure to any new recruit's thoughts of independent thinking, the plan was not to break down Craig Edmonds; rather, to find a way to instil the confidence and self-assurance that he had had twenty years earlier.

That said, the four weeks was still a brutal shock to a forty-year-old alcoholic whose only exercise had been to stumble a few blocks each day to buy booze and occasionally food.

Thanks to all the walking Craig had been doing in the hills behind the house, he had already built up some stamina and was no longer getting winded every time he got out of bed.

After eating a breakfast of oatmeal, blueberries, honey

131

and almond milk in a makeshift dining room at the back of his barracks, Craig showered and headed out to one of the athletic fields on the base. The track was closed whenever Craig was training so that there was no interaction with anyone else but his trainer.

Staff Sergeant Jance Fall met him at the bleacher end of the oval track and gave him a quick once over. It was obvious that she wasn't impressed with what she saw.

Craig pretty much did the same and decided that he was glad he didn't have to come up against Sergeant Fall in the field of battle. The woman was beyond formidable. At a smidge over six feet and weighing in at a well-muscled one hundred and seventy pounds, Jance would never be called petite, not that she had ever wanted that. She had wanted to be a Marine from the age of ten. Now thirty, she had risen to the rank of staff sergeant quickly and knew that she couldn't rise a lot farther without additional educational accreditation so she could apply for officer candidate school. The fact was, she didn't want to be a commissioned officer. She was happy doing exactly what she was doing, especially as it guaranteed three squares a day and a roof over her head.

Having been raised in New Orleans and evacuated during Katrina, she knew how it felt to be homeless. The government had given her and her family temporary housing but at the same time, through lots of subtle ways, they were constantly reminded that a black family without a fixed address of their own, hardly counted for much of anything.

Jance enlisted when she was seventeen and had considered the Corp to be her home ever since. The great thing was that the Corp went out of its way to ensure that she kept on feeling that way. They'd always been straight-up truthful with her, and she'd done the same back to them.

This assignment was one of the few times that she was tasked with work that she didn't understand. She had become one of the Marine's best trainers. Even though she'd never held a weapon in her hand before her seventeenth birthday, by the time she was twenty-five she could outshoot just about anyone they tried to match her with.

One look at the man standing in front of her and she knew there had to be one hell of a back story to justify trying to get his sorry ass in shape. She'd rarely seen a soldier that had deteriorated as much as Edmonds. She had read his file, at least the part she was permitted to read, and knew that he'd been an MOS 0311 (Marine speak for a sniper or 'killer-shooter'). But that had been twenty years ago. Why they wanted to focus that much attention on a jarhead that looked like he'd been living rough for way too long, just didn't make sense.

Bringing an old shooter back to the Corp that was filled with young talent that had fresh fire in their bellies was just fucked up. Then again, hers was not to reason why, etc. She just had to find a way to get the dinosaur back on his feet.

"Your expression says it all," Craig stated as he offered his hand.

"So does yours," Jance replied. "They tell me I have four

weeks to get your body and your mind back in shape."

Craig nodded.

"Have you done any track work since leaving the Corp?"

"No Ma'am?"

Jance studied him for a few moments.

"I'll tell you what. Let's you and I try for one mile on the track and see what exactly I have to work with. That's four laps give or take a foot or two. Think you can handle that?"

"Not well," Craig replied honestly.

"We're not aiming to beat any records today, so we'll take it real easy. We'll start off with a slow jog and see how you do."

Craig took off the Corp sweatshirt he'd found in his footlocker, stepped onto the synthetic track surface and tried to do a few knee and leg stretches. He was embarrassed at how hard even that motion was to perform.

"Slow and steady," Jance said as she began a gently trot.

Craig ran alongside her and was shocked at how foreign it felt to be running. He hadn't even run across a street in at least fifteen years and felt it in every muscle and bone. Even with the forgiving surface of the track, each stride felt percussive and damaging. Halfway around the first lap, he was in pain. His breathing, which he thought had improved with his hikes, was raspy and shallow.

He had to bend over and hold his knees just to get enough air in his lungs to make a difference.

Jance retraced her steps and stood next to him just as his body was wracked with a wave of phlegmy coughing.

"Oh, this is going to be a veritable delight," she said as

she shook her head from side to side. "One thing is for certain, I sure as shit am glad that I'm not you."

*

That night, Craig fell asleep the moment his head hit the pillow.

He was back in Iraq and was being driven down a back street in the Baqubah neighbourhood just north of central Bagdad. The road wasn't paved, and the fine sand was even getting through the Humvee's air filtration system.

In the dream, Craig felt confused. He didn't know where he was being taken and couldn't understand why he was wearing only shorts and a t-shirt.

The Humvee took a right turn onto an unmarked gravel road then pulled up in front of a single-story, concrete building with a flat roof and no visible windows.

"Good luck Gunny," the driver said.

"Good luck for what?" Craig replied. "I don't even know why I'm here."

"You're here to verify your kill-count," the driver replied. "You knew you had to do this at some point, so just get it over with and you can get on with your life."

Craig stepped out of the vehicle and was shocked at the heat and the force of the Shamal wind that was peppering him with fine sand. He turned his head to avoid getting any in his eyes and saw that the building's door was open. He turned back to say something to the driver, but the Humvee was gone.

Craig approached the entrance.

"Hello?" he called out.

Receiving no reply, he stepped up to the doorway and peered inside.

"Hello?"

The wind was making it hard to hear anything, but for a brief second, Craig thought he heard a young girl crying. The inside of the structure was completely dark. Even the light from the doorway didn't seem to be able to penetrate the gloom.

Craig stepped in but stayed close to the door. He heard a rustling sound from deep within the blackness then glanced back to make sure his exit remained clear.

The doorway was gone.

He couldn't see a thing and tried to feel for where he knew the wall must have been, but there was nothing but air. Craig had to make a concerted effort not to panic and kept telling himself that he had to be safe, otherwise they wouldn't have simply dumped him there.

As Craig tried to decide what to do next, a smell reached out from the darkness. It was putrid and reeked of rotten meat and dry earth. It was so intense that Craig started to retch violently and was doubled over by the spasms.

It wasn't until he noticed a dim illumination deep within the dark interior that he was able to get himself under some degree of control.

A tiny flicker of light was suspended in mid-air above the veiled form of what looked to be a young woman. She was kneeling with her head bowed. A black scarf covered her hair and draped all the way to the dirt floor.

"Hello," Craig called to her.

The woman didn't move.

Craig walked slowly towards her, wishing he had some sort of weapon. He couldn't help feeling that he should be in full dessert kit and armed to the teeth. Having nothing on but a pair of shorts and a t-shirt made him feel practically naked.

Craig stopped a few feet away from the woman. He noticed that her arms were especially thin, almost as if she was severely malnourished.

"Don't be scared. I'm not going to hurt you," Craig advised.

The woman slowly lifted her head.

"Not going to hurt me?" her frail voice repeated as the black scarf fell to the floor.

The flickering light suddenly intensified, clearly illuminating the woman. Her skin was grey and seemed to be pulled tight against her distorted facial bones. In the middle of her forehead was a single black hole where the round that killed her had entered her brain.

Craig tried to step back but was unable to move. As he looked on in horror, the woman turned her head giving Craig the full view of the exit wound. A piece the size of a grapefruit had been blown out of her skull. What remained within was black and lifeless.

"I'm sorry," Craig managed to say as he gasped for breath. "I was just doing my ..."

Before he could say any more, the light above the woman

extinguished and another one took its place a few paces to the left.

This time it was a teenage boy. He too was kneeling but wasn't wearing a scarf. Craig could see the damage to his young head without needing to get any closer.

"Jesus," Craig gasped just as the boy looked up at him.

Suddenly, dozens of flickering lights appeared, each one revealing a kneeling corpse beneath it.

Craig started to back away but sensed more lights coming on behind him. Soon he was surrounded by countless, illuminated bodies that, one by one, raised their heads and looked directly at him with dead, unseeing eyes.

Craig felt his mind start to drift away, trying to save his sanity from the horrific reality. Just as he felt that he could somehow cope with it all, the corpses all stood up, then as one, began to shuffle towards him.

*

Craig woke up screaming.

The barracks was in complete darkness, and it took him almost a minute before he pieced together where he was and that the whole thing had been a dream.

Still shaking from fear and with his t-shirt soaked through with sweat, Craig stumbled to the far end of the building, to what would normally have been a communal latrine.

He flipped on the lights and blinked until the neon bulbs stopped flickering. The space was designed to be used by as many as thirty men at a time with no privacy of any kind. To see it empty just seemed wrong.

Craig splashed cold water in his face then studied his features in a worn mirror. He did not like what he saw. Somehow, getting clean and sober had made him look even older. At least when his main diet was alcohol, his face had held a puffiness that disguised the wrinkles and sagginess.

"You look terrible," he said to his reflection.

The neon lights began to flicker, and the ceiling ballasts began humming. Craig's mirror suddenly darkened. He leant closer to see what was wrong with it when a pair of wizened arms reached out and grabbed him by the head.

Craig tried to break away, but it felt as if he was wrestling with steel girders. As he struggled, Craig could distinctly smell a mix of something fetid and ancient. Something that couldn't possibly be alive.

The claw like hands began dragging Craig's face closer to the mirror which had stopped reflecting altogether. Instead, within the scarred, stainless-steel frame, a figure began to form. Though Craig had never, at least in the current timeline, seen Beyath, he knew that it was her.

She was naked and her blackened skin, if that's what it was, was pulled so tightly against her bones that she looked more like the creature from the Ridley Scott film, *Alien*, than anything that had ever been human.

As Craig's face reached what should have been the surface of the mirror, Beyath's mouth began to open. Within her maw, were rows of pointed black teeth. Her tongue looked like a strip of shoe leather as it whipped from side to side.

Craig felt Beyath's jaws clamp against his head as the razor-sharp fangs sunk into his face.

*

Craig woke up screaming.

Again.

CHAPTER 19

For the first week, Jance focussed on getting Craig back into a condition where a slow quarter mile wouldn't cause him to hack up a lung.

She started by having him walk four times around the track four times a day. On the fourth day, she had him walk his first circuit then increased the pace to a slow half-jog until Craig made it the full way around the track. At which point she had him complete the session with two more laps at a fast walk.

Between track work, Jance pushed him through some not very demanding sets of push ups, sit ups and chin ups. On day one he'd managed one of each, though the chin-up did require a little help from her.

By the end of week one, Craig could run a slow half mile once a day and manage five reps of the ground exercises, even though the chin ups were still giving him trouble. Over the years, Craig had seemingly lost almost all upper body strength.

Jance decided on another tack.

At the end of his second Friday session, she used Velcro straps to tie his wrist to the bar and had Craig, instead of trying to pull himself up so that his chin was in line with the bar, simply raise his knees to his chest and hold the position for five seconds. She made him do five sets of what seemed like a ridiculously simplistic exercise, then called it a day.

With his arms and shoulders feeling like they were on fire, he returned to his private barracks, had a quick shower and changed into civies.

"How's it going?" Connor asked as Craig walked through the front door of their shared house.

"She just tied me to the chin up bar and made me lift my knees up in the air."

"Sounds to me like you were having trouble lifting yourself up."

"Maybe," Craig replied.

"You're gonna feel that tomorrow."

"Tomorrow? I feel it now."

"Trust me. That's nothing," Connor said with a grin.

"What have you got planned for the weekend?" Craig asked.

"This is one of the last ones you'll have with any free time, so I thought the three of us would do something a little unusual. It'll test your calming abilities, your reflexes and will give you a chance to put some of those muscles into practical use. It's supposed to be gusty as hell tomorrow so it should be a blast."

"Care to give me a clue?" Craig asked.

"No. I don't want you stressing about it all night. Trust

me when I say that you will have fun and leave it at that."

"You do realise that I'm now capable of stressing over what I don't know as well as what I do know, don't you?"

"But you're handling it. That's the difference," Connor replied.

"That's debatable."

"Why don't you go say hello to your mother," Connor suggested. "She's on the patio. I'll bring you a tomato juice."

"With vodka?" Craig asked.

"With a lemon wedge." Connor answered.

Craig pulled a face then stepped out through the sliding back door.

"I'm making chili for dinner so don't fill up on crisps," Connor called after him.

"What the hell is a crisp?" Craig asked.

"Sorry. Potato chips," Connor replied in an exaggerated American accent.

*

Craig was deep asleep and dreaming that he was on a passenger jet that was lost and trying to find its way back to the runway. It was somehow taxiing along Wilshire Boulevard in Los Angeles, then made a sharp turn on Western before having to stop at a red light.

Connor shook him awake.

"Come on lad, It's time for your little surprise."

"I was having a nightmare," Craig said as he tried to open his eyes.

"That's normal considering what you're going through, though the shouting was interesting."

"I was shouting?"

"At the top of your lungs. But you're awake now, so grab some breakfast and toilet time so we can get a start."

"Can you at least tell me where we're going so, I know what to wear?" Craig asked.

"You've only got jeans and T-shirts, so I'd say, go with that."

It took Craig an inordinate amount of time to get dressed as his arms were so sore and stiff that he could hardly use them.

After a quick breakfast, Julie drove as Connor gave directions. They descended out of Camp Pendleton and took the 5 freeway south. They got off at Harbor Drive in Oceanside, then pulled up next to a place called the Oceanside Broiler.

"I'm not hungry," Craig said as he looked at the shabby looking eatery.

"That's good, because we're not here to eat."

Connor led the other two to a security gate and used a key fob to open the lock. They walked down a steep ramp to a floating jetty. On either side were slips for both sail and power boats. Connor checked the key ring and confirmed it said Q Dock-Slip 29.

"This is it," he exclaimed happily.

Craig looked down at a small sailboat that looked to have been shat on by every passing seagull for its entire long life.

"I'm not going out on that," he stated categorically as he

stared up at the top of the mast.

"I took you sailing once on Lake Powell, remember?" Julie reminded him.

"I do. And do you remember that I almost drowned?"

"I remember that you were standing at the front showing off and fell in, but I can't say I remember the drowning part," Julie replied.

"Well, I could have drowned," Craig replied indignantly.

"Come on then, let's get this fine vessel out of the harbour and see what she can do," Connor said as he jumped on board.

After retrieving the tired-looking seat cushions from the lazarette, Connor proceeded to ready the sails. The one on the boom was easy. All he had to do was removed the stained cover as well as a couple of bungie cords that were holding the mainsail in place.

Getting the jib ready was even simpler. Connor explained that it was self-furling, so it was basically always rolled up and attached to the jib halyard. Neither Craig nor Julie knew what he was talking about so just nodded back at him.

Next, Connor lowered the 15HP Johnson outboard into the water. He checked the portable fuel tank and gave the black primer bulb a couple of hard squeezes. He then pulled the manual choke halfway out and attached the kill switch 'key'.

"How the hell do you know how to do all this?" Craig asked.

"Let's just say that part of my training involved small craft operations."

Craig nodded as if Connor's words meant something.

It took three tries, but finally, with a burst of blue smoke, the outboard fired up. Connor checked and saw a steady stream of water shooting out the back of the engine, meaning the cooling system was working. He kept it in neutral until he'd squared away the lines.

"Julie, would you please go forward and free up the bow line. Don't do anything else. Just hold it until I say so, then I want you to give it a gentle toss onto the jetty."

"What do you want me to do?" Craig asked.

"Until we are out of the harbour, I'd like you to sit right there," he pointed to a spot in the cockpit. "And try to keep from being in the way."

Connor then freed up the stern line and looked towards the bow to make sure Julie was ready. He could see that she was doing exactly as requested and was standing at the bow while holding the dock line in her hand.

"Right," he shouted to her. "Give it a toss onto the jetty but try not to let it fall in the water."

"Now?" she asked.

"Now."

Julie gave it a light throw and the line fell in a tidy pile only inches from the cleat.

"Beautiful," Connor said to her. "Why don't you come back here for a while."

Even as she made her way astern, the bow began to gently drift away from the dock. Connor threw his line ashore then immediately put the tiny engine into gear.

The boat moved out of the slip and Connor, using the

wood tiller, guided it into a graceful starboard turn.

"Julie, can I give you another assignment?"

"Yes, captain," she replied with a smile.

"On either side of the boat are two fenders."

Julie looked over the side and saw the sausage-shaped devices that kept the boat from rubbing against the dock.

"I see them," she announced.

"I'd like you to please lift each one over the lifeline so it's not dangling into the water once we start to heel."

Julie didn't need to be told twice. By the time she'd finished they were approaching the breakwater and open sea.

"You'd best sit back down until we clear this channel," Connor advised. "Though you can't tell from here, there's usually a cross-current at the mouth of the harbour which can make for an interesting ride for a few minutes."

Craig looked forward and couldn't see anything but a light chop. He decided that Connor was just showing off to his mother.

Then, as they reached the harbour mouth, it felt as if they were in the middle of a whirlpool. The little boat was tossed from side to side as four-foot waves hit her from all directions at once.

"Maybe we should go back," Craig suggested just as a wave drenched him.

"This is nothing," Connor reassured him. "We'll be through it in a couple of minutes."

Sure enough, as they left the breakwater in their wake, the chop evened out and though still rough, the waves were coming from the same direction and could be easily anticipated.

Connor waited until they were clear of the harbour entrance as well as any other shipping, then, swapping places with Julie, he unwound two wraps of the starboard jib sheet from its winch.

"What do those do?" Craig asked.

"I thought you were a Marine?" Connor joked. "Shouldn't you be a little more familiar with boats?"

"I wasn't that sort of Marine," he replied.

"Craig, did you see what I just did? I'd like you to do the same with that winch behind you, but in your case, I'd like you take it off the winch entirely and lay it loose on the sole … the floor."

Craig did as requested, but just as he leaned over towards the winch, a huge wave violently rocked the boat sending him to his knees.

"Okay Julie," Connor said as he pointed to a wind direction meter mounted at the front of the cockpit. "This arrow here shows the wind direction, and this pointy thing is our bow. What I want you to do is to slowly steer the boat so that it's pointing right into the wind."

Julie started to pull the tiller the wrong way, saw her error and recovered immediately. Within seconds she had the bow facing into the wind.

Connor released the furling line from the cleat lock, then began pulling on the jib sheet as fast as he could. At the bow, the jib unrolled from the reefing stay, revealing a triangle of dirty, white sail.

After getting the main sail up, both it and the jib were flapping in the stiff breeze while the boat remained under the power of the outboard.

"See that red, curly chord attached to the engine?" Connor asked Julie.

"This one?" she said pointing to the kill switch.

"That's it. I'd like you to simply pull it out. Then I want you to turn the boat slowly to port … left."

Julie followed the instructions, and the little engine went silent. Connor Immediately winched in the jib and it started to fill with air. Before long the boat was heeling and moving forward under its own power. The lack of engine noise coupled with the sound of the Catalina's bow slicing through the water was a strange sensation after the noise and smell from the outboard.

Connor let out the main sheet so that the sail could fill enough for the tell-tails to lie flat against the canvas. The boat heeled even farther and speeded up at the same time.

Because the boat was heeling to port which was the same side Craig was sitting on, he was being pushed hard against the fibreglass seat-back and was clearly pinned down.

"You may find it more comfortable sitting on the high side with us," Connor suggested, laughing at Craig's situation until he saw that all the colour had drained from the other man's face.

Suddenly Craig began convulsing.

"He's having a seizure!" Julie shouted as she crawled over to Craig's side of the boat. She tried to put her arms around him but the motion of the bow rising and falling through the swells kept knocking her off balance."

While Connor pointed the boat back towards the marina, Julie finally managed to get both arms locked around Craig so that his thrashing was minimised.

"Please hurry," she called to Connor.

*

While his body continued to spasm, Craig's mind took him back to the Al Asad airbase outside Bagdad. He had just finished a special op where he'd been providing cover for a rush transport out of the country. He wasn't sure why they'd needed a shooter just to sit in the back of one of the Humvees, especially as there wasn't much he could have done even if they did get attacked.

Next to him in the rolling hot-box was a guy in his thirties. It turned out that he was the special cargo everyone was protecting. He was dressed in camo, but it looked store bought rather than government issue. His hair was brushed straight back and looked as if there might even have been some product involved in keeping it in place.

Despite every attempt to look civilian, the guy had CIA written all over him.

"How the fuck do you guys put up with the heat?" he asked.

"We can handle the heat just fine. It's the bullets and shrapnel that spoil the place," the driver shouted back.

"How long have you been in the suck?" Craig asked him.

"Long enough to know I don't ever want to come back."

They ended up having as much of a conversation as you can when one person is protecting their identity and the reason for being there.

As they got closer to the gates to the airport, the man sighed and turned to Craig.

"I heard this morning that my son was born last night."

"Shame you weren't there," Craig said back to him.

"You know it."

They drove through the security gates and out to sector D where some of the 'special' aircraft were parked.

They drove right up to a 747 operated by Universal Cargo. The plane seemed to have been waiting for their passenger. The moment he stepped inside, the door swung closed, and the giant aircraft started to taxi.

Craig said he'd walk back to where he was barracked and let the Humvee drop him off on the tarmac. For some reason, Craig wanted to see the plane take off.

Unlike a commercial airport outside the war zone, planes taxi as fast as is safe and get in the air as soon as they can. The jumbo jet reached the end of the runway then powered up its four jet engines.

Despite its size, it lifted off surprisingly quickly and tried to gain as much altitude as it could. Craig knew that they wanted to get out of missile and gun range as soon as possible, but the 747 looked like it was climbing way too steeply. Suddenly it tilted to the right and almost seemed to come to a complete stop in the air. Even though Craig wasn't a pilot, he could still recognise a stall. The jet banked sharply the other way and dropped sideways, crashing onto the area between the active runways.

Craig had to have been at least a mile maybe even two from where it hit, but he could feel the heat from the explosion. He turned away from the burning wreck and headed back to his barracks, trying not to think of the new mother and child waiting excitedly for the man back stateside.

CHAPTER 20

Connor and Julie sat in the makeshift waiting-room of the base's 'private' treatment centre.

"It was too soon to take him off the base," Julie said.

"It wasn't exactly a stressful outing," Connor replied.

"It obviously was for him. Don't forget that a few days ago, he couldn't walk to the car without getting out of breath. He should have stayed in the house and rested some more."

"He's a Marine," Connor stated.

"He was a Marine. Now he's an alcoholic."

"A recovering alcoholic. There's a huge difference," Connor said offhandedly. "I'm living proof of that."

Julie tried to hide her surprise, but apparently not very successfully.

"You look as if I just admitted to eating puppies for breakfast," Connor said.

"I'm sorry. I just assumed that with you being Craig's minder, you would be …"

"Be what?" he asked with a smile. "A saint? I'll have you

know that I haven't had a drink in over thirty years, and if it makes you feel any better, having suffered from the same afflictions as Craig makes me the perfect person to guide him through the ordeal."

There was a lengthy silence between them.

"I didn't mean any disrespect, I just never considered you as someone who has to … or at least had to … climb into a bottle to avoid confronting your demons."

"You'd be amazed how many soldiers go down that road rather than having to face what they've done and what they've seen. Alcohol never requires you to question your actions or relive the darkest moments of your life. In my day, there was no talk of stress syndromes within the military. Breakdowns were basically forbidden. Which, in retrospect, explains the high rate of suicides and drug addiction back then."

"How did you get help?" Julie asked.

"I didn't get help. Help got me," Connor explained. "Very like Craig, at least in the timeline we're hoping to resurrect, a young woman I met just after my discharge must have seen some good in me. She dedicated herself to getting me help and staying by my side through the worst of it. It shouldn't come as much of a surprise to you that Northern Ireland in the 80s wasn't exactly the most nurturing environment for someone trying to stay away from alcohol. The mere fact that I was in counselling made me a target for just about anyone looking for a punch-up."

"I had no …"

"Nobody ever does," he replied, cutting off her words.

"What happened to the young woman who helped you through all that?"

"She married me," he replied.

"How does she feel about you doing the work you're doing now? I would have thought she'd keep you away from anything this … dangerous."

"She probably would have but she was killed in the IRA bomb attack in Brighton in 1984," he replied.

"I'm confused," Julie said. "When we first met, you said that you knew Craig in the original timeline, and that if it hadn't been for your wife not wanting you to time-walk anymore, you would probably have gone on that mission instead of my son."

"I did say that, and it's true. The problem is, in this timeline, because Ahote never existed past 1978, I was never recruited to work with him. So, instead of Lisa, that was my wife's name … instead of Lisa spending most of the 80s with me, living on the International Dimension's estate in Scotland, I was still active in the military, and because of my special knowledge of the IRA, got assigned as extra security for the Conservative Party Conference in Brighton.

"As a treat for Lisa, I was able to finagle a temp job for her as a night, room-service waitress at the hotel where I was stationed. As I was on the same shift, we could at least get an occasional glimpse of each other. Normally I wouldn't have bothered, but I knew how much she loved Thatcher and would enjoy being involved in all the shenanigans."

"I should probably know the answer to this, but … what happened in Brighton?" Julie asked.

"Lisa was in the basement of the hotel having a break when, at 2:54 in the morning, an IRA bomb brought down one entire chimney column which collapsed through the centre of the hotel. I was one of the first people who reached the rubble pile and was the one who found her. Amazingly she was still alive, at least she was for a couple more minutes."

Julie was about to say something when Dr Gainer appeared.

"He's resting now," he reported.

"What happened?" Julie asked. "One minute he was fine, the next, he started having a seizure."

"He's a broken man, both physically and mentally. I told Connor that if he was pushed too quickly something could snap and it did."

"How bad is he?" Connor asked.

"If you're asking if I can get him back on his feet for this one mission, then the answer is yes."

"And beyond that?" Julie asked.

Dr Gainer shrugged. "It'll be a miracle if he doesn't have a complete psychological breakdown before all this is done with."

Julie was ready to ask more questions, but Connor cut her off.

"Thank you, Doctor."

Julie waited until Dr Gainer had left the waiting area before turning on Connor. "What did the doctor mean about his having a complete breakdown?"

"I told you everything I knew about Craig's condition

when I flew out to talk to you. You've seen him. He's a wreck."

"Yet, you're going to use him anyway, no matter what it does to Craig."

"We have to. There's nobody else. Please believe me when I say that I would do anything to not have to put him through what's ahead."

Julie studied Connor for a moment.

"I believe you."

They sat in silence for a few minutes as each battled with their own internal thoughts.

"Did I understand you correctly earlier?" Julie asked. "Did you say that your wife died thirty-seven years ago as a direct result of what Craig is currently involved with?"

"Yes," Connor replied. "That's another reason why this mission is so important to me. If we can somehow defeat Beyath before she is able to take Margaret and Ahote, the damage she has done to the timelines will be reversed and the original one will be reset. Lisa will have been with me in Scotland on October 12th, 1984, and though the Brighton bomb will still have taken lives, hers won't have been one of them."

"I don't think I can get my head around this."

"For what it's worth," Connor explained. "Up until Beyath started messing with the timelines, it was far more straightforward."

"For you maybe," Julie said, shaking her head. "May I ask one more question?"

"Of course"

"If in this timeline, Lisa wasn't around to save you from your addiction, how did you get yourself clean?"

"I got help," Connor said.

"From who?"

"From the Church. For some reason, they took an interest in me and managed to get me clean and sober before I did any more damage to myself."

"So, you believe in God?" Julie asked.

"Heavens no! But I do believe that there are some decent people down here on earth and I was lucky enough to run into a few of them."

CHAPTER 21

Weeks later, after recovering from his mini meltdown, Craig had the chance to show off his real talent, at least the one he'd had when he was last on active duty.

With bootcamp completed, the withdrawal symptoms mostly behind him and his PTSD under medicated control, Connor decided that it was time to get Craig onto the shooting range.

Connor wanted to start off with some rifle practice and presented Craig with something he was very familiar with. It was a well-used, M40A3 with a M8541 Sniper Day-Scope. Craig had used an identical rifle throughout most of his time in Afghanistan and Iraq.

Craig cradled it in his arms and was overwhelmed with conflicting emotions. It felt very familiar, yet at the same time, almost alien. Since his breakdown and subsequent discharge, he hadn't touched any firearm. He couldn't. Even watching a firefight on TV would open the memory wounds and take him to a frighteningly dark place.

Holding the Remington and smelling the mix of gun oil

and steel took him back to times and places he never wanted to think about again.

"Try a few shots," Connor suggested, as he handed him a preloaded magazine.

"NATO 7.62?" Craig asked.

Connor nodded.

Craig automatically slammed the magazine into place. He wasn't even consciously aware of doing it, it was so deeply ingrained in his muscle memory.

Connor had chosen a small rifle range just off 15th Street within the camp. It was little more than a cored-out piece of land with a level surface at one end and a rough, hill-backed area down-range. Shooters were expected to bring their own targets. Connor had 'borrowed' a rickety sawhorse and assembled it at the far end of the range. After clipping a sheet of paper onto the wood frame using oversized crocodile clips, Connor produced a can of black spray paint and added a dark splodge roughly the size of a human head.

Once Connor was behind him, Craig extended the bi-pod legs then lay down on the rough earth.

"Distance?" he asked Connor.

"This is your show. You're the one who needs to gauge his own distances."

"I'm going to say it's around two-fifty," Craig said to himself.

Craig chambered a round with the bolt action just as he'd done thousands of times before. He sighted the black painted area, blinked once, then breathed out.

He fired.

Connor lowered the binoculars he'd used to verify that the target had been hit.

"You missed."

Craig looked through his scope and confirmed that same fact.

"It must be the scope," Craig stated.

"Yeah, that's the likely reason," Connor replied with a smirk. "Try it again."

Craig took much longer for the second shot. He waited until both his heartbeat and breathing had slowed considerable before firing.

He missed again.

"I don't know what's wrong," Craig said.

"I do. You can't fecking shoot."

Craig scowled and got to his feet. He folded in the bi-pod legs and walked towards the target stopping fifty feet further along the range.

He fired a single shot.

"You missed," Connor called after him.

Craig continued walking towards the target, firing every twenty-five feet or so.

All were misses. He stopped about a hundred feet from the target and emptied the rest of the magazine. None hit the target.

Craig stormed back to where Connor was standing and tossed the rifle to him.

"I suck. You better have a back-up plan that doesn't involve me, or we're all screwed."

"Tell me when your little pity party is over so we can

continue," Connor replied.

"Continue what? In case you haven't noticed, I can't hit a thing."

Connor tossed the M40 back at him then handed him a fresh magazine.

"Try again. I have a feeling you'll do better."

"I don't see why." Craig said, sulkily.

"Trust me and give it one more go."

Craig flipped out the bi-pod legs and again lay on the ground. It was obvious that his heart wasn't in it. He didn't even bother modifying his breathing or heart rate. He simply fired.

"Better," Connor said.

Craig checked his scope and verified that he'd hit the dark area, just left of dead centre.

Confused, he fired off six more shots, one after the other. Craig didn't even wait to hear Connor's spotting report and checked his scope. There was only one hole on the target. It was too big for one round to have made. It was the size of a silver dollar.

"Nice work, Marine," Connor said from behind where Craig was lying. "Seven for seven, all dead centre."

"But ... how ...?" Craig couldn't understand what had just happened. Same weapon, same distance yet he'd missed every shot with the first magazine and had bulls-eyed all seven on his second try.

He looked back at Connor and saw that he was grinning like a deranged Cheshire cat.

The penny dropped.

"The first magazine had dummy rounds, didn't it?" Craig asked, already knowing the answer.

"It wasn't as if I was going to hand over a fully loaded M40 to a depressed alcoholic without first checking that he wasn't going to point the gun at himself, or worse, at me."

"I thought we agreed that you weren't going to play any more games with me?" Craig asked.

"That wasn't a game we just played. That was me making sure you weren't a danger to anyone."

Craig let his words sink in.

"Time was, I would have felt the difference in weight from the rounds."

"That time was many years and many bottles ago. The important thing is that you seem to still be able to shoot."

"Paper," Craig commented.

"You'll have no trouble pulling the trigger if you're facing that fecking witch."

"I'll hardly be facing her if I'm going to be shooting at this kind of distance."

"You're very unlikely to have that luxury, but because your skill was in long range targeting, I wanted you to get a feel for a long gun before we start working on your handgun skills."

"Does anyone really believe that a gun is going to stop her this time. She seems to have upped her game."

"To be honest with you, none of us have a clue what she's going do when we try to stop her taking Margaret. The biggest problem is that back in 1968, there was no International Dimensions so we can't hope to get any help with manpower or equipment. It's basically just going to be you and me."

"That's if I can do this time-walking trick," Craig commented.

"It's way more than a trick, and as I've already told you, you supposedly already have the knack, you just don't know it."

"Strangely those words do little to make me feel better. Telling me that I will be good at something I've never done before doesn't exactly sound like the best scenario for attacking Beyath."

"I couldn't agree with you more. Hopefully, next week, once we get to Sedona and you start working with Ahote's father, things will start falling into place."

"Was that falling or failing?" Craig asked with a forced smile.

"Hopefully the former," Connor replied.

*

That night over dinner, Julie advised that she was going to head back to her home in Mesa, Arizona the following morning. She could see by the look on Craig's face that he wasn't happy with the news.

"You don't need me hovering over you anymore. I think it's best for you to focus on your training for your last few days here. Once you are in Sedona, I'll only be two hours away from you, so I can always come up if you need me."

"I'm not sure how that will fit in with his training,"

Connor chimed in.

"We'll work it out," Craig said, smiling.

As Julie took some plates to the kitchen, Craig turned to Connor. "Why can't my mother visit me in Sedona?"

"Because the location of the safehouse and the identity of some of the people who'll be there is highly classified."

"I thought Julie was cleared to know everything?"

"She's cleared to know everything about you," Connor replied. "Not everything about International Dimension."

"Oh," was all Craig could say.

"What you need to be focussing on is making sure that Jack and Hania are able to teach you how to time-walk as well as Ahote."

"Who's Hania?" Craig asked.

"Hania is ... or was, Ahote's father and is the only person besides Jack and you who can time-walk in this timeline."

Julie reappeared and began scouping fruit salad onto dessert plates.

"I hope I didn't open a can of worms by suggesting I come up to Sedona to visit," Julie said.

As Connor was looking down at his plate and couldn't see her face, Julie winked at Craig.

CHAPTER 22

The rest of the week was filled with handgun training using an outdated, 45 calibre, Colt 1911. On the second to last day, Craig underwent an extensive psychological and physical examination to try and determine just how much he could accomplish without breaking.

"There's not one single hole that that doctor didn't stick a camera into," Craig complained as he got in Connor's car after the final test.

"I hope you asked for some copies of the pictures. I hear they make lovely Christmas cards."

After one last night in the house, Connor and Craig gathered their meagre belongings and drove to the base airfield. Another private, unmarked jet was waiting for them. This time it was an Embraer 300E.

"I expected something a little bigger," Craig remarked.

"Sedona is in the mountains and has a short runway, so we had to downsize," Connor commented. "I hope you can forgive us."

The flight took just over an hour. It was Craig's first visit to Sedona, at least in the current timeline, and he was stunned by the raw beauty he could see through the aircraft window. The Embraer banked left over Bell Rock then joined the traffic pattern for the Sedona Rock Creek airport, runway 21.

The first thing Craig noticed as he stepped out of the plane was the sky. It was a shade of blue that, even as a boy growing up outside Phoenix, he'd rarely seen. The vibrant colour against the red mountains was as striking as was the temperature. The air had to have been at least twenty degrees cooler than at Pendleton and smelled clean with only a trace of raw earth and pine in the background.

A car and driver were waiting and drove them through the north end of town. They stayed on 89A until they reached Old Indian Road then turned right and wound further into the red hills until they reached a private drive with a rusted chain-link gate blocking any access.

The driver entered a code into his phone and the obstruction swung silently open. The property beyond the gate had been kept as natural as possible. The road was unpaved but well-graded so, despite raising a cloud of dirt in their wake, the going was relatively smooth.

They rounded one last bend and saw the house. Craig had assumed that a gated estate was bound to contain some sort of lavish home.

Instead, fifty metres ahead of them was a log cabin perched close to a sheer drop down into the valley that had been carved out of solid stone by the humble Rock Creek.

Not only was the house underwhelming, but it also

appeared to be in poor repair. The slate roof was missing tiles and looked to be sagging badly on one side. The only window facing the driveway was filthy and cracked.

"You've got to be kidding," Craig said. "We can't stay here. The place is a dump; even for me."

"I have to admit, it's not exactly what I was expecting. Most of the InDem properties are comfortable to say the least. This place is ..." Connor searched for the right word.

"Shit?" Craig offered.

"That'll do."

The driver stopped the car in front of the only door, and the moment Craig and Connor stepped out of the vehicle with their duffle bags, he put the SUV in gear and, without a word, drove back down the dirt road.

Connor and Crag looked at each other with real concern.

"Well, that was rude," Connor said.

"What do we do?" Craig asked. "Go in?"

"We might as well. Normally I'd knock but I'm afraid that a good rap on that door could bring the whole structure down."

Craig pushed the door. The rusted hinges squealed in protest as it reluctantly swung open.

Craig stepped in and looked around what appeared to be the only room. He wasn't impressed. The entire house was about three hundred square feet. There was a ratty looking sofa against one wall, a log burner in one corner and a rickety dining table with two chairs. On the wall that would have looked out onto the Oak Creek valley had they bothered to install a window, there was a floor to ceiling, framed, promotional poster for a hot air ballooning event that, according to the wording, took place in 1987.

It was faded, torn and the frame's glass was cracked and discoloured. Craig couldn't understand why anyone would want to keep such a tacky item.

"This can't be the right place," Craig stated. "I thought we were going somewhere where I could learn how to time-walk. This place doesn't even seem to have a toilet."

Craig noticed that Connor was smiling.

"What?" Craig asked.

"Nothing. It's just that I've seen posters like this before."

"And that makes you happy?" Craig asked.

"I think it's going to make both of us happy. The thing you have to remember about old poster is that you have to learn how to appreciate them."

"What the fuck are you talking about?" Craig said getting frustrated. "It's a crappy old poster that along with the rest of this dump should be set alight and burned to the ground."

"You could do that," Connor agreed. "Or you could do this."

Connor stepped up close to the poster and lay both his palms against the cracked glass. The poster suddenly retracted a few inches then slid silently into the wall. The two were then faced with a brightly lit alcove decorated in brushed steel and highly polished maple.

Connor stepped inside. Craig didn't.

"Are you going to join me or do want to spend your time in the shack?"

"Join you where? You're standing in what looks to be a

nicely decorated closet. Why would I want to join you in there?"

"I think you'll find it's a little more than that," Connor said, grinning.

Craig shrugged, stepped inside and the door immediately slid shut. There was a whirring sound then, only a few seconds later, the door opened again.

Connor stepped out of the 'closet' and into the most striking space he had ever seen. Craig followed him and stared, open-mouthed at his surroundings. The room had been carved out of the hillside. Natural woods and fabrics had been used to make the space look comfortable, modern and yet somehow cosy, which couldn't have been easy considering that it had to be at least a thousand square feet. Apart from one narrow section which housed what Craig realised was the elevator shaft, the wall was made entirely of glass and looked out and down upon Sedona in the far distance.

"Why didn't we see this place from the road?" Craig asked. "We had to have been facing this part of the cliff."

"You were; however from the outside, you would have seen only red rock. The technology is what's currently being used to design the next generation of stealth fighter."

Craig spun around and came face to face with a distinguished looking man in his early sixties. He was immaculately dressed, was wearing what Craig could tell were seriously expensive clothes and spoke with a refined English accent.

"I know you," Craig blurted out. "You look so familiar.

Were you on TV?"

"I have been retired from public view for a few years now, but for a time, I did have some degree of notoriety."

Craig gave him a puzzled look.

"Craig, before you say anything else stupid, I'd like to introduce you to Edward Jenkins. He was the Prime Minister of the United Kingdom from 2006 till 2014."

"On what show?" Craig asked.

Connor shook his head. "I guess there was still one last bit of stupidity waiting to be set free. Edward wasn't in a TV show. He was the actual Prime Minister of the country.

"Shit!" Craig said. "Sorry about that. I was right though; I knew you from TV. You were on the news all the time."

"Regrettably, yes," Jenkins replied. "How was your trip from Pendleton?"

Connor was about to reply when Craig asked, "What are you doing here, and what is this place?"

"You didn't explain any of this?" Jenkins asked Connor.

"This is my first time here as well, so I'm as surprised as Craig. I knew we were going to a safehouse, but I never expected anything like this," Connor replied.

"Well, Mr Edmonds, you are standing in one of International Dimensions strategic launching points, which as Connor just mentioned, is also a safehouse."

"What makes it safe?" Craig asked.

"Nobody knows it's here."

"And you need that because …?" Craig asked.

"There are times when we need to meet in complete privacy outside the UK. This property, like many of the others, is located within an area that contains one of the Earth's energy vortexes. Have you not felt a sense of peace and contentment since you landed here?"

"I've been a bit busy being pranked, but now that you mention it, I do feel relaxed."

"That's because of the local vortex," Jenkins explained. "What most people don't know is that these vortexes exist because they are centred around an active dimensional portal, or time-space rift."

"Suddenly I'm not feeling as relaxed anymore," Craig responded.

Jenkins laughed. "You will once you come to terms with what all this means. Before that, why don't I give you a quick tour. Connor, the parcel arrived earlier today, and I placed it in the den."

"I'll go check it out," he replied.

"What's the Prime Minister of England got to do with hunting down a witch?" Craig asked.

"I'm not the Prime Minister anymore, and International Dimensions is devoted to far more than the Beyath situation, though, with her having taken Ahote out of the timeline, our work has become far more difficult."

"How did you get involved?" Craig asked.

"It's a long story, but I'll make you a deal. If, after you face off with Beyath, you are unable to revert the timeline, I will explain everything to you. However, my hopes are that you will be successful, and once Ahote is back and your grandmother-in-law is safe, you will have no need to know anything about any of this."

"What if I don't come back at all?" Craig asked.

"That is not an option I wish to contemplate," Jenkins replied. "Let's start the tour with the lower floors so we can end up back here in time for lunch."

The complex was comprised of three floors. The lowest one was set out like a barracks with one giant room filled with row after row of army cots taking up most of the space. Showers and toilets were at the very back and a canteen with a full kitchen were built into the rock on the far, right-hand side.

There were no windows and the wall where they should have been located, housed a giant video screen which, as Jenkins demonstrated with his iPhone, could be used for any viewing function. Craig's favourite though was when Jenkins put in on *exterior theme* mode and selected Arctic Winter. It looked as if they were standing before a giant picture window staring out at a violent blizzard. Craig even started to feel cold, such was the definition of the playback.

"Why do you need a space for so many people?" Craig asked.

"Because the dimensional rift is so strong here in Sedona, we use this complex as a prepping area for incursions," Jenkins explained.

"You make that sound so normal," Craig replied.

"Sadly, it has become a more frequent need. Imagine if social media informed everyone about an incredible new fishing ground where you were guaranteed to catch as many fish as you want."

"The place would become overwhelmed in no time,"

Craig commented.

"Well, to a lesser, but more sinister, degree that's what we are fighting. Somehow, knowledge that our world is a wonderful hunting ground has spread interdimensionally. Our job is to ensure that the hunting trips are either stopped before they enter our dimension or are disrupted before the entities can stray too far from the portal."

"Why isn't everybody aware of this?"

"Mainly because the entities ensure that they remain concealed so as not to frighten off the prey."

"And when you say prey ...?

"I mean us," Jenkins replied. "Humans."

Craig stared, dumbfounded.

"Anyway, that's enough small talk," Jenkins continued. "Let's show you the next floor."

Unlike the stark, military-like décor of the lower-level barracks, the next one housed twelve identical suites that looked out over the red rocks and the valley. They each contained a modern, luxurious bedroom with an adjoining sitting area. An ensuite bathroom, was fitted with a rain-forest shower, a jacuzzi tub, and had the same view as the bedroom.

"Isn't this all a little grand considering the way the troops have to sleep on the lower floor?" Craig asked.

"When the soldiers are here on mission, the upper floors aren't in use. The top floors were designed specifically so that our patrons as well as leaders of supporting countries can meet here in complete comfort and security in order to discuss current and future strategies."

"Where do all the aides and assistants stay?"

"In most cases, because of the highly secretive nature of the topic, the leaders come here unescorted."

"How does that work?" Craig asked. "Don't they need interpreters and stuff?"

"Again, because of the sensitivity of the subject matter, there are no peripheral personnel. As for coping with the different languages, we all seem to be able to understand each other perfectly well."

Craig mulled that over.

"So which level do Connor and I get to sleep in?"

Jenkins laughed.

"We will all be here on this floor," he replied. "Let's finish off the tour so that we may have lunch. I don't know about you, but there's something about the vortex here in Sedona that makes me perpetually hungry."

"I could eat," Craig agreed.

Beyond the incredible living room, the main floor contained a chef's kitchen, a formal dining room that could seat twelve, a meeting room with every digital conferencing toy imaginable and, at the back, there were six bedrooms for the supporting staff.

"How do you ensure that the staff keep what they see and hear to themselves?"

"They're not just staff. They are all highly trained operatives of International Dimensions."

"You seem to have thought of everything," Craig commented.

"If that was the case, we wouldn't be where we are

today. What Beyath managed to do to the timeline had never been imagined. Partially because we thought she was dead, but also because, which in retrospect was stupid of us, we believed that she could only move through time in a linear fashion. Her twenty-five-year cycles of feeding had gone on for centuries without ever straying from their linearity. Not one of our computer modelling forecasts ever came up with a variant where she could skip back and forth though, thankfully, we believe that she can only do so within her original timeline."

"Why is that important?" Craig asked."

"It's important because, so far, she has always managed to get back into the mirror and resurface in a different time. It's believed that, if she is killed outside the portal in 1968, she will cease to exist in any form, within any timeline."

"How will you know?" Craig asked.

"We might not. Sometimes, we just have to act on faith as well as science."

"I suddenly feel like a lab rat," Craig replied, shaking his head.

Jenkins wasn't sure how to react to Craig's odd comment.

"You mean way more to us than that," Jenkins stated. "Let me show you one last room."

They walked down a short corridor and stopped at a closed door. Jenkins knocked.

"Come in," Connor replied from within the room.

Jenkins opened the door and stood aside so that Craig could enter. It looked more like a study in an English manor house. Wood panelled walls held framed paintings by local Sedona artists. A fire burned in a stone hearth. It took Craig a moment to realise that it was, in fact, a holographic fire and was giving off neither heat nor smoke.

In front of the fireplace were two leather armchairs. Connor was in one, but Craig couldn't see who was in the other one because the chair back was facing him.

"Craig," Connor said gesturing to the other chair. "I'd like you to meet your guide for the next phase of your training."

Jack Winston rose with difficulty from the other chair and faced Craig.

"So this is our saviour," he said with obvious sarcasm. "As you probably already know, I am, or was, Ahote's son."

Craig looked at the sweaty, dishevelled and severely overweight man and was not impressed. After shaking the stranger's hand, he surreptitiously wiped his palm on his jeans.

"Pleasure," Craig mumbled.

"Then there's the other half of the training team," Connor said as he gestured to the back of the room where a dark sofa sat in shadows. "I'd like you to meet Ahote's father, and Jack's grandfather. Craig, this is Hania. It will be his timeline you will use when travelling back to fight Beyath."

Craig stepped closer and almost gasped when the man leaned forward into the light.

He was the oldest human being Craig had ever seen.

CHAPTER 23

Later that day, when they were alone, Craig looked at Connor with great concern.

"Ahote's son was bad enough, but that old man looks like he could drop dead any minute."

"He doesn't need to be that strong, you will be the one doing most of the work. He just needs you to join your spirit with his so you can travel back using his life-force memories."

"How do you know this is going to work?" Craig asked.

"We don't."

"That was reassuring," Craig said. "Let me ask that a different way. How many people have time-walked using a second person's memories?"

"You know the answer to that. Sitting in that study are the only two people who even know how to time-walk and neither of them have tried using another person's spirit force to go back."

"Why can't Hania go back like Ahote used to do. I know he's old now, but if he walked back to 1968, he'd be middle aged."

"Unfortunately, the stress of the time-walk would impact his current body, not the one in the past. Maintaining the connection, especially while hosting you within his own time bubble would most likely kill him."

"That brings up a good question. Even if Hania isn't the one who creates the time-walk, what would happen to me … to us, if he did die here while we were still in 1968?"

"Nobody knows," Connor replied. "The best case scenario is that the time-walk bubble would immediately cease to exist and both you and I would find ourselves right back here in present day Sedona."

"And the worst case?" Craig asked.

"It's completely theoretical as nobody has ever done this before."

"What's the worst case, Connor?"

"It's possible that if your host dies, and as you never existed in 1968 …"

"Go on."

"You would cease to exist altogether. In any time."

"Nice," Craig said shaking his head. "What about you?"

"I would either revert to my actual age in 1968," Connor replied. "Which means I would be eight years old and basically live most of my life over again from that time on, or, according to the brainiacs that try and work out all this shite, I would find myself back in present day, as you see me now, but with no memory or experience of having worked with you or International Dimensions in any time-line."

"Neither of those options sound that appealing," Craig

responded.

"Can't argue that," Connor said, smiling.

Craig felt anxiety building up at the base of his spine. Chills began fluttering across his back as he started to hyperventilate.

"Have you taken all your meds?" Connor asked.

Craig nodded.

"Wait here for a minute," Connor said as he stepped out of the room. He needed to speak to Jenkins.

Craig lowered his head between his knees and felt his grip on his emotions start to slip. He'd had the sensation a lot over the past years, but this was the first time since his treatment and giving up alcohol. He felt his eyes begin to tear. He tried calming his breathing but sensed that he was spiralling out of control.

Connor reappeared.

"Let's get out of this dump and get you some fresh air," he announced.

"I thought I couldn't go out in public?" Craig asked.

"That was while we were at Pendleton. Too many people could have recognised you and started asking questions. I just checked with Jenkins, and he didn't see any harm in us checking out the town."

"Can I have a drink?" Craig asked.

"Do you really want one?" Connor asked.

"No. I just wanted to hear what you'd say."

"I'd say, 'dry your eyes, you sniffling mess and let's go have some fun'."

By the time they walked out of the log cabin, a red jeep

Wrangler was parked in front of it with its engine running. There was no sign of how it got there.

Connor seemed to know where he was going and headed south on 89A until they reached the 179. He turned left and after a few hundred feet pulled into the parking lot for the Tlaquepaque Arts and Shopping Village.

"I think you'll like this place, and we may even be able to find you something to help with those left-over nerves of yours."

"At a mall?" Craig asked.

"It's a little more than a mall."

Connor led Craig through Tlaquepaque's hacienda style archway to a central plaza built around a percolating, multi-tier fountain. Soft, Native American flute music gave the area the perfect aural backdrop.

They walked from one art gallery to another, each one seemingly more impressive than the last.

Craig had never experienced authentic tribal art before. His only point of reference was the cheap reproduction crap sold at the tourist shops in the wrong part of Old Scottsdale.

After about fifteen minutes, Craig realised that he was feeling calmer. The beauty of the paintings, the pottery and the sculptures was having a profound effect on him. He'd never in his life considered that art could be enjoyed at such an emotional level. One where the spectator could actually feel the passion and deep respect that the artist held for what he was creating.

After walking out of the last gallery within that section of the plaza, Craig felt as if a new door had been opened within his consciousness. One that he hoped he could nurture into remaining a constant part of his life.

Connor led him to an inviting looking Mexican restaurant tucked away at the back of the faux village. The hostess showed them to a table on the terracotta-tiled terrace.

"What can I get you boys?" a waitress said only a few seconds later.

Craig looked up at her and felt his heart do a back-flip. The waitress was tall, had long dark hair held back with a turquoise hair clip. Her eyes were startlingly blue, especially against her darkly tanned face. There was a trace of Native American genetics in her nose and strong chin which just added to her striking appearance.

Danielle looked down at Craig and felt her universe shift as well. There was something about Craig's eyes and the way he was looking at her that sent a warming shiver along her back and neck.

"What's your name," Craig asked.

"You go first," she replied.

"I'm Craig, and this wreck of a man is Connor."

"Well, hi there, Craig and Connor," she replied. "I'm Danielle."

For the longest time, Craig and Danielle simply stared at one another. If Connor hadn't ordered when he did, he wasn't sure if they'd have stopped.

"I'll have a Coke."

Danielle tore her eyes away from Craig.

"Sorry," she said, flustered and blushing.

"I'll have the same," Craig replied. His voice sounded

raspy and dry.

Danielle headed back inside to get their drinks, but just before entering the restaurant, she turned and glanced back at Craig.

"Don't do anything stupid," Connor said.

"Why not? She's gorgeous."

"You're married and have two children. You're up here to prepare for the hardest battle you have ever fought in your life, so that you can get that family back."

"Look," Craig said. "I know that in a different timeline I supposedly have a family, but I'm not in that timeline, in fact, from what you've told me, my wife has never existed in the here and now. You can't expect me to be faithful to someone who I have never met."

"I just think that you should be careful. What if this mission works out and you do return to your wife and kids? What if there is some spark of memory about you having been with someone else?"

"I thought you said that I would have no memory of any of this because none of what we are doing in this timeline will ever have actually occurred."

"I did say that, but the fact is, nobody that I'm aware of has the slightest clue as to the chemistry of this whole alternate timeline crap. In fact, because of your experiences with so many different timeline variants, you are probably the world's leading expert on the subject."

"But I don't know anything about it. You're the one who had to explain everything to me."

"Exactly," Connor nodded. "Nobody understands what

impact these fluctuations in time are having on us or what part of each variant we may still retain in our memory."

"I don't feel as if I have any part of it in my memory. God knows I've tried to think about my other timelines, but I get zip. Not even a glimmer of anything."

"That doesn't mean that there isn't some repressed memory in there somewhere."

"So, you're saying that I shouldn't be interested in Danielle because of a repressed memory about a wife I have never had in this lifetime, just in case when I go back to a different one, some flicker of remembrance may possibly flit through my head?"

"Yes," Connor replied, emphatically.

"Here's your Coke, Craig," Danielle said as she leaned close to him to place it on the table.

Her bare arm touched his, sending a tingle all the way up to his shoulder.

"Do you want to meet up sometime?" Craig said, ignoring everything that Connor had just tried to tell him.

"I'm here every lunchtime except Sundays," she replied as she placed Connor's drink in front of him.

"I was thinking more like something a little more private."

"I'll tell you what," she said in a lowered voice. "I get a break every day from three to four in the afternoon. If you happened to be here at that time, I might let you walk me around Tlaquepaque."

"Deal," Craig replied, grinning as he watched her walk away.

"Just don't blame me if this whole thing literally comes back to haunt you," Connor stated.

"Will I be allowed to come back here one afternoon?" Craig asked.

"We'll have to discuss that with Jenkins, but considering that there's a good chance that neither of us will survive this mission, I doubt he'll refuse you something as basic as wanting to spend a few minutes with a beautiful woman before you die."

"So, you agree?" Craig said. "She is beautiful."

CHAPTER 24

The next morning, Craig's final stage of training commenced in earnest. He, Connor, Jack and Hania met in the conference room so that Jenkins could outline the specifics of what was expected from Craig and how he imagined that could be achieved.

As Jenkins talked about the part where Craig would have to time-walk within Hania's timeline, Jack started fidgeting and shaking his head at almost everything he was saying.

"I'm sorry," Jack interrupted, having reached a point where he could no longer accept what was being said. "This sounds like something from a Marvel movie. To begin with, time-walking is nearly impossible. In fact, from what you told me, the only two people left on earth who can actually do it are sitting in this room. Me and my grandfather. We're talking about a phenomenon that is intrinsically tied to a tribal ceremony that hasn't been practiced in over a hundred years."

Connor tried to remind him about Craig's supposed abilities, but before he could say anything, Jack continued,

186

"Then there's the small problem that my grandfather doesn't have the strength to open the time-walk bubble and then sustain it."

"We know that," Jenkins responded. "It was never the intention to have Hania do the time-walk himself."

"Well then you're screwed," Jack interrupted. "I have no intention of doing it. I gave all that up when my father disappeared."

"We are all very aware that you have refused to time-walk for this operation," Jenkins said, forcing a smile. "You are only being tasked to instruct Craig on the art of walking. And, If I may remind you, you are too young anyway to act as the walking guide back to 1968. You would have been a very young child back then. Besides, as time-walking limits us to only the guide and one guest, we require that both be trained soldiers, in the hope that Beyath can be successfully overpowered."

"If I'm not time-walking, and my grandfather is only permitting his timeline to be used as a pathway, then please explain how you plan to go back?"

"Craig will guide the actual time-walk," Connor stated.

Jack turned and stared at Craig. "Have you ever time-walked before?"

"Not that I'm aware of," Craig replied. "But I'm told that in my original timeline, I had some potential skills."

"That's ridiculous," Jack stated. "You either can or you can't. I began training when I was only three years old. It took me my entire childhood to master it. There's no way you can be expected to do it after a few weeks' training, especially as you have to have been born with the ability. It's not something you can simply be taught."

Craig simply shrugged.

"There is a way," Hania said in barely a whisper. "If he already has the light of the travelling spirit, he will be capable of acting as a guide."

"Look at him," Jack said, pointing at Craig. "Does he look like someone who could master the most spiritual art of our ancestors?"

"You did," Hania replied. "And look at you."

"That's it," Jack got to his feet. "I told you when you first contacted me that I wasn't going take any more shit from my family."

"Sit down Jack," Hania voice sounded much stronger. "If I can prove to you that this man has the light, will you, for once, be a help to your people instead such a ch'osh."

"I am not a worm," Jack stated emphatically.

"Then stop your wriggling and help us."

"Only if you can show me that this man," he again pointed at Craig, "is going to be able to learn anything."

Hania looked over at Craig. "Please come over here and sit next to me."

Craig did as he was told. Hania turned in his chair and faced him. He reached out his hands and laid the palms on the top of Craig's head.

"Close your eyes."

Craig closed his eyes.

"Think of nothing. Imagine a field of wheat undulating as a breeze passes across it. Then imagine that your mind is slowly covering the image with black paint from the bottom to the top. Focus only on what you can see above the paint. Be aware as it slowly covers the image of the field."

Craig concentrated hard on the visual that Hania had described. The paint had so far covered almost two thirds of it. As he continued to focus, the final view of the field vanished and all he could see was a black nothingness.

"As you stare at the blackness, imagine yourself moving into it," Hania instructed. "Feel your body grow lighter and more aware of all the senses beyond your vision. Feel yourself start to float. You feel safe. You are at peace."

Jack looked on and shook his head. He had seen the hypnotic effects of his grandfather's voice many times when he was a child. He wasn't remotely impressed and sat back down at the table. He reached for his coffee mug and took a sip.

"You are warm and comfortable," Hania whispered.

There is a moment of complete silence.

"Danger!" Hania suddenly shouted. "Save us all!" he yelled even louder.

Craig, his eyes still closed, was feeling immense peace and calm until the old man's words caused him to jerk backwards as his mind was filled with a flash of white light.

Hania turned to face his grandson.

"Satisfied?" he asked.

"At what?" Jack asked before it dawned on him that he was still standing. He had not yet sat down and had not reached for his coffee mug.

Jack looked across the table in complete amazement.

Craig had time-walked not only himself, but Jack and everyone else at the table. He had taken them back at least thirty seconds in time.

Jack sat back down.

"Maybe I do still have some things to learn," he mumbled.

"We all do," Hania said as he nodded to his grandson.

*

Later that day, Craig had his first one-on-one session with Jack. They sat in an alcove within the massive living room. He had assumed that there would be some friction between them considering his having distanced himself from all tribal affairs and traditions when he was nineteen. However, after Hania's little demonstration earlier in the conference room, Jack seemed far more invested in helping the operation.

"Until I saw what you could do without any training whatsoever, I never thought this plan had a chance of working."

"But now you do?" Craig asked.

"Now, I at least believe that there is some minute possibility of success. I have to be completely honest with you, Craig. Until today, I didn't give a flying fuck about International Dimensions and their objectives. I have spent my entire adult life believing that my father walked out on me. To find out that he didn't and was, in fact, killed in action, forces me to re-evaluate my whole existence. The idea that you, with my help, could revert history so that

Ahote never disappears, is almost too much to accept."

Jack had to take a moment to blow his nose and blot his tearing eyes.

"The idea that I could actually see him again is ..." Jack couldn't find the words.

"You do realise that if we succeed, you will have no memory of your father not having been around?" Craig explained. "You will have simply lived your entire life with Ahote being a part of it."

Jack managed to nod. "The thing is," Jack said in a raspy voice. "I haven't lived a good life. I'm sure you've been told that, but, in my own defence, believing that your father thought so little about his son, that he was capable of abandoning him, isn't exactly the best foundation on which to build a life. I'm sure the shrinks would say that I've been trying to satisfy what was missing through women and booze, but it's way more complicated than that."

"Have they told you everything about me?" Craig asked. "We may have more in common than you think."

"All they said was that you are a recovering alcoholic. Not that that isn't enough."

"When I was five, my parent's killed themselves in our home while I was sleeping twenty feet away," Craig explained.

"Jesus. I think you may just have me beat."

"I don't believe there's a ranking for the worst ways a child can lose one or both parents. Sure, I was a lot younger than you when your father vanished, but my parents had become raging alcoholics years before selfishly deciding to take the easy way out. In a weird way, though their death was undoubtably traumatic for me, I'd actually lost them years earlier."

"We sure as shit aren't the best poster boys for adjusting to what life threw at us, are we?"

Craig laughed. "No, we're not."

"It's so unfair. If this mission works, my life will be reset, and I'll grow up whole. At least I hope that's the case. But if you manage to reset the timeline and Ahote is never taken from us, you'll still carry the same pain as you have now."

"Not really," Craig replied. "In the original timeline, I meet a woman who saves me from myself and my fucked-up memories. The pain of losing my parents will always be there, not far from the surface, but between Jenny, my wife, my kids and my adoptive mother Julie, I end up in a good place."

Jack nodded his understanding, but a thought kept whirring around in his head.

"What if you could actually get rid of the pain completely?" Jack asked.

"I tried that with tequila. It's not a good long-term option."

"You are going to go back to 1968," Jack said. "What if, before you face the old witch, you track down your parents and have a little talk with them. Maybe you could somehow set them on a different path."

"That's a great idea, but they hadn't even met in 1968. I don't even know where either of them lived back then."

"You could research that now and have that information

before you time-walk. You could actually track them down and ..."

"Let me stop you there," Craig said, smiling at the other man. "That's a wonderful idea, and I really want to thank you for thinking of it, but, if I do track down my parents before they ever meet and try to explain all this and what will happen to them, there's every likelihood that they will then go out of their way to ensure they never meet. If that happens, I will have just caused myself to not be created. Then what?

"From what I understand, I have a wonderful life to go back to," Craig continued. "I have a wife and two great kids, a decent job and am in control of my addictions and PTSD. If you don't mind, I think I'll settle for what I once had rather than for an option that has never existed."

"It's your life," Jack replied.

"Yes, all versions of it."

CHAPTER 25

"Let's discuss what happened with you and my grandfather," Jack said. "What exactly did you do to make yourself go back in time?"

"That's the big problem. I have no idea. Hania talked me into what I presume was a state of light meditation, then suddenly started screaming at me. The next thing I knew, you were no longer sitting, and I was having a serious case of *déjà vu*."

"Except it wasn't *déjà vu*, was it?" Jack asked. "I don't know if anyone has explained it to you, but many cases of *déjà vu* are in fact moments when people involuntarily time-walk and re-live the last few moments of their life."

"I thought you and your grandfather were the only time-walkers left in the world?"

"We are the only ones left who can do so intentionally and control the specifics of the walk. I have never heard of anyone who has the unconscious ability to be trained to expand it into a controlled time-walk. Hardly anyone outside my tribal family is even aware that such a talent even exists.

For obvious reasons, it's one of the most closely guarded secrets of our ancestral heritage.

"Imagine if militaries, or even terrorists, could find a way to walk back in history and change events in their favour. People have always hypothesised about going back in time and killing someone like Hitler so that millions of lives could be saved. But what if, instead of a good outcome, history is changed to benefit evil. Let's stay with Hitler for a moment but reverse the outcome. What if someone was able to go back and kill Churchill as a child? Would the bulk of the UK's forces have perished at Dunkirk instead of being rescued? Could killing him have resulted in Britain falling to the Nazi forces? Would Hitler, with the UK under his control, have lost interest in the Russian front and focussed on the USA?"

"I get all that, but why has nobody ever put two and two together?" Craig asked. "Why haven't the people who have the latent ability to time-walk worked out that they have jumped back a few seconds instead of just assuming it was a trick of their mind?"

"Because," Jack replied. "It is a thousand times easier to accept that one's mind has just played a trick on you than believing that you have just gone back in time. We always go for the easier solution. The one without stress or consequence. Why do people accept explanations that an errant weather balloon is the cause of an entire town seeing a UFO streak through the night sky? It's because, the balloon explanation lets them sleep at night. If the masses were to suddenly believe in alien visitations, not just as a potential concept, but as a confirmed fact that beings from a different planet had just done a fly-by over our world, the consequences would be psychologically catastrophic throughout every culture."

"I get that," Craig said. "But we're talking about something far simpler than alien life."

"Are we, though?" Jack responded. "The world believes in a clear-cut, linear existence. Time, as a constant is a comforting panacea. Take that away and you remove the stability of life's most fundamental framework. Thankfully, the human brain, for the most part, will always accept the weather balloon response and therefore keep our fragile minds cocooned within the safe haven of an unimaginative mind."

"Is it true that you haven't time-walked since you were nineteen?" Craig asked, changing the subject.

"Yes. When I left the reservation, I turned my back on all tribal beliefs and traditions, including time-walking. When my father disappeared, for some reason I felt the need to rebel against everything he'd done and believed in."

"And now?" Craig asked.

"Now I know differently. Now I know that he didn't abandon me at all and that he'd actually been trying to make the world a better place."

"So, in all this time, you've never once tried it just to make sure you still had the ability?"

"Why would I?"

Craig nodded his understanding.

The two sat in silence for a moment.

"That's bullshit," Jack said suddenly. "Of course, I went

back. I was doing drugs and all sorts of stupid shit and one night, I actually time-walked to before my father vanished."

"Did you speak to him?"

Jack's eyes misted over.

"No," he said. "I watched from a nearby hill as my dad and my younger self sat outside at night. He was pointing out a meteor shower and explaining what we were looking at."

"Why didn't you say something? You could have stopped him from being taken."

"Back then, I didn't know he was taken. I thought he'd simply had enough of me and my bullshit and had gone off to have a better life. What could I possibly have said to him that would have made a difference? 'I'll try and be a better son?' Besides, as long as my younger self was close by. I could never have got close to my father."

"I'm sorry," Craig said.

"Instead of trying to talk with him, I walked back to present day and vowed never to time-walk again."

"So, you couldn't see him anymore?"

"No, so I didn't start using it as an escape. The one thing that nobody understands is the temptation that can exist to use time-walking as a way to remould your own existence. For some reason, despite the drugs and the booze, I recognised that messing with my timeline in order to get things right would only make things worse."

"But aren't we planning to do just that?" Craig asked. "To go back in time to make things better?"

"Yes, but we are going back to fix something that was

done specifically to hurt us. We're planning to use time as a way to put things back the way they were, not to remould our own histories. We will be using it so that we can have the life that was stolen from us by some messed up old witch."

"How do you know you can still do it?" Craig asked.

"I just do," Jack replied. "It's not like a muscle that's become atrophied. Once the pathways in the mind have been reconditioned to allow the opening of the time portal, it stays that way."

"But, how do you know that?"

"I just do."

"I don't mean to harp on this, but just saying you do, doesn't seem to be enough of a certainty considering what's at stake."

"What do you mean?" Jack asked. "I'm not the one who's going to walk you back, you and my grandfather are doing that. I'm just here to teach you."

"You're here to teach me something you haven't done in forty years. What if you leave out some parts? What if you ..."

"Let's go for a quick walk," Jack suggested.

"Now?"

"Trust me," Jack said as he closed his eyes. Moments later, Jack grinned at Craig and stood up.

"Come with me."

Jack led Craig past the dining room and to the closed conference room door.

"Peak inside," Jack said, smiling.

Craig did as instructed and saw that the meeting with Jenkins was still going on.

"So what?" Craig asked. "They're still talking."

"Look closer."

Craig sighed in frustration and opened the door a little wider, so he had a better view of the entire room. He felt his insides turn to ice as a shiver ran up the length of his spine. Jack was standing on one side of the mahogany table as Hania whispered into Craig's ear.

"We're in there?" Craig whispered as he closed the door. "How can we be in there if we're standing out here."

"Because, my doubting friend, you and I have just time-walked two hours into the past. That's this morning's meeting seconds before you jumped back."

"How ...?" That's not possible?"

"Of course, it is. I just guested you in your first formal time-walk. At least your first one in this timeline."

Craig was busy studying the palms of his hands as if expecting them to dissolve in front of him.

"Pretty cool, huh?" Jack asked.

Craig reached out and touched him to make sure he was real.

"I guess you can still do it," Craig said, stunned.

"I guess I can," Jack replied, grinning.

CHAPTER 26

"So, how do you do it?" Craig asked.

"Actually, it's quite simple. You concentrate on a date in the past, then count back from ten and just before reaching zero, you blink three times, very quickly."

"Seriously?" Craig was astonished at how easy it sounded.

Jack rolled his eyes. "Of course not. It's a transcendental process that was handed down through tribal elders for hundreds, maybe even thousands of years. Did you really imagine it involved counting backwards and blinking?"

"How the hell am I supposed to know? You're the one charged with training me, not making fun of my ignorance on a subject nobody in the entire world is even aware of."

"Fair point," Jack agreed. "I'm sorry. I really don't know why I did that."

"Cause, you are an ass?" Craig suggested.

"That could be it."

"How about you start over, and you tell me exactly what I'm going to have to learn?"

"Okay. The corner stone of the whole process is to be able to self-hypnotise yourself."

"I thought you were going to be serious," Craig barked.

"I am. This is the real deal. The first thing I had to learn as a child was to put myself into a trance-like state."

"Was it easier as a child?" Craig asked.

"No. It was a hundred times harder. I was five years old. My mind was so full of a million different thoughts that clearing it was a fucking nightmare. Thankfully, as I got older, I was able to compartmentalise my thoughts and by the time I was fifteen, I could clear my mind in a millisecond. Once you train yourself to basically let go of all detritus that's swirling around in there, it becomes second nature to transition one's brain waves from the alpha stage to the theta level, then to the point when your brain is creating only delta waves yet you remain fully awake."

"I don't know what any of that means," Craig announced.

"When you are awake and your brain is in full activity mode, it's creating alpha waves. Your synapses are firing all over the place. You are worrying about money, what's in the fridge for dinner, does your car need servicing, why is my knee sore, etcetera. Some people refer to this state as monkey-brain."

"I get that a lot when I'm trying to sleep. I'll even get tunes stuck in my head while I'm stressing about just about everything you could imagine."

"That's because your brain has never been trained to work in any other way. It's a muscle and it needs to learn how to control its thought process."

"How the hell do I do that?" Craig asked.

"Let's try a simple exercise which will give you some idea of what you will have to learn. I will guide you this time, but starting tomorrow, you are going to learn how to guide yourself."

Craig checked his watch.

"Do you have somewhere else you need to be?" Jack asked.

"Actually, yes. I need to be in Tlaquepaque by three o'clock."

"That only gives us forty minutes," Jack replied. "Guiding you to the beta state for the first time will take a lot longer than that."

"I'll tell you what," Craig replied. "How about we stop for today and let me do what I have to do, then, from tomorrow on, I will work whatever schedule you need me to work?"

"That sounds fair. I think we covered a lot of preliminary ground anyway. How are you getting into town?"

Craig looked dumbstruck. "I hadn't even thought about that."

"I'll tell you what. I'll drive you there. It will give me a chance to grab a couple of cold ones. How long are you going to be? I can wait if you like."

"I'll hopefully be an hour. Will that work for you?" Craig asked.

"Sure. Find me a nice bar and an hour will go by in no time."

"I'm surprised that they don't have a problem with you drinking while you're working here?" Craig said.

"They probably do, but I made it clear that they would have to find another instructor if they tried to stop me. Besides. I'm not the one who needs to stay sober."

"Don't you want to get ... I don't know ... a little cleaned up before you're reunited with your dad?"

"Won't make a difference. That will happen in a different timeline. If all goes well, I'm hoping I never became the drunk I am now. If the mission fails, I will probably drink even more."

"That's reassuring," Craig commented.

"That's just the way it is," Jack responded.

Craig gave Jack directions to Tlaquepaque and introduced him to the Mexican restaurant.

"Will this suit your purposes?" Craig asked.

Jack eyed the array of beers on tap at the bar and nodded happily.

"This will do very nicely. Where are you off to?" he asked.

"Hopefully, for a walk around the art shops."

"I think I'm getting the better part of this deal," Jack said as he strode over to the bar and swung his substantial girth into one of the stools.

Craig checked his watch for the tenth time in as many minutes.

"Expecting something important to happen?" Danielle asked.

Craig spun around and did his best to look calm and collected. Neither of which was how he was feeling at that moment.

"That pretty much depends on you, doesn't it?" he

replied.

"Oh god! What a cheesy line. Loosen up Craigie or I'll have to find someone else to show around Tlaquepaque."

Craig was flummoxed by her having called him Craigie. The only other person who'd ever called him that was his adoptive mother, Julie, and she'd stopped calling him that almost three decades earlier. The weird thing was that even though he'd hated it as a child, there was something about the way Danielle said it that he kind of liked.

"Sorry Danny," Craig replied with a smirk.

Danielle grinned and punched him in the arm.

Despite Craig being in his forties, he felt like he had at school when at the ripe old age of seven he had developed his first crush on Diana Olson.

"Let me just clock out and we can get going. Meet me out back in about two minutes."

Danielle turned away, said a few words to the restaurant manager who was standing next to the hostess station, then vanished into the back of the building. As Craig walked out into the bright sunshine, he couldn't help noticing the man give him a long appraising glance.

Craig walked to the back entrance of the restaurant. Gone were all attempts at creating the pueblo atmosphere. The back of the place was plain, tan-coloured stucco and looked as appealing as a dead fish.

A reinforced service door opened, and Danielle appeared. Behind her, Craig could hear the sounds of a busy kitchen.

"Before I give you my patented VIP tour of the place, I

need to know if you've already done any exploring?"

"The guy I was with yesterday gave me a brief tour," he confessed.

"The old Irish guy? That doesn't count. He looked about as interested in Native American art as I am in Vogon poetry."

Craig burst out laughing.

"I'm impressed," he said. "There can't be that many women who quote The Hitchhiker's Guide to the Galaxy on a first date."

"Is that what this is?" Danielle asked, amused. "I think of it more as your one and only chance to impress me. If you pass that test, we might … I repeat … might, start using the D word."

"I stand corrected and accept the challenge to impress."

"Good. Let's start at the far end of the plaza, then we can make our may back here in time for my four o'clock shift."

"Is an hour long enough for you to complete my evaluation?" Craig asked.

"I've been known to reach a determination in less than five minutes, mind you, those quick tabulations are usually because I'd worked out that the guy was a pig or a creep; sometimes both."

"So, I'm not your first?" Craig joked.

"You're my first today. Does that make you feel better?"

CHAPTER 27

Danielle chose a small shop that specialised in hand carved wooden sculptures and boxes. Craig had never seen anything like them. There was something almost sensual about the way the artists had matched curved form with the natural grain of the woods.

He became fascinated by a carving of an egg made from highly polished walnut. Just holding it in his palm seemed to make him feel relaxed and at peace. Danielle noticed the caring way he was handling the piece and couldn't help smiling. She gently took it from him and laid her palm on the top. She rotated her hand and, much to Craig's astonishment, the wooden egg opened. Though invisible to the naked eye, it was in fact made up of two pieces that seamlessly fitted together.

Craig could happily have spent the entire hour in that one shop, but Danielle urged him to follow her to the next one on her tour. It was three doors down and was substantially bigger than the first one. It had to be to hold the artwork that was on display.

On the walls were paintings of the mountains that surround Sedona. Most captured vivid storms as they crested the valley. The smallest canvas was twelve feet by eight feet. On it, a single lightning bolt striking a tree provided the only light source of the piece.

The artist had somehow captured the raw power and majestic beauty of nature on one simple canvas. Craig felt his eyes mist up as he stood in front of it in complete awe.

"I've never seen anything like that in my life. It's so ... real and yet, somehow ..." he couldn't think of the right word.

"Alien?" Danielle suggested.

"That's it. It's almost too vivid, as if it could only occur on another world."

"You're deeper than I thought," Danielle commented.

"Is that a problem?" he asked.

"I don't know. I'm usually scared of the deep end. A person could drown in all that water," Danielle replied as she looked into his eyes.

Craig didn't know how to respond. For the past twenty years he'd spent his life focussing on keeping himself self-medicated with enough tequila to deaden his senses to the point where he felt almost nothing. Danielle had the exact opposite effect on him. He was nearing sensory and emotional overload.

It's not that he'd not had a few relationships since drinking his way out of the Marines, but there'd been no emotional connection other than two people wanting to forget the world through sexual release.

"You still with me?" Danielle asked, smiling. "You look

like you took a little detour there for a moment."

"I'm with you," he replied. "It's that painting. It's messed with my head."

"I think we both know that your head was already messed with before we even stepped in here."

"How can you tell?" Craig asked, aware that her comment was not a jibe, rather a statement of fact.

"It's your eyes," Danielle said as she stepped closer. "There's a lifetime of pain just below the surface."

"I feel I should plead the fifth. Anything I say now is only going to send you running for the hills."

"We already live in the hills. It wouldn't exactly be that long a run."

"You know what I mean," Craig replied.

"I've had my share of life disasters as well," Danielle said. "You can ask either of my previous husbands. I would prefer to find out all about your dark side now. If I can look past it, then I know we're on the right track. If I can't, isn't it better to finish this now before it gets to a point where things could get more complicated?"

The owner of the store who was sitting behind a rough-hewn wooden desk tucked in the far corner, gently cleared his throat.

"Sorry Brian," Danielle said, realising that the two of them had been taking up precious floor space and might want to take their discussion elsewhere.

"Why don't we find somewhere a little more private. If I'm going to unload my cargo plane full of baggage on you, I'd prefer to do so in a less public place?" Craig suggested.

Danielle led him to a small piazza tucked at the end of a narrow alley. A fountain gurgled against one wall and an oversized wind-chime provided a melodic background.

"You're sure you want to hear this?" Craig asked.

"I'm still here, aren't I?"

Craig took a deep breath then gave her an abridged version of his life from the time his parents carried out their murder-suicide pact, through his time in the Marines, and ended with his alcoholism and subsequent, recent, recovery. He didn't mention anything about the mission or his alternate timelines. Craig felt that his history was dark enough without bringing in any supernatural elements.

"I'm so sorry," Danielle said, clearly moved by Craig's story. "I'm amazed that you're as together as you are."

"It's all a veneer. Under this calm, mature façade is a trembling mass of insecurities and regret."

"Join the club," Danielle replied, smiling. "What are you doing in Sedona?"

"I'm working with Connor, the Irish guy. We're consultants on a construction project in the Middle East."

"You don't look like a builder," Danielle commented.

"I'm not. We're advising on the security requirements to keep the site safe."

"Sounds like a bad CIA cover to me."

"It's not," Craig insisted.

"Then why meet here in Sedona?" she asked.

"The money guy has a home here."

"Still sounds pretty thin."

"Sorry," Craig smiled. "I can't help it if the truth sounds

hollow."

"What are they planning on building?"

"Condos."

"Where exactly?" Danielle fired back, trying to catch him out.

"Oman," Craig volleyed.

"Were in Oman?"

"Sohar. It's halfway between Muscat and Dubai," Craig replied. "Satisfied?"

"I don't know."

"Well, while you're making up your mind, why don't you unpack your baggage for me."

Danielle looked at her watch.

"Don't even think of trying to get out of telling me your sordid history," Craig said. "You've got over twenty-five minutes before you have to be back at work."

"Damn," Danielle said, grinning. "Okay, if you're sure you can handle it."

"I was a Marine sniper. I'm pretty sure I can handle your life story."

"We'll see just how dedicated you really are," Danielle said as she settled back on the bench. "I'm going to give you a Reader's Digest version ..."

"Are they still around?" Craig interrupted.

"I have no idea," she replied, laughing. "I was raised just outside Provo, Utah. My family were ... and I assume still are, devout Mormons. I was planning on becoming a veterinarian but, apart from that, my life was exceedingly ordinary until I turned seventeen and my father announced that I was to be married.

"I remember joking with him that that was highly unlikely as I hadn't yet met anyone that I was remotely interested in. His voice went all cold and weird and he told me that the elders at their temple had decided that I was to wed one of their sons and that it was important that I comply, otherwise they could make things difficult for my father. I was horrified. I had heard of such archaic traditions within some of the fundamentalist branches of the LDS, that's Latter Day Saints for the uninitiated, but not somewhere like Provo. Anyway, three days later I met the man they intended for me to marry. He was old. He had to have been at least forty."

"Excuse me," Craig said gesturing to himself.

"To an eighteen-year-old, forty is ancient. It wasn't even as if he was a Bradley Cooper kind of forty. He was fat, had greasy, receding hair and was a pig farmer. Once we were married, I was to live on a fucking ... excuse my French, pig farm fifty miles from my home and school. I was informed that the farm would be my new home and, as for schooling, I was smart enough already to do what was needed around the house and in the bedroom."

"Good God!" Craig said. "Was that even legal?"

"I don't know. Maybe if I'd stuck around, I would have found out."

"You ran away?" Craig asked.

"I didn't run. I fled with dignity and grace. Thankfully, I had a really good friend who lived in Glenwood Springs in Colorado."

"I know the place. There's a great hotel there."

"That's the Colorado Hotel." Danielle nodded. "It's gorgeous. Erica's dad was the general manager and I used to go stay with them at least once year. I told them what was being planned for me, and Erica and her mother drove all the way to Salt Lake and met me there. They drove me out of Utah and let me stay with them at the hotel. Her dad even managed to get me a job cleaning rooms until I decided what I wanted to do."

"Did your family come after you?" Craig asked.

"You'd think they would, but they didn't. I was terrified that they would somehow turn up and drag me back, but Erica kept reminding me that I was, by that time, eighteen and that they had no right to do that. Two months later I got a letter … not an email, mind you, an actual letter from my father. He said that he was happy that I'd left and found a safe place to stay. He told the elders that he had no idea where I was and hadn't communicated with me just in case they were monitoring him."

"That all sounds horrible," Craig said.

Danielle just shrugged.

"Anyway, I finished school but didn't have the funds or the grades to study and become a vet, so I stayed working at the Colorado Hotel. That's where I met my first husband, Jimmy. He worked for the liquor supply company that had the hotel contract. He used to come by once every two weeks and meet with the beverage and restaurant managers. By that time, I was working as a waitress at the Coppertop Bar within the hotel and one day we just started talking."

"Travelling salesman meets attractive waitress," Craig commented. "What could go wrong?"

"Well, as you just pointed out, there were a few red flags, but I missed every single one of them. Within a month he was staying in my apartment ... and before you ask, no, we were not sleeping together."

"I'm greatly relieved," Craig replied, grinning.

"Three months later we were married. Erica's father insisted we use the hotel for the service and the reception. I should have been concerned when I saw the guest list. For obvious reasons, my side was very short, but Jimmy's had even fewer names. I guess I was too carried away with the planning and everything to wonder why he had so few friends and family.

"The wedding was beautiful, despite their being only eighteen guests. We had to have an abbreviated honeymoon because Jimmy had some big sales convention he had to go to, so we ended up going to Telluride for a long weekend. It was fantastic. Jimmy was sweet and gentle and took my cherry on a four-poster bed in a five-star hotel."

"Took your cherry?" Craig laughed. "Do people still say that?"

"I just did," she replied. "Anyway, when we got back to Glenville Springs, he had to rush off so he could swing by his apartment in Denver before flying to Vegas for the convention. I never remember missing anyone so much in my entire life."

"How long was he gone?" Craig asked.

"That's the thing. The convention was supposed to be

three days, yet he was away for six."

"Oh, oh," Craig said.

"Big oh, oh," she concurred. "That started to be a thing. He would go away on a sales sweep that should have taken him two to three days but would be gone for twice that long."

"Did he say why?"

"Sure. Each time he said it was because he got stuck doing an extra sweep to a different part of the region or his appointment got postponed by a day or two."

"Without telling you?"

"He claimed that he couldn't get phone reception on the road and got so tired at the end of each day that he just passed out in some motel and slept though."

"And you bought that?" Craig asked.

"I was nineteen by that point, and he was twenty-seven. I had no experience with men whatsoever. Now it sounds pretty dumb, but I just thought that that was how guys behaved."

"So, what was he really doing?"

"Well, one day while I was sitting alone in our apartment ... again, the phone rang, and I saw that it was Jimmy calling. Imagine my shock when I answered it and found myself speaking to a woman."

"He had a girlfriend?"

"No. A wife."

"What!?" Craig shrieked.

"It turned out he had three wives if you included me."

"You must have freaked out."

"That's putting it mildly. It wasn't even as if I could just walk away and erase all traces of the debacle. I had to meet with countless police officers and then appear for the prosecution at Jimmy's trial. Just as an extra kick up the ass, it turned out Jimmy wasn't even his real name. It was Ralph."

"You promised me a train wreck, and gosh darn-it if you haven't delivered on that promise," Craig said in a southern drawl. "You said that you were married twice. I hope the second one wasn't as bad?"

"It wasn't particularly good. I met Brad five years later when I was working at the Auberge Hotel right here in Sedona. I was the assistant manager, and he was my boss. We did a whole lot of flirting for months before going out and getting drunk and crossing the line that, in retrospect, shouldn't have been crossed. I wouldn't say we fell in love. It was more like we fell in lust. There was a lot of sex and hardly any conversation."

"Nothing wrong with that," Craig offered.

"There wouldn't have been, except that we decided, for some unknown reason, to run off to Vegas and get married," Danielle said with a sigh. "It took two whole months to find out that we hardly had anything in common, and once the bad dynamics of the marriage entered the picture, working with him as my boss was untenable."

"Ouch."

"It was really weird. The guy had been a blast to work for until the moment we got hitched. From then on, he basically became a complete bully. By the three-month mark, we both knew that the marriage was a bust. The problem was that I still reported to him at work."

"That must have been fun," Craig said, cringing.

"It was horrible. It was as if he blamed me for everything that happened. Not only did he treat me like a second-class citizen, but he also started writing me up for what he called 'work-place infractions', including acting disrespectfully to senior management."

"Were you, in fact, disrespectful to senior management?" Craig asked.

"You bet your sweet ass I was. I wasn't going to take any shit from him."

Danielle checked her watch.

"Crap. Out of time. I'll understand if you don't want to see me again." Danielle said. "I did warn you that I came with some pretty low-class baggage."

"My project is going to take up most of my time ..."

"Here we go," Danielle said, shaking her head.

"During the day," Craig finished. "So, I was wondering if I could see you after work for one of those real dates I keep hearing about?"

Danielle looked at him, long and hard.

"Don't fuck me over, okay." she said, her tone decidedly serious.

"Ditto," Craig replied.

CHAPTER 28

The next morning, Craig met with Jack in one of the conference room break-out spaces, and the training started in earnest. Though he hadn't been aware of it, Tia Lash, the woman at Pendleton who had introduced him to mindful meditation, had primed his mind for what Jack was going to teach him.

"When you were in Camp Pendleton, you started to learn about meditation, correct?" Jack asked.

"Yes, but it was just to help me de-stress and not think about drinking."

"It was more than that. You were shown how to shift your mind to the beta-wave state."

"I wasn't shown how to do it," Craig corrected him. "That woman talked me through it."

"Nevertheless, she started moulding your mind to accept a hypnotic state. That's going to make this much easier. This is the first time I've ever tried to teach anyone much of anything," Jack admitted. "I'm glad that she at least got you started."

"If that's meant to be reassuring, It's not. Why isn't your grandfather doing the teaching? Isn't he the one that taught you and your father?"

"Yes, but you've seen him. He's old. Very old. I think they're saving him for the walk itself."

"How about you? Do you feel up to this?" Craig asked.

"I wish I'd had a few less beers yesterday, but apart from that, I'm good to go."

"Still not feeling reassured."

Jack smiled. "I want you to close your eyes and think of a time and a place where and when you felt the most at peace."

Craig closed his eyes and tried to recall any time when he'd felt stress free and relaxed. Even after Julie had adopted him and gave him a wonderful home, the psychological damage had already been done as a result of his parent's murder-suicide pact.

That sort of memory doesn't just drift away as one gets older. Instead, it finds a dark corner somewhere in the back of the brain and slowly festers away until it has robbed the host of the ability to ever feel completely safe and secure. The fact that, after his parent's death, he'd suffered even more mental anguish at the hands of a vengeful city employee, only helped to loosen a few more screws within Craig's fragile, psychological framework.

Craig concentrated on the numerous times in his life when he should have felt peace, but none of them seemed to offer quite the calm serenity that Jack was hoping he'd find. While trying and failing to find some degree of zen at the memory of his tenth birthday party, a completely different mental image crept into the foreground.

Abraham's Oasis was not that far from one of the main US airbases in Iraq. It was a small patch of palm trees and water miles from the mighty Euphrates River. It was fed by an underground spring and was surrounded by harsh inhospitable desert.

Craig had heard talk of the place when he arrived in-country but had never gone there until the day when he'd shot his first female terrorist. Al Qaida had just started using woman to detonate roadside IEDs, believing that the soft American soldiers wouldn't be able to intentionally kill a woman.

It was the first time that Craig had been faced with this new threat and it had shaken him to the core. Through his and his spotter's scopes, they could see the convoy approaching and the young woman at the side of the road pull a cell phone from her pocket.

"Shit," the spotter had said.

Though Craig felt the same way, he knew that he was the only thing stopping a convoy of his fellow soldiers from being ripped apart by the roadside bomb that the girl was about to detonate. He took the shot but didn't keep his scope trained on the target after the round left his rifle. It was one thing to fire the kill shot. It was something else entirely to watch a woman head snap backwards as the back of her skull was blown away.

When Craig got back to the base, he'd begun feeling, though he didn't know it at the time, the onset of the mental fatigue that would torment him for the rest of his life. One of his bunk mates, a black, mountain of a man from Mississippi, could tell that Craig was in a bad place and had suggested he drive out to the oasis.

On the pretext of scoping out a route for an upcoming convoy training exercise, Craig had signed out a Humvee and had driven the three miles into the desert.

He had walked into the centre of the green haven and sat on the bank of a crystal-clear pool of water and had started to cry. After a few moments he had looked up and seen a flock of flamingos fly overhead, then, in a graceful show of aerial skill, they circled once before landing on the still water.

Craig had watched them for almost an hour. They were a glorious shade of reddish pink that he'd never seen before. Eventually, the birds had lifted off and flown in formation across the darkening sands.

The image of the flamingos and the oasis was the only thing Craig's mind could produce that brought back any semblance of a peaceful moment. Despite the horrors of the war and his recent killing of the woman, that moment by the spring-fed waterhole was the closest thing to a happy memory that his mind could muster.

Though surprised at his own brain's choice of setting, Craig tried to recall the sense of harmony he'd felt on that day, in that location. He forced himself to recall the sounds of the palm fronds as the Shamal wind swept across the tiny oasis. He felt the heat from the sun as it reddened his forehead and arms. He heard the sounds of the birds as they landed upon the chilled pool. He could even smell the vegetation and slight tanginess of the spring water.

"You are at peace now," Jack said in a calm, slow voice. "Your body is completely relaxed. You are safe. Nothing can harm you here."

Though Craig could clearly hear the other man, his words didn't lift him out of the memory bubble he'd created.

"I want you to feel every sense of where your mind has taken you. I want you to close your eyes within the memory. Your other senses will continue to work but your eyes need to close.

In his memory, Craig closed his eyes.

"I want you to feel your body grow lighter as you listen, hear and smell your surroundings. Your body is growing lighter and lighter. You can no longer feel the ground beneath you. You are now floating amidst the memory image."

Jack said nothing for thirty seconds.

"Through your mind's eye, you look down and can see the place from above. It is just as peaceful and safe as it ever was, but now you are floating above it. I want you to sense both the memory location and where you are in reality. Your mind will remain in the peaceful place while your body sensations will be here, in Sedona."

Craig didn't even have to concentrate that hard. He was suddenly seeing the oasis yet sensing the interior of the break-out room within the compound.

"Craig, I want you to know that your real self is here in Sedona while your mind is still in your peaceful place. But slowly, I want you to wish that your body could join you in the memory. You are still floating, your eyes are still closed in the safe place, but your body is here in Arizona. It needs to be together with your mind. Have your memory pull your body into it. Think how much you want your entire being to be present in your safe and happy place. Think it. Wish it."

Craig did exactly as he was told. It was hard at first to focus on the memory to the point where it could interact with his body, but after a few moments, he felt his physical self grow lighter. Craig wished even harder, almost commanding his body to meet up with his mind floating above the oasis.

"Now, I want you to feel yourself grow heavier as you float above your safe place. You sense yourself slowly drifting back to the ground. Your mind and body are in perfect harmony, and you know that when your feet touch the ground, both your mind and your body will be one."

Craig, his eyes still closed, felt himself gently floating back down to solid ground. His senses were filled with the sounds and smells of the oasis.

"The moment your feet touch the ground, your body will join your mind and you will be as one within the place of peace and harmony. You will be safe, and you will be completely in control of yourself and your surroundings. You will feel nothing but harmonious freedom."

Craig could sense that the ground was getting closer.

"You will reach the ground in a few seconds. Your body is ready to join your mind. They are about to become as one."

Craig felt his feet touch the ground. He opened his eyes

so he could see Jack and thank him for the amazing experience.

Jack wasn't there. In fact. The room where he'd been sitting was gone as well. Instead, Craig was standing on the bank of the clear pond within Abraham's Oasis in Iraq. The Humvee he'd driven that day, twenty plus years earlier, was parked in the distance about fifty yards away. He looked down and saw that he was wearing desert fatigues and military issue boots.

Craig then did what any normal human being would do.

He screamed, seconds before everything turned bright white.

CHAPTER 29

"It's okay," Jack's voice said. "You're back. You're safe."

It took Craig a moment to fully grasp that he was, in fact, sitting opposite Jack in the Sedona safehouse.

"What the fuck just happened?" he asked, his voice shaky.

"You just completed your first space-time, astral projection."

"I did what?"

"You went back to a moment in your life when you felt peace and safety. Where did you go exactly?"

"An oasis in Iraq, but does that mean that I just time-walked?"

"No. You sent your mind back, but your body stayed right here."

"What's the difference?"

"In a time-walk, you can travel back to whenever you want, and your mind and body will always stay together. Once you have created the time bubble, you will be able to move anywhere within that time period. Astral projection allowed you to take your mind back into a younger you, however your body stayed routed here. It is however a very transient state and can only last a few minutes at most before your younger mind rejects the intrusion."

"Is that why I jerked back here so fast?"

"No. You returned because you were terrified and wanted to return. It's that simple. When you want the trip to end, it ends."

"What about in a time-walk?" Craig asked. "Can I end it whenever I want?"

"Yes and no," Jack replied. "You can terminate it when you like, however it is essential that you are back in a place where it is safe to end the event and return to present day."

"In case the place where I'm ending the walk doesn't exist in the present?" Craig asked

"Very perceptive of you," Jack smiled, impressed. "You could theoretically end a time-walk anywhere you want, but you would have to be 100% certain that, your location in the past, still exists in a suitable form in present day. You don't want to come back to 2022 and suddenly materialise in the middle of a crowded mall, or worse, within a slab of concrete. That's why we will use the old cabin as a departure and re-entry point. It was built in the late 1800s so it's the perfect launch-pad for a time-walk."

"Launch-pad?" Craig asked. "Is that what Hania calls the starting point?"

"No. That's what I used to call it when I was kid. I thought it sounded pretty cool."

"Except you couldn't tell anyone about it."

"Correct."

Craig tried to get his head around what he'd just done, and the seemingly never-ending rules and parameters involved in time-walking.

A thought then struck him. "There must be some way that I could go back with that astral projection thing and stay longer. I mean, back then I was super fit and would be far better suited to go up against Beyath in my old body than this one."

"While that may be true, it can't happen," Jack explained. "The you, back whenever you project to, will always, though subconsciously, reject the second mind that has suddenly entered your younger head. It's just the way things are. Also, with time-walking, you are able to take a guest with you on the journey. That's something else that would be impossible during astral projection."

"Then why have me do it at all?" Craig asked.

"Because the process of creating the time-walk portal starts with opening the minds-eye to be able to project your consciousness back in time. Think of it like math. The first thing you must master before you attempt anything else is simple addition. That's the initial steppingstone. Astral projection is like addition."

"What math subject is the equivalent of time-walking?" Craig asked.

"Algebraic geometry," Jack replied.

"I don't even know what that is."

"Exactly," Jack smiled.

"I don't like it," Jenkins said to Connor as he paced the room.

The two were in the den, and as Connor watched the other man wear away a swath of carpet pile, he couldn't help agreeing with him, if only partially.

"The man's got a wife and children," Jenkins stated. "That's all that counts."

"I agree," Connor replied.

"I assumed you would."

"But," Connor continued, "his family exists in a different timeline. In this one, he has nobody. From what I've been able to piece together, he's never had any significant relationships in this lifetime."

"This lifetime doesn't count. That Beyath creature intentionally altered it, purely to cause Craig pain and misery."

"To be fair, Craig had tried to kill her twice."

"The word fair is not part of the lexicon of war," Jenkins insisted.

"We're hardly at war," Connor replied.

"Of course, we are. What do you think we've been doing if not battling the forces of evil? We have no idea of the total death toll from dimensional incursions but estimate the number of people killed each year to be well into the thousands. And what really scares the hell out of me is that the numbers are rising. Each year there are more reports of missing people that have all the ear marks of a dimensional abduction. Add to that the fact that there are twice the number of rift portals now than there were ten years ago. Have you ever considered what would happen if the intruders became organised and came into our dimension in force? So far, with the exception of Beyath, they all appear to come here just for sport, but what if one day they set their sight on not just a single assault, but an all-out invasion."

"What would be the point?" Connor asked.

"Perhaps to take over our entire planet," Jenkins suggested.

"There's nothing to show that as being a possibility, is there?" Connor asked.

"Pearl Harbor, 9/11 … our history is filled with unexpected attacks that shocked the world. At some point, we must start treating these incursions as what they very well might be; a prequel to something far bigger."

"You're right, of course, but what does any of that have to do with Craig and the waitress?"

"Perhaps on the surface, very little. However, he is our only hope at reverting time back to the version we had before Beyath took Ahote and then Craig's in-laws. We need him to have the necessary fire in his belly when he goes back to battle the witch. At the moment, his life is a wreck. The possibility that we have given him whereby he can return to a timeline where he has a wonderful life, is the entire incentive on which this fragile foundation has been built. If he falls in love with … what's her name?"

"Danielle." Connor replied.

"If he falls in love with this Danielle woman, what would be the driving force to get him to do what we require, especially when it will result in him losing his newfound love. Don't forget, we are asking him to go back in time and eradicate the only version of his life that he has ever known. Up to a few days ago, that seemed a fair request, especially with the promise of a beautiful wife and children at the end of the mission. We have assumed that by showing him pictures and videos of himself in the original timeline, he fully believed us and is ready to do whatever it takes to get that life back. But, what if, deep down, there's doubt in his mind? Doubt about all of this, especially the part where we promise that his mission, if successful, will bring him the security and love that he's never had. Doesn't that sound a little familiar? Male Islamic suicide bombers are promised that they will be given seventy-two virgins in the afterlife once they've carried out their lethal mission."

Jenkins watched his words hit home. "Aren't we, in some way, doing the same thing with this Marine, and isn't it possible, that somewhere deep in his soldier's mind, he might just know that? What if he starts to doubt the whole alternate timeline scenario while his attachment to Danielle grows stronger? How do we know that this man, especially considering the life he's had, will be there for us when we really need him?"

"Because he's a Marine," Connor replied without a moment's hesitation.

"Was a Marine," Jenkins shot back.

"Sir, if there's one thing I know and live by, it's that once you are a Marine, you are always a Marine."

"That's all very well and good, but how does that help the

situation with Craig and this Danielle woman? Do we keep him locked down until the mission?"

"If you want to ensure some level of distrust and frustration, then by all means, try that," Connor replied. "Personally, I believe that Craig will complete the mission to the very best of his ability. If in the meantime, he begins a relationship with Danielle, I can't help wondering if there is anything wrong with that. I know he has, or at least had, a different life in an alternate timeline, but that's only according to our records, not through personal experience."

"Are you suggesting that there are inaccuracies in the detail we have of the original timeline?" Jenkins asked.

"No, I'm not. It's just that as far as Craig is concerned, it doesn't relate to him. I feel that at this point, we just let him keep seeing her. If it makes him even remotely happy, then, what's the real harm?"

"There are simply too many hypotheticals," sighed Jenkins.

"Of course, there are," Connor stated. "We're dealing with alternate dimensional timelines as well as time-walking. The entire premise is insane. Everything we do is beyond the realms of accepted science as it currently stands. If the global population ever found out the shit that we're involved with, there'd be no containing them. So, when you say, there are too many hypotheticals ... I have to say, so what? It was bad enough when we were only dealing with alien hunters sneaking through rift portals. Once a sixteenth century witch who was feeding on the lifeforce of her own bloodline showed up, this all became complete and utter insanity."

"An insanity that we have to navigate on a daily basis if we are going to keep this planet safe … at least this version of it," Jenkins said. "Which is why we can't risk losing an operative like Craig or Ahote."

"Craig's not an operative in this timeline. He's no more than a shell of the original man."

"A shell who happens to be one of the only people in this world capable of time-walking. At least we hope he can," Jenkins remarked.

"Just out of idle curiosity, does International Dimensions have a plan B if this one goes to shite?"

"Would I be this worried about the mental stability of one man, if we did?"

CHAPTER 30

Two days later, Craig was obsessing over whether he was going to be permitted to leave the safehouse to go into Sedona. He knew full well that Connor was concerned about Danielle becoming too much of a distraction. If he was troubled, Craig couldn't even imagine what Jenkins must have been thinking.

When he asked for a car after he'd finished his day's training, he fully expected to have his request denied. Instead, a black Jeep Wrangler and driver were waiting for him outside the log cabin. He would have preferred to drive himself, but twenty years of competition-level drinking hadn't lent itself to maintaining a clean license. Craig had lost his when he was twenty-eight and had never seen the need to reapply, not that he would have succeeded.

Danielle had suggested they meet at a funky, cowboy bar and restaurant on highway 89A only a few miles from the safehouse. Craig was dropped off at the front entrance and walked through a pair of swing doors just like the ones in classic western TV shows and movies.

Inside, the place was throbbing. A long wooden bar sat between two dining areas. Instead of bar stools, the clientele had to mount suspended saddles that looked well-worn and very easy to fall from, especially if intoxicated.

Before Craig could ask the hostess where to sit, Danielle's head popped up from the crowd at the back of the right-hand section. She waved until she finally got Craig's attention as well as those of a few men who were clearly on the 'hunt'.

"I thought you said somewhere quiet," Craig said once he'd battled his way through the masses.

"I forgot that it was taco Tuesday," Danielle replied.

"Which means?"

"Two for one tacos, duh," she said in an exaggerated, valley-girl voice.

Danielle had managed to snag a booth despite there only being the two of them. Groups of four who were waiting to be seated did little to veil their displeasure at the gross breach of dining etiquette.

"We're getting glared at," Craig announced.

"Let them look. It's a first-come-first-serve world we live in."

"You should tell them that," he joked.

Danielle started to rise from her seat. "You know ... I think I will."

Craig gently pushed her back down. "I was just kidding."

"So was I, but I wanted to see what you'd do. I don't usually allow physical contact on a first date, but on this occasion, I'll let it pass."

A waitress appeared at the table and asked what they wanted to drink. Craig was suddenly hit with an almost overwhelming craving for a Cuero shot and a beer back.

"I'll have a draft root beer," Danielle ordered.

Craig was surprised. "Just cause I'm not drinking, doesn't mean that you can't have one."

"Haven't touched a drop of the hard stuff in over ten years. No reason to leap off the semi-wagon at this point."

"You didn't tell me," Craig replied.

"You didn't ask," she said, smiling.

The waitress cleared her throat.

"Sorry," Craig said. "I'll try one of those root beers as well."

"Do you know what you want to eat?" she asked.

Craig looked to Danielle for inspiration.

"It's taco Tuesday. The choice has been made for us," she stated. Danielle turned back to the waitress. "I'll have the Taco Grandes with fish."

"Beans and rice?"

"Absolutely."

The waitress looked down at Craig.

"I guess I'll have the same."

"Good choice," she said as she entered his order into what looked to be an oversized iPhone.

Once she was gone, Danielle patted Craig's arm. "So, they let you out, huh? I thought you were worried about that."

"I was, but they must not have minded."

"Then why were you so concerned?" she asked. "Surely

going out on a date after a day's work is hardly that earth-shattering a concept."

Craig wasn't immediately sure how to respond. Danielle was right, it shouldn't have been a big deal, but he hadn't exactly given her the whole story about why he was in Sedona. Especially the part about time-walking and alternate dimensions. Probably because Danielle may not have fully understood the part about his having a wife and kids in a timeline that he was supposed to restore.

"The other consultants all like to stay in at the house so they can discuss anything that may have come up during the day and requires more detail or explanation," Craig replied, lying through his teeth.

"So, you should be there," she stated.

"Probably, but I wanted to see you."

"Why? You don't know anything about me."

"That's why I wanted to see you," Craig answered. "So, I could find out more. Then, I would be in a better position to decide if I want to spend any more time with you."

Danielle smiled. "Trust me. The more you get to know me, the more you're gonna want to hang around."

"You're that sure of yourself?"

"Someone's gotta be," she stated.

"So, tell me some of the basics. We jumped past that and went right into baggage exchange."

"Okay. I was born in Utah, but I already told you that. When I was a teen, before the whole fixed marriage thing, my dream was to run into Brandon Flowers so that we could fall head over heels in love, and I could spend my life touring with him and the band."

"A Killers fan, huh?"

"Big time. Then I heard that he got married and started having kids and that somehow diluted the fantasy aspect of my plan."

"It would," Craig said, smiling. "Are you still a fan of the band?"

"That, nobody can take away from me."

"Favourite song?" Craig asked.

"*Are We Human*," she replied immediately.

"Album?"

"Live at the Albert Hall. What's your favourite band?"

"When I was a kid and then a Marine, I was a big Springsteen fan, but after the breakdown and subsequent tangle with Señor Cuervo, I didn't really have any urges to listen to music."

"That's sad. I think I'd at least like to imagine that in your darkest moments you still had music to help you through."

"Music couldn't even have made a dent."

"Okay, then," Danielle said, determined to change the subject. "What's your next question for me?"

"Favourite food?" Craig asked.

Danielle gestured to the surrounding dining area. "Tex-Mex. You?"

"Probably pizza. But it has to be a good one."

"There's a place just past Bell Rock that makes the best pizza I've ever had. Maybe if you decide that I am worthy of another date, we can go there."

"I like your optimism," Craig said with mock sincerity.

"What about hobbies?"

"What about them?" she asked.

"Do you have any?"

"I like to shoot," she replied. "Going out into the desert and spending an hour or so shooting up tin cans, is my idea of a perfect afternoon."

Craig felt a chill spread up his back. He at first thought it was the first sign of an anxiety episode, but after a few moments realised that they weren't those kinds of chills. These were the happy ones.

"A girl ... sorry, woman, who loves The Killers, Tex-Mex and shooting ... I have to say, your chances of a further meeting are increasing by the second."

"Oh, be still my heart," Danielle joked.

"Are you any good?"

"That's a bit personal," she shot back, grinning.

"At shooting," Craig said, trying not to smile. "Are you any good at shooting?"

"You already told me that you were a sniper in the Marines so don't think you're going to get me into a shooting challenge."

"I can't believe you think I'd do something that petty and childish," Craig stated.

"But that's exactly what you were going to do, wasn't it?" she asked, smiling.

"Oh, yeah. No question about it." He grinned back.

They spent the next hour and a half digging deeper into each other's past. They both felt comfortable opening up their lives as if they'd known each other for years. Even with the tangy, taco sauce still covering their mouths and chins, they kept on talking.

At the end of the evening, before making for their cars, they hesitated outside the restaurant entrance. There was a moment of pure electric chemistry as they stared into each other's eyes.

Like a couple of stumbling teens, neither seemed able to make the next move. Finally, Danielle stepped forward and gently kissed Craig on the cheek.

"Please don't turn out to be a schmuck," she whispered.

Craig watched as she made her way to a tired looking Toyota Corolla. She looked back once, smiled then got in the car and drove off.

Craig missed her immediately. It had been half a lifetime ago since he'd felt any sort of emotional bonding.

As he stood alone in the parking lot, it dawned on him that the life that Connor and International Dimensions were promising him must be filled with the same degree of power-packed feelings. If they were correct and he was happily married with two great kids, such sensations must be a common occurrence, but to an ex-Marine sniper who'd spent the last twenty years living out of a tequila bottle, it was almost too much to believe, especially as he only knew the one life.

The one with Danielle in it.

For the first time, it hit him hard that he was going to have to make a very difficult choice. Possibly one that no other human being had ever had to make before.

His choice would be to accept what he had at that

moment and build on it, or lose everything he currently knew on the gamble of a promised, alternate lifetime.

It was one hell of a choice.

CHAPTER 31

The next three days were spent in intensive training with Jack. The one big change was that, instead of it just being the two of them alone in the break-out room, Hania was also present for the sessions. He never said a word and simply watched quietly from his chair, his face completely expressionless.

Jack had created a series of exercises so that Craig could expand his limited time-walking abilities. By the end of the first morning, Craig was able to step back a full ten minutes rather than the few seconds he'd managed before. By the end of the day, he could jump back and forth for longer and longer periods. Though impressive, Craig was still nowhere near able to walk to a specific time and remain there indefinitely, as was essential for accomplishing the mission.

It wasn't until midway through the following morning when Jack showed him the trick of starting a time-walk a millisecond before he was about to astral project. Craig was shown how, if he timed it correctly, at the very instant when the projection would occur, he could force himself to jump back much farther than he'd ever imagined possible.

The effect was instantaneous and terrifying, at least the first few times. He would open his eyes, and everything was changed. Depending on how far back he went, the décor within the house changed just like in the movie adaption of H G Wells' *The Time Machine*. Buoyed by this newfound ability, at the end of the day's session he tried to walk back as far as his mind could imagine and found himself on a cliff ledge a few feet from the broken-down cabin, sitting where the safehouse would one day be built.

"I thought that it was impossible to go back beyond one's lifetime?" Craig asked when he was finished with the walk.

"It is. You couldn't have gone back farther than your lifetime," Jack stated.

"Then explain to me why I ended up halfway down the cliff on a ledge where this house should have been?"

"The safehouse was built in 1992," Jack explained patiently. "You would have been around thirteen at the time, hence you were able to send yourself back to a time before this place was here."

"I don't see why I have to keep going back and forth," Craig grumbled in frustration. "I understand it's practice and all, but it seems like overkill. I mean, I'm only going to have to jump the once, right?"

"It will only be once, but it will still be one hundred percent your responsibility to not just get yourself and Connor to exactly the right time and to remain there as long as is needed, but to also bring the two of you back if things go wrong. Despite what you may think, you do not have the ability yet to have that level of control."

"How close am I?" Craig asked. "I feel like I must be getting close."

"You're not close," Hania said, his voice barely above a whisper. "Your mind is like mush. You have to focus."

"I am focussing," Craig insisted.

"No, you are not," Hania replied.

"I'm doing the best I can," Craig barked back.

"Your best is not good enough. You have to focus and cleanse your thoughts of unneeded contemplations."

"That's what I've been doing," Craig insisted.

"No. That's not what you have been doing. You have been thinking of someone else. Someone to whom you are growing attached. There can be no room for distractions while time-walking. If your mind wanders for even a second during the transitional phase, it can be highly dangerous for you and your guest."

"Dangerous how?" Craig asked.

Hania just shook his head.

Jack responded for him. "You could inadvertently launch your mind into a non-linear time dimension in which you have no control whatsoever."

"How do I get back from something like that?" Craig looked to Jack then Hania.

"That's the problem," Hania stated in a serious tone. "You don't."

*

After that day's training, Craig's driver pulled into the parking lot of a generic strip mall less than a mile beyond Bell Rock. Two doors down from a chain, hardware store, was Red Rock Pizza. From the outside, Craig wasn't impressed even though Danielle had told him that they made the best pizza she'd ever eaten.

After glancing at himself in the vanity mirror, he stepped out of the jeep and entered the restaurant. Craig's first reaction was disappointment. The inside was as uninspiring as the exterior. Brown Naugahyde booths were set against one wall and five hi-tops filled the rest of the space.

Just as Craig was starting to doubt Danielle's claims about the place, a waft of baking dough, oregano and spicy tomato sauce reached him. The result was pure Pavlovian instinct. His mouth began to water, and his stomach started growling.

Craig spotted Danielle in the last booth as she poked her head above the partition and waved him over.

"I'll give you this much," Craig said as he slid in opposite her. "It smells good."

"You wait."

Danielle was wearing a pale-blue, western-style shirt with pearl buttons and an embroidered collar. He couldn't help noticing that the top three were undone affording him a view of her perfect neck as well as a tantalising hint of cleavage.

Craig felt his mouth go dry and for the first time in what seemed like decades, he could feel himself getting aroused.

"You look nice," he said, his voice just a smidge higher

than usual.

"So do you," Danielle replied, mimicking his higher register.

Craig could feel his face redden at her having noticed the effect she had on him.

"I ordered their home-made lemonade. I hope that's not too presumptuous of me?"

"Just sitting with a woman who uses words like presumptuous, won me over," Craig replied, grinning.

"What's good here?" he asked.

"It's really up to you but I would recommend having pizza," Danielle said with a straight face.

"Cute." Craig shook his head. "Let me try again. If I was to have pizza here, which one would you recommend?"

"Wow. Choosing the right pizza for someone you hardly know is a serious responsibility. What if I said Hawaiian with extra pineapple?"

"Then we'd have a real problem."

"Good answer," Danielle smiled. "I know it doesn't sound very adventurous, but you should try the Margherita pizza. It's amazing."

"What are you having?" Craig asked.

"I'm having spaghetti. I can't stand pizza."

"You're kidding?"

Danielle sighed. "Of course, I'm kidding. You already know that I love pizza. I'm having the Margherita. I always do."

Before Craig could respond, a waitress arrived with their lemonades and took their order.

"How's the planning going for your hotel in Jordan?" Danielle asked once the waitress left them alone.

"It's condos and they're in Oman, but nice try."

"Just checking that your story still matches what you originally told me," she replied.

"Why don't you believe that that's what I'm doing here?"

Danielle took a moment to study him while she tried to find the right words.

"It just seems a little strange that a massive development in the Middle East would rely on the input of a Marine sniper, who, by his own admission, had a breakdown and became a full-scale alcoholic. Don't take this the wrong way, but I just can't see what you bring to the table. There must be some heavy-weight consulting companies that specialize in security for construction projects in the Middle East. Unless I'm sorely mistaken, your tours in Afghanistan and Iraq hardly make you an expert in Oman."

Craig couldn't help but smile. Danielle had seen through the cover story that Connor had provided with ridiculous ease.

"Maybe I'm just that good," Craig suggested.

"Maybe, you're just that full of shit," Danielle shot back. "Look, if I'm reading the room correctly, you and I are becoming something of an item."

"Go on," Craig replied, nodding.

"I'm too old and have had too many shitty experiences with lying men. I'd like to think that you might feel it beneficial to be straight with me. I don't think that starting off a relationship with a lie is a particularly good first step."

"I agree."

"Then tell me the truth."

"I can't tell you the truth. At least not in any detail. What I will say is that I am being trained for a project that I can't discuss."

"Why you?" she asked.

"I have some skills that are a perfect match for what this operation requires," Craig replied.

"Your shooting skills?" she asked.

"Among other things."

"I take it that these other things are the part you can't talk about?"

"Pretty much."

"Please tell me that you're not screwing with me. That you don't have a wife and kids a couple of counties over."

"I swear that I don't have a wife and kids," Craig replied trying to sound as sincere as possible. The problem was that she had inadvertently drawn blood with her comment, especially as that's exactly what he had, but instead of counties, they were an entire timeline away.

"Do you want to try that again, but this time as if you mean it?" Danielle asked, concerned.

"I do mean it," Craig replied. "I just wish I could tell you everything."

"So do I."

The pizzas arrived and Craig, relieved at the distraction, pulled away a slice and bit off the thin end.

"Oh my God," he managed to say, his mouth full. "This is delicious."

"Why would I lie?" Danielle said as she bit into her slice. There was something in her tone that gave the question a little more bite than Craig liked. It almost felt like the rest of the question was 'so why would you?'.

They ate in silence, partially because of the fantastic food, but also because neither knew exactly what to say at that point.

After devouring their pizzas, both attempted some light small talk to get things back on the rails, but a sense of tension hung in the air and made any real conversation stilted and overly complex.

Craig paid the bill and the two stepped out into the clear, high-desert air.

"I'm sorry I fucked up the dinner," Craig said as he looked out towards Bell Rock.

"You didn't. If anyone screwed things up it was me," Danielle offered.

"Can we give this another try? Soon?"

"You make it sound like the evening's over," Danielle said, stepping closer to him.

"Isn't it?"

"Not if you don't want it to be?" she whispered conspiratorially.

"But I thought ..."

"Stop thinking and follow me back home." Danielle leaned into him and kissed him gently on the mouth before walking to her car.

Craig had so many thoughts vying for attention that he stood routed in place for a good few seconds. It wasn't until

Danielle honked that he ran to his waiting ride.

His driver followed her to a small townhouse development in the town of Oak Creek. There were no streetlights, and the surrounding red hills were capped by a dark purple sky and a shimmering starfield.

Danielle's townhouse was at the junction of a paved road and raw, high-desert scrubland. They pulled up alongside her faded blue Toyota and Craig sat in the jeep as he tried to get his heartbeat to settle down.

Craig jumped as Danielle knocked on the passenger window.

"You planning to come in or are you happier out here?" she asked, smiling.

Craig grinned sheepishly as he climbed out of the vehicle and walked alongside her.

"Should I wait?" the driver asked, having lowered his window.

Craig, not wanting to seem too overconfident about how the rest of the evening would progress, suggested that he stay and wait for him.

"That was very gentlemanly of you," Danielle said as she took his arm. "Most men would have probably told him that he wouldn't be needing the car anymore tonight."

"I'm not like most men," Craig replied.

"God, I hope not."

As they walked towards Danielle's front door, Craig glanced up at the dark hills. "It's kind of creepy up here."

"Just what every girl wants to hear from a man she's bringing home for the first time."

"I just meant …"

"I know what you meant. I'm teasing. I do that when I get nervous."

"I thought I was the nervous one," Craig admitted.

"I'm putting a lot of faith in you being the decent guy I think you are. Of course, I'm nervous. Despite my chequered past, this is still a big deal for me."

"There's no reason to be scared," Craig replied.

"I never said I was scared, why are you?"

"Yeah, a little."

Danielle smiled as she inserted her key and opened the door.

CHAPTER 32

The townhouse was small but cosy. The furniture, though inexpensive, was cleverly eclectic and gave the place a personal feel. Danielle switched on a standing side lamp then flipped a switch on the wall. A fire instantly came to life within a glassed-in hearth.

"I've never been able to decide if that is seriously cool or really cheesy," Danielle stated.

"I'd have to say cool, but in a sleazy, bachelor-pad kind of way," Craig said, while nodding his approval.

Danielle burst out laughing.

"You're right. That's exactly what it seems like. Thank you for putting it into context."

She stepped towards him and kissed him. Craig wrapped her in his arms and kissed her back. She tasted of pizza sauce and mint. As their kissing grew more intense, Danielle bit down gently on his lower lip causing Craig to softly moan.

Danielle stepped out of the embrace and instructed Alexa to play *Sting Duets* and headed for the kitchen.

"I've got orange juice, diet Sprite or fizzy water."

"Soda water would be great," he replied as he tried to position his erection in such a way as to make it less obvious to her and more comfortable for him.

Craig wandered round the living room looking at some of Danielle's photos and ornaments as Sting and Melody Gardot's voices filled the air. In every picture, Danielle looked happy and carefree as if the camera had managed to capture a moment of exquisite joy.

"You seem to have lots of friends," Craig commented.

"I do seem to have quite a few. Just lucky I guess," she called back from the other room.

"Who's the guy in the cowboy hat?" Craig asked, feeling as if he'd seen him before. "He seems to be in a lot of the pictures."

"That's Freddie. He's the manager of the restaurant where I work," Danielle said as she handed Craig his water.

"Did you two have a thing?"

"A thing?" Danielle said, amused. "What a quaint way of saying it. The answer is no. I always thought we would, but he never seemed to want to move from friendship to something else."

"What's he going to think about you and me?"

"I have no intention of telling anyone about us until I am certain that there really is an us."

Craig nodded. "That sounds like a safe plan."

"Feeling safe is important."

"And do you feel safe with me?" Craig asked.

"If I didn't, you wouldn't be here, and I certainly wouldn't offer to share some of this."

Danielle produced a thin, hand-rolled joint from her shirt pocket and a lighter from her jeans. She carefully lit the end. After drawing in as much smoke as she could, she placed her lips only a millimetre away from Craig's and gently blew. He inhaled deeply. For a moment their eyes were rivetted on each other, then Craig started to cough.

"Pretty smooth, huh?" she asked, smiling.

"Exceptionally," Craig replied between coughs and wheezes. "I'm not even sure I should be doing this."

"That's okay, I'll smoke the rest if you don't want it."

Craig took the joint from her hand and took a deep toke. Danielle touched her lips to his as she slowly inhaled the cannabis smoke. She pressed her lips harder against his and gently opened her mouth.

As their tongues touched, Craig could feel the grass taking effect. It was strong stuff. He'd only ever indulged when in-country in Afghanistan and Iraq and assumed that he'd smoked the good stuff out there. It was nothing compared to the single hit he'd taken from Danielle's stash.

She took his hand and led him to her worn leather sofa that faced the fire. She snuggled up next to him as the two shared a couple more hits on the joint. At one point, Danielle produced a small remote-control unit from the coffee table and pointed it at the hearth. She pushed a button and the flames got bigger.

"No way," Craig exclaimed, amazed.

"That's not all," she said with stoned pride. "Watch this."

She pressed another button and the flames changed from the normal fire colour to dark green, then to bright blue.

Something about the remote-controlled fire resonated in his cannabis infused brain and he started to laugh. Seeing him hooting with laughter as tears ran down his face, Danielle lost it as well and the pair giggled for almost five minutes straight before Danielle slid over and sat on Craig's lap, facing him.

The two grew silent as Danielle slowly removed her shirt then leaned forwards and kissed him.

Whether it was the pot, the passion, or both, but the kiss was different. It was all consuming. Craig moved his hands up Danielle's back and unsnapped her bra. She leaned backwards allowing him to gently lick each nipple until the tingling sensation was almost too much for her.

Danielle eased herself down onto the floor and looked up at Craig with pure lust and desire. She reached for his belt buckle and slowly separated the two halves. She unzipped his jeans revealing his engorged penis straining against his white briefs.

Danielle started to pull down the top of his underwear.

"Wait," Craig said, his voice raspy. "I have to tell you something first."

"What could you possibly need to tell me at this exact moment?"

"I need to tell you why I'm really in Sedona. You have to know before we go any farther."

With the mood shattered, Danielle got off her knees, put on her shirt, shouted for Alexa to turn off the music and sat facing Craig.

"Go on," she said, her voice was calm but with an icy trace.

"I'm sorry," Craig said as he zipped up his jeans. "I should have said something before now ... before we ... you know."

"Yes, I do know."

Craig nodded. The happy, carefree sensation of the pot had changed and was starting to make him feel a little claustrophobic.

"This is going to be hard," Craig said as he tried to think of the best way to tell Danielle what she needed to know.

"Telling the truth shouldn't be that difficult. Not unless you really are a bad person."

"It's hard because I don't see any way of telling you why I am here and where I will soon be going without it sounding like the world's worse lie."

"Try me," Danielle said.

"First of all, I need to tell you a story about a 16th century witch called Beyath."

"Oh fuck," Danielle said as she subconsciously held a throw cushion against her chest. It had never dawned on her that Craig was anything other than what he said he was. A broken man. But with his first few words of the 'true story' she suddenly had to question his sanity and her safety.

"Maybe we should do this another time," she suggested, suddenly wanting to get him out of the house.

"I'll tell you what," Craig said, holding his hands up in a show of surrender. "Let me show you one simple thing. If after that, you don't want to hear any more, I'll leave."

"Just so long as you stay right where you are. I'm not

feeling like having you too close to me at this exact moment."

"That's fine. I don't want you to be scared, okay?"

"Too late for that."

"Here we go," Craig said as he closed his eyes.

Danielle stared at him, wondering what the hell he was doing.

The next thing she knew, they were sitting on the sofa laughing hysterically at the remote-controlled fire as Sting's voice acted as an aural backdrop.

Then Danielle stopped laughing.

"What the fuck?" she said, jumping to her feet. What did you do to me?"

"Nothing. I just walked us back in time."

"The fuck you did," Danielle said, looking around the room and noticing a few oddities. The cushions on the sofa had been thrown to the floor when the kissing had become passionate. They were now back in place where they had been earlier. The fire was bright blue yet a second earlier it had looked like a regular fire. Danielle ran her hands up her chest and felt her bra back where it had been before Craig had removed it. What made the whole thing ever creepier was that the Sting Duets album was playing from a point that had past, many minutes earlier.

"It can't be real. There's no way anyone can do that."

"Yet, I just did," he replied in a calm voice.

"Prove it," she demanded.

Craig closed his eyes.

Danielle was back in the armchair facing the sofa. The music was off, and the fire was the right colour.

"You're back in present day," Craig advised. "Will you now try to believe what I have to tell you?"

Danielle nodded.

CHAPTER 33

Craig told her the story of Beyath and how she'd preyed on the family of a deputy sheriff in Southern Utah. He told her how, together with a Native American by the name of Ahote, they had walked back in time to 1996 and thought they had killed the witch. He then explained how Beyath had, in fact survived and taken Ahote, then, out of pure vengeance, she had killed the deputy's in-laws before the woman who would become his wife had even been born, thus robbing the man of his entire family.

Danielle listened patiently and waited until Craig had finished the explanation.

"Let's say I believe all that. I'm not sure I understand what all that has to do with you?"

"The sheriff's name was Craig Edmonds," he said with a sigh.

"That's weird. You two ..."

Craig waited for the penny to drop. He knew it had when Danielle's face paled, and her hand shot to her mouth.

"That was you. You're the deputy sheriff. You're the one

who lost his wife and children."

"Yes and no," Craig replied. "All that happened in a different timeline. In this one, I can honestly say that I have never had a wife and family, just as I told you when we met."

Danielle stared at him long and hard as she tried to put the pieces of the complex matrix together in her head.

"So, you never met … what's her name, by the way?"

"Jenny, and no, because, as Beyath killed her grandmother long before she was ever born, she has, in reality, never existed in the only world I've lived in."

"You do see how this could easily be construed as being the biggest bullshit story in the history of bullshit stories, don't you?" Danielle asked.

Craig nodded.

"So, I still don't get why you are here."

"I am one of the only people alive who can both time-walk and has the skills to fight Beyath."

"What are you saying, she's here … now?"

"No, that's why the time-walk is necessary. I'm going to take Connor back with me to 1968, the day that Jenny's grandmother was killed. We plan to destroy Beyath before she can do any more damage."

Danielle cocked her head to one side as a thought hit her. "If you kill the witch before she kills your grandmother-in law, doesn't that mean that you will, in effect, re-set everything? That your original life will be restored, and you will have your wife and children back?"

"Theoretically yes, but no one knows for sure how all that will actually work. It's hoped that this alternate life will simply be erased and the other me will simply continue life with his family as if nothing ever happened."

"Won't he … you … whatever, remember what happened?" she asked.

"Not according to the people who know about this stuff. That version of me will never have been impacted in any way. In fact, because Beyath would be destroyed before she first threatened my supposed family, I won't have ever encountered Ahote and will be totally unaware of time-walking, alternate dimensions and …"

"Crazy old witches?" Danielle finished the thought.

"Exactly. Crazy old witches."

"Let me get this straight. If you are completely successful on this mission, you won't be coming back to me?"

"If it plays out like they say it should, you and I will never have met."

"I guess that's better that my sitting here waiting for you to return," she sighed. "What if it doesn't happen that way?"

"What Connor and I are going to attempt is absurdly dangerous. There's every chance that Beyath could end up killing us both."

"I don't like that option either. Are there any ones where you and I get to be together?"

"Absolutely. Beyath might not appear at all, which pretty much ensures that this will remain the only timeline in which I will live. Alternatively, we might just scare her off or wound her so that she retreats into her dimension leaving this timeline intact."

"I have to be the only woman in history to have to go

through what will most certainly be the strangest waiting period imaginable. Just exactly how long will you be gone?"

"The training is expected to be finished in just over ten days."

"You don't have an exact schedule," she asked, surprised.

"We don't need one. It's not as if the past is going to change because we take longer to visit it."

"Once the mission starts, how long will you be gone?"

Craig smiled. "That's the cool part of time-walking. Even though I might be back in 1968, we'll return within seconds of having gone back."

"So, you will actually come back here, to Sedona?"

"That was more of a figure of speech. Don't forget, if this works according to plan, this timeline will simply cease to have ever existed. Craig Edmonds will continue on with his life in Kanab, Utah as if nothing ever happened, because, to him, nothing ever did."

"That sucks," Danielle said.

"Actually, I've been giving a lot of thought to not going back and changing the timeline. I mean, why spoil what we have now?"

"You can't just not go," Danielle stated. That witch has killed or erased too many people. You don't have the option of letting her continue just because you're falling in love with me."

"I didn't say I was falling in love with you."

Danielle gave him a questioning stare.

"Okay, so maybe I am falling in love with you, but that's even more reason to stay."

"Not reason enough. I should probably mention at this point that I feel the same way about you, but we can't ride off into the sunset together knowing that by doing so, we are responsible for countless deaths so far, and countless more if that ancient bitch is allowed to stay alive."

"But ..." Craig started to say.

"No buts. Here's what's going to happen. You are going to go back to wherever the hell you are staying and keep training. I don't want to see you again until such time as your timeline and mine actually mesh together cleanly. I have to protect myself, and that's why I don't want to talk to you, see you or even hear about you until you've completed the mission."

"That's not exactly fair," Craig said.

"Fair!" she said raising her voice. "What part of this whole thing has been fair?"

Danielle's eyes reddened.

"How could you let me fall for you without telling me all this? I've got to tell you, I'm almost hating you at the moment."

She leaned over and kissed him once then pointed to the front door.

"Please go."

Craig wanted to say more but saw the look of fragility in her eyes and knew that he had to give her the space she needed.

As he shut the door behind him, he could hear her crying as he walked towards the waiting jeep.

The drive back to the safehouse was surreal. Despite the

sadness that had enveloped him after Danielle's words, Craig couldn't ignore the impossibly bright, night sky filled with stars stretching back to the formation of the entire universe.

Something about the experience of being on the empty road with the heavenly lightshow framing the darkened mountains, made him realise just how small and insignificant the earth really was and just how important it was for everyone to do what they could to preserve it. That included ridding the world of a demonic force that used the planet as a feeding ground.

Craig knew that he would continue the mission as planned and would do everything in his power to destroy Beyath and put right the chaos that she'd created. If somehow the end result was that he was able to return to Danielle; all the better.

*

Danielle stared out into the night as tears clouded her eyes while she watched the taillights of the jeep dwindle then disappear. Though telling Craig that she didn't want to see him until everything was cleared up had been the right thing to do, she was missing him already and prayed that he would have the driver turn around and bring him back to her.

Finally, Danielle closed the vertical blinds and, after turning off the downstairs' lights, made her way upstairs. It wasn't until she entered her bedroom that her mood began to lift. Just seeing the intricately carved mirror that had been left on her doorstep the previous day sent a shiver of pleasure through her body.

As she approached it, she heard a rustling sound coming from the attic.

She knew that it was just some night critters looking for a warm place to nest.

What harm could come from that?

CHAPTER 34

The next week passed quickly. Craig made no more trips to town and focussed on the training. Much to the surprise and delight of the rest of the team, Craig even insisted that they start earlier each day and work right up to dinner time.

Craig learned how to control every aspect of time-walking, but knew that he was still basically a novice when it came to the subtleties of the art.

Hania continued to monitor each session and never said a word or changed his blank, serene expression. It wasn't until three days before the tentative mission start-date that Hania interrupted his grandson and announced that it was time for Craig to start using his timeline instead of Craig's own.

Hania announced that at six o'clock the next morning, Craig would meet him in the run-down cabin above the safehouse and, working together, Craig would be able to travel back to a time before he was even born.

Craig hardly slept. His mind had gone into monkey-brain mode and was filled with dozens of unrelated and random thoughts. No matter how hard he tried to focus on one thing, a swarm of battling mental impressions destroyed any possibility of focus. What made it even worse was that Cher's lyrics, *Do You Believe in Life After Love,* was stuck firmly in his head and would not leave. The weird thing was that Craig wasn't even a fan of Cher or the song and had no idea why it had chosen to nest in his already troubled brain.

Suddenly, Craig had a craving for a drink. All the other thoughts and even the song crept to the background as Craig unconsciously visualized a half full bottle of Cuervo and a shot glass. He could even taste the sour flavour of the tequila and feel the bite as it hit the back of his throat.

Craig felt stress chills crawl up his back as he started to sweat. He had never felt the need for a drink so much in his life, and that was saying something. As a practicing alcoholic for over twenty years, he'd had more than his share of terrifying cravings, but none as bad as the one he was having at that moment.

Craig prayed for the night to end and for the crushing desire to go away.

Then something made him open his eyes. Standing at the end of his bed was a spectral figure of a man. A weak golden light outlined the body and after a few seconds, Craig was relieved to see that it was Hania. What wasn't a relief was that the old man seemed to be translucent.

Craig watched in shock as the figure floated into the air and moved above the bed, towards him. A ghostly hand reached out and touched Craig's lips then almost instantly, the vision vanished.

Craig wasn't sure which part unnerved him the most; the apparition or the fact that the second the hand touched him, Craig tasted the sweetest tequila he'd ever imagined. It was smooth and warming without any of the usual burn that accompanied his normal tipple.

Craig didn't feel remotely intoxicated, yet the craving for a drink was miraculously gone. So were his jumbled thoughts. In their place, all that remained was a sense of peace and calm.

Craig closed his eyes and fell immediately to sleep.

*

The next morning, Craig met with Hania at six sharp. He felt well rested, and his mind was clear yet surprisingly focussed.

"Was that you last night?" Craig asked the old man.

"I don't understand the question?" Hania answered.

"Did you come to my room last night? I thought I saw you there."

"You were dreaming. I never left my room."

Hania could see that his answer troubled Craig.

"This visitor you dreamed of; did he help?"

"Actually, yes. He helped a lot. But you're sure it wasn't you?" Craig asked.

"I think I would remember something like that," Hania said as he turned away, not wanting Craig to see the smile that briefly crossed his lips. "At least you seem calm this morning. Let's begin."

"From here?" Craig asked, surprised as he looked around

the derelict cabin.

"This is a good place for us. The house below is too new. This one is well over a hundred years old so will have existed back to when you will be walking."

"How far back are we going?" Craig asked.

"I thought that for the first trip we should go as far back as possible. Once we have managed that, we will spend the rest of these few remaining days with you practicing date specific time-walking. First, please bring those chairs over here in the middle of the room."

Craig looked round the cabin and noticed a pair of hand carved wooden chair stacked one atop the other at the far end of the room. After trying to rid them of as much dust as possible, he placed them where Hania indicated.

"What now?" Craig asked.

"Now we sit."

The two sat facing each other.

"Do you understand how this will work?" Hania asked.

"I think so. You will create a time-walk environment and when I concentrate on a time in my past, I will instead, somehow be able to access your timeline memories instead of mine."

"You say that as if it was an everyday occurrence. I hope you realise the power with which you have been gifted."

"I do, but once this mission is complete, you don't have to worry. I have no intention of ever using it again."

"I'm glad you believe that," Hania replied.

"Why did you say that? It sounded as if you think I will."

"Oh, I'm certain you believe what you say, however, if

there is one thing that life has shown me, it is that we should never plan a future that is rarely within our control."

"Are you talking about this mission or … later on?"

"Yes," was all Hania replied. "But let us not concern ourselves with tomorrow, as first we must focus on yesterday."

Hania closed his eyes and began to close his mind to all extraneous thought. Craig, not sure what he was supposed to do, closed his eyes as well.

"Think of your earliest thought," Hania said, his voice low and soft.

Craig found his mind taking him back to the little house in Apache Junction where he'd lived with his birth parents before their death. The farthest he could stretch his memory was to his fourth birthday party when it had still been a relatively happy home and his parents had surprised him with a brand-new, red tricycle. His mother had baked a chocolate, angel-food cake. The ceiling of their small kitchen was festooned with balloons that had been filled with helium and were being swirled around the slow-moving ceiling fan.

Craig felt a wave of happiness and loss.

"Think back further," Hania whispered.

"I can't. That's as far as I …" Even as he said the words, it was as if a massive door opened in front of him and new memories began spilling in, flooding his mind. They were strong, vivid recollections, but Craig immediately realised that weren't his. He suddenly had the memories of the old man.

268

"Now think as far back as you can," Hania instructed.

Craig concentrated and found that he could clearly remember standing on an open plain as a man that he knew to be his, or rather, Hania's father, gave him his first bow and arrow. Craig understood that he was now remembering Hania's birthday. His eighth birthday. He could also distinctly remember the happiness he felt back on that day. He'd had other 'play' bows to use since he'd turned five, but what his father had handed him on that day was an adult bow. A hand-carved hunting bow.

"Now time-walk back to that memory," Hania said.

Craig started the astral projection process then as soon as he felt his mind begin separating from his body, he used his inner strength to bring his mind and body together, thereby forming the time-walk bubble.

There was a momentary sensation of dizziness then nothing. Craig opened his eyes and saw that Hania was looking intently back at him.

"Nothing happened," Craig said, disappointed.

Hania just shrugged. "I would not worry. This, like everything else in life, takes patience and practice. Let's get some air then we can try again."

They stepped out of the cabin into a sparklingly bright, sun-drenched day. The only sounds were that of early morning bird song and the wind as it passed through the dense pine trees.

"Beautiful day," Craig commented.

"Extraordinary," Hania said as he stood with his back to Craig while looking down the valley towards Sedona.

Craig followed his gaze and suddenly felt unsteady and, quite frankly, terrified.

Sedona was gone.

CHAPTER 35

Craig looked down Oak Creek Canyon and saw that where the city of Sedona had previously been visible in the distance, now there was only what looked to be farmland and a few homestead dwellings.

"Beautiful, isn't it?" Hania said. "Or should I say, wasn't it?"

"It's gone. I mean there's nothing there but a couple of scraggly looking farms."

"This is how it will look until the 1940s and '50s when people realise that this area is worth visiting."

Craig silently turned and faced the cabin. It looked exactly the same as it had when he first arrived at the safehouse.

"What year is this?" Craig asked.

"I received my first hunting bow in 1926. That was the memory you focussed on and that's the year in which we are now standing."

"But the cabin looks exactly the same," Craig stated.

"I'm told that it was built in the 1870s and abandoned

soon after. It's looked like that for a century and a half."

"That's not possible. It would have turned to dust by now," Craig insisted.

"It would indeed, had it not been for Ahote and I returning here to repair it and provide maintenance," Hania explained.

Craig stared back at the view and shook his head. "We're really here? I mean mind and body?"

Hania nodded. "Why don't you walk around the property for a while so you can get a feel for where and when you are. I would join you but … I'm … feeling very tired."

Hania suddenly stumbled and looked about to collapse. Craig grabbed hold of him before he could fall.

"We need to go back," Craig said.

"No. I am fine."

"You're obviously not fine. Here …" Craig helped Hania sit on a large bolder. "What's wrong with you?"

"I'm old," Hania answered with a weak smile. "Age is the one guaranteed fatal disease."

"We should still get you back to the safehouse so you can be checked out."

"Going back will unfortunately not make me any younger."

A thought hit Craig.

"In a time-walk, shouldn't you be the age you were at this time in your life?" he asked.

"I would be if it was my time-walk, but it was yours, not mine."

"Then shouldn't I have grown younger?" Craig asked.

"You cannot grow younger than the days you have lived. That's the thing about sharing another's timeline. You travelled back in my memory, but because it was a split time-walk envelope, neither of us reverted to an earlier self."

"I still think ..."

"Please, humour me," Hania said. "Walk around and get a feel for the time and place. You will need to understand that you are not simply visualising this moment. You are actually living it."

Craig looked around the property and nodded. He spent the next fifteen minutes walking a full circle around the old cabin. He stopped at one point and lifted a stone. He examined it then threw it hard against a bigger rock. It behaved exactly as a thrown stone would.

When he returned to Hania, the old man was standing again and seemed to have more colour in his face.

"You look better," he commented.

"Looks can be deceiving," the old man replied. "We can go back now if you've seen enough."

"May I ask you one more question?"

"You may."

"When I go back in your timeline but take Connor with me instead of you, what will you be doing?"

"I will be in a meditative state for the duration of your mission so that my timeline envelope remains open to you."

"What if you can't maintain that state?" Craig asked. "I mean, if I'm back in 1968 and you, for some reason, can't meditate any more, what happens to us?"

"All I can say is that I hope you like 1968."

"Why wouldn't we just jump back to when we started?" Craig asked.

"Because that's not how it works. If you visited the past via astral time projection, the event would always default to you returning from when you started. Time-walking is not temporal. Your body and mind exist in the time you have travelled to. There isn't a different version of yourself waiting in present time while you gallivant around in the past. All of you … both mind and body … are in the past. If the link is broken, that is where you will remain."

Craig stared at Hania, trying desperately to choose the next words carefully.

"Are you healthy enough to do this?" he finally asked.

"Not even remotely," Hania replied as he gently patted Craig's back. "That's what makes this so exciting."

Before Craig could respond, Hania added, "I've made it this long. I am relatively certain I can manage a few more weeks. Now, take us home please. I do believe that my bladder is trying to get my attention."

"You could always go right here," Craig suggested.

"I've tried my entire life to live by one simple credo," Hania stated.

"And, what's that?" Craig asked.

"Never piss on the past," Hania replied. "Now, if you don't mind, please take us back to 2022."

*

274

Three days later, they all met in the conference room. Hania and Jack advised Jenkins that they felt Craig was as ready as he could be considering the obvious time constraints. They believed that he was capable of keeping a time-walk environment intact and had become completely comfortable using Hania's timeline as his target guide.

Not that he would ever admit it to anyone else, but Craig was actually happier using someone else's timeline. As the nucleus of the gift relied on the walker being able to focus their mind on a specific event within their lifetime, one that correlated with the date that the time-walk was targeting, it was essential that the person's memory be intact and available to recall.

Between Craig's PTSD and subsequent alcoholism, his memory wasn't that good. Even when in deep meditation, remembering any one specific day was almost impossible. There were also quite a few mentally redacted periods, some as long as a full year, when he couldn't visualise anything.

Thankfully, Hania, once in a meditative state, could recall the most seemingly inconsequential events within his life and mentally compute the day, the date and sometimes even the time. Craig then only had to focus on Hania's targeting and walk back to that moment in time.

"Thank you both," Jenkins replied. "We couldn't do this without your help."

"I think we have you to thank as well," Jack said. "If you hadn't brought me into this ..."

"Kicking and screaming," Connor added.

Jack shrugged. "Yeah, there was a little of that, but to be fair, I didn't really understand what was going on. If you hadn't shown me that my father hadn't abandoned me, I would never have reconnected with my grandfather. This time together has changed my entire outlook on life."

Hania nodded his agreement.

"What about you Craig?" Connor asked. "How do you feel? You're the one who's going to be in the driver's seat. Are you are up for this?"

"When you guys basically kidnapped me in Los Angeles, I wouldn't have believed I could ever get back into any semblance of good health. I know I'm still in bad shape and that it's gonna take years to see any real recovery, but you've put me on the right road. In answer to your question ... yes, I feel I am ready for whatever that creature throws at us."

"That's a pretty brave statement considering we have no idea what she can actually throw at us," Connor commented.

"Just so long as Hania is able to keep his memories intact, I feel that between us, we can deal with whatever she can come up with."

"I certainly hope so," Jenkins replied. "There's a lot riding on you two ... you three ... sorry Hania."

Jenkins looked over at the old man just as his eyes rolled back in his head and he started to swoon forward.

Jack and Connor both managed to stop him from falling and slowly eased him to the ground.

Hania was out cold.

CHAPTER 36

When Hania woke up in his bed within the safehouse, Craig, Jack and Connor were standing over him, all looking very concerned.

"What happened?" Hania asked.

"It appears that you fainted," Connor replied.

"Ah," Hania said, nodding. "I do that occasionally."

"Care to tell us why?" Jack asked.

"I'm well over one hundred years old. It's a miracle that I'm here at all. The fact that I sometimes faint or get cramps or lose my balance seems to me to be a fair trade-off for my longevity."

"So, there's nothing wrong with you?" Connor asked.

"Of course, there is something wrong with me. I'm dying."

The three looked at him in shock.

"Don't worry," Hania said. "It's non-specific. At my age there really is very little that works as things were meant to work. My plumbing's shot, my wiring's obsolete and my skin no longer fits properly. One good sneeze could probably see me off."

Hania could see that his words had not pacified the other three.

"I can say, however, that I would like to believe that I will know with some advance warning when the time comes for me to be taken up into the heavens. So far, I have not had that warning, so, please, don't concern yourself about me. I will keep my timeline intact until the mission is complete."

"No more fainting for the next few days," Jack said gently.

"I'll do my best," Hania said with a weak nod of his head.

"Do you think you'll be strong enough by tomorrow?" Jenkins asked.

"Of course. Why do you even ask?"

The three looked down at Hania's frail condition as they did their best to hide the seeds of doubt that were sprouting in their minds.

*

After dinner, Connor suggested that Craig contact Julie as it was the last chance to speak with her before the mission.

"I was thinking that tomorrow we could stop by her townhouse in Mesa. It's only just down the road from Scottsdale."

"That's a nice thought, but tomorrow for you will be 1968. Julie will be a young child and the townhouse will most likely not even be built yet. Contact her now, while you can."

Connor left the room leaving the communal laptop open

to the Zoom app.

"I'm sorry I haven't made it up to Sedona during your training," Julie said once the video chat was connected. "I have to be honest with you. My nerves can't take seeing you when, in a matter of days ... well, you know."

"Yes, I do know," Craig replied.

"I have to tell you that seeing you in Pendleton, sober and ... closer to the old Craig, was a wonderful gift."

"If all goes well, that's how I will always be. All the pain you've suffered watching me tear myself apart will never have happened."

"I understand that, but I still can't bear the fact that you will soon cease to exist," Julie said as she dabbed a Kleenex to her eyes.

"That's not true. This timeline will vanish but will be replaced by the original one. The one where things turn out okay."

"You can't guarantee that, can you?"

"I can guarantee that I'll do everything in my power to make sure that that's what happens," Craig insisted.

"Will that be enough?" she asked.

"It has to be."

*

The video call didn't last much longer. Neither knew quite what to say after the initial exchange. Julie attempted some half-hearted small talk about local gossip and political disillusionment, but with both of them knowing what was at stake the following day, words seemed somehow redundant.

While both desperately wanted the original timeline to be restored, they were scared at losing the one they had, no matter how bad it had been.

It was complicated.

When they said their goodbyes, both tried to sound upbeat and positive, but neither was that convincing.

*

Connor found Jenkins sitting alone in the panelled study, a large snifter of brandy in his hand. When he looked up, Connor was shocked to see that the man looked to have aged ten years.

"You wanted to see me?" Connor asked.

"It's been confirmed. She was taken four days ago."

"Oh shit," Connor said as he stood across from him. "Are you sure?"

Jenkins picked up a remote and pointed it to a large screen monitor. A video was frozen on a shot of a small eclectically furnished bedroom. At one end was a large, empty frame leaning against the wall. On the floor next to it, a pile of mirror pieces told the whole story.

"You still don't think we should tell him?" Connor asked.

"To what end?" Jenkins replied.

Connor tried to find the right words.

"Say what you're thinking, Connor."

"I'm thinking that if he knew that Danielle had been

taken, he might just be a bit more focussed on ensuring the success of the mission, considering …"

"Considering that he really would have nothing left in this timeline?" Jenkins finished the thought.

"Basically, yes."

Jenkins took a slow sip of his drink before answering.

"I think it could be a big mistake to tell him. He's fragile enough. We have no idea what news like that could do to him. I say we keep this to ourselves."

"I don't like what we are becoming," Connor said as he turned and walked out of the room.

"Neither do I," Jenkins said. "Neither do I."

*

Craig couldn't sleep. For a change, he wasn't being bombarded by dozens of confused thoughts at the same time. It wasn't even thinking about Danielle that was keeping him awake. As he lay flat on the bed with his eyes open, he was thinking about the mission and his part in it.

When Craig was an active Marine, he'd had countless sorties depend solely on his own actions. That had never fazed him. Even when the first tendrils of PTSD brought on icy chills that at times were so bad that they caused him to physically tremble, he never doubted his own abilities.

This time was different. He was out of shape, and despite all the smoke that Jenkins and Connor had blown up his ass about how good he'd done at Pendleton, he knew that he wasn't even remotely fit for this assignment.

Craig knew that when push came to shove, Connor would be the one who would end up killing the witch, at least he hoped that would be the outcome. Spending a few weeks on a Marine base and playing soldier did not a fighting man make. From what he'd heard about Beyath, she was formidable. Hell, she was way beyond that. She was superhuman, if indeed there was any part of her left that was human.

Craig tried to get his thoughts into some sort of controllable order, but one realisation kept fighting its way to the surface. It was something that Craig had never had to deal with the entire time he was a Marine. Something that is trained out of you from day one, turning young recruits into formidable fighting machines.

Craig was scared.

CHAPTER 37

Craig and Connor met Hania in the old cabin. They were both dressed in vintage, used clothes which, once they went back to in 1968, would be current if not exactly fashionable. A third rickety chair had been added to the original two so that all three could sit facing each other. The single room was cold, and the smell of the pine needles and dust was thick in the air.

"This is your play Craig. It's up to you now," Connor said.

Craig took a moment to calm his breathing.

"Hania, are you ready?" he asked.

The old man nodded.

"Let's get started," Craig said as he looked at the others one last time before closing his eyes.

Craig led himself into a deep meditative state and then to the moment just prior to astrally projecting when Hania opened his memory, and his mind could lock on to the time-walk target. They had learned the previous night that on the day that Margaret was taken in 1968, Hania had been forty-nine years old and had been at a tribal conference in Omaha

Nebraska. The specific memory that took him to that day was that during the morning session, the discussion had been focussed on the fact that Native Americans were starting to receive property tax bills for their own tribal land.

The tribal nations were furious and discussed various ways to fight back against such an outrage. The most vocal person in the room was a Seminole tribesman from Florida who suggested that the nations force the US government to permit gambling on tribal land to offset these new costs.

Hania remembered those almost prophetic words as clearly as if they'd been said only last week and was thus able to not just target the date, but also the time of the meeting which had taken place from 10am to midday.

Craig felt a moment of dizziness then the sensation of floating. He opened his eyes and saw that while Connor was still sitting facing him, there was no sign of Hania. Nor should there have been. The old man was to remain in 2022 and clearly had done just that.

"Are we here?" Connor asked.

"I think so. I'm not sure when else this could be."

Connor got to his feet and opened the cabin door. A Ford Bronco was parked outside. It was filthy but looked to be in good condition.

"That's a classic," Craig said as he stood beside Connor.

"Actually, it's only one year old. It was bought off a lot in Phoenix."

"How is that possible?" Craig asked. "Ahote couldn't have bought it."

"Theoretically he could. This is ten years before Beyath

took him, however, the complexities of communicating with someone who ceased to exist in 1978 would have been a nightmare."

"So, who came back?"

"Hania. He did a lot of prep work for us."

"But he's ancient," Craig stated.

"Not when he time-walked back to 1968. He was only middle-aged. He's been coming back for a few days at a time."

"How could he have had the stamina?"

"He was only gone a matter of a few seconds each trip relative to 2022."

"Fuck," Craig said as he held on to the sides of his head. "This is all so weird."

"That's an understatement."

Connor walked over to the fireplace and looked down at the rough wooden floor. He smiled then brought his heal down onto one slightly discoloured plank. It sunk causing the other end to rise up. He raised the piece of wood, revealing a hollowed-out area beneath the flooring. In it were several oilskin bags.

"What the …" Craig said as he watched Connor open each one and place the contents on the rickety wood table in the middle of the room.

The keys to the car, the insurance policy and what appeared to be driver's licences for each of them were in the first bag.

"How could he possibly have had driver's licenses created for us?" Craig asked.

"There's a pretty good chance that those may be modern day fakes, but they'll be good enough to satisfy anyone should we get stopped."

"That's a big gamble."

"It's 1968. There were no computers, no cell phones and no technology to whip up a perfect counterfeit licence. Any policeman who sees one of these will automatically assume that it's legit."

Craig continued watching as Connor removed a pair of mint condition Colt, 45 calibre 1911s from the second bag.

"I don't see why we couldn't have brought something a little more modern back with us," Craig asked. "I mean if Hania could bring back fake drivers licenses, why not guns?"

"Simple," Connor replied. "The driver's licenses were made using old, repurposed credit cards from this era. The plastic and the photo were the same as would be found in this time period. A newer handgun, however, especially something like a Glock, is made from material that didn't even exist in this day. Plus, the fact that if we or our car were ever to be searched, finding a type of gun that no policeman had ever seen in his life, would no doubt cause a little bit of trouble."

"Good answer," Craig said with a weak smile.

Alongside the handguns were maps, toiletries, additional clothes, a couple of newspaper pages and a surprising amount of cash.

"There would have been no way to create a forged credit card that actually worked. Even in '68, they still have a verification gizmo that's attached to a phone line."

"So, cash it is," Craig said, nodding. "I have no trouble using that."

Connor slid one of the guns over to Craig as well as his fake driver's licence and half the money.

"What about ammo?" Craig asked.

"The mag's full," Connor replied.

"We're going to need more than that."

"Why? If you can't kill her with fifteen rounds, I don't think reloading is going to be much of an option."

"What about practicing?" Craig asked.

"If you can't shoot now, a few hours of practice really isn't going to matter," Connor pointed out. "Let's not waste any time and get on the road. We'll drive to Scottsdale, find a motel then have a quick look at Margaret's house."

"Why don't we just introduce ourselves to her and get her the hell out of there?"

"Tomorrow is when she was originally taken. That means that Beyath is already in the house but hasn't finished the transition to our dimension. If we warn Margaret and she leaves the house, Beyath is just as likely to vanish back into her realm which would pretty much end the mission right then and there."

"So, we're just going to leave her there while that monster gets ready to kill her?"

"That's exactly what we are going to do," Connor replied. "We know that she's safe today, so, let's just have a look at the place and decide how best to involve Margaret before one o'clock tomorrow. That's the last time she was ever seen."

"By whom?" Craig asked.

"A couple of people saw her in the local supermarket. That was between twelve-thirty and one o'clock. The sheriff's report shows that her car was parked at her house when she vanished, so we know she made it home."

"That poor woman," Craig said with a sigh. "What ever happened to her husband?"

"You mean your grandfather-in-law? You don't want to know."

"Really? That's the part of all this that you don't want to tell me?"

"Okay. Six months after Margaret and his unborn child vanished, he drove himself into a freeway support pillar at ninety miles an hour," Connor advised.

"I wish you hadn't told me," Craig said, shocked by the revelation.

"I told you," Connor reminded him. "The point is that if we're successful, none of that is ever going to happen, so let's just focus on the here and now, agreed?"

"That would be much easier if the here really was now, wouldn't it?"

"Don't be a wise-ass."

CHAPTER 38

Connor drove out onto 89A heading south. As they neared Sedona, they were shocked at the difference fifty plus years had made. Not surprisingly, none of the sleek, modern shops, galleries or resort hotels existed in 1968. In fact, at the junction of 89A and 179, one of the busiest intersections in the town, there were only a few buildings and hardly any traffic.

It wasn't until they reached the south end of town that one of its most iconic buildings came into view. The ultra-modern Church of the Holy Cross was perched among the red rocks and was visible for miles.

"What's that doing here in 1968?" Craig asked.

"Believe it or not, it was built in the fifties," Connor replied.

"How the hell do you know that?" Craig asked.

"While you were spending all your free time with that waitress, I was soaking up a little local culture."

"Her name is Danielle," Craig said, tersely.

"Whatever."

"It's not whatever. Her name is Danielle," Craig insisted angrily.

"I meant no disrespect," Connor said, surprised by Craig's outburst.

"I know that everyone else thinks she is nothing but an inconvenient distraction, but she means something to me."

"Understood," Connor answered.

"I'm serious. She's the best thing that's ever happened to me."

Connor swerved the car off the road in front of a tired looking motel.

"Look, I know she means a lot to you, but now is not the time to talk or even think about her. You need to be stone-cold focussed on what's going to happen tomorrow. Anything else just jeopardises the entire mission."

"I wasn't thinking about her," Craig shouted back at him. "You brought her up!"

Connor replayed the conversation in his mind then smiled. "You're right. That was completely my fault."

Craig was surprised by Connor's admission. He wanted to say more but didn't know how exactly to clear the air. Instead, he harrumphed and went back to staring out the window.

Connor shook his head and pulled back onto the road.

The drive to Scottsdale took just over two hours. The scenery was stunning and being able to see it without all the new construction that had taken over so much of the modern landscape made them both feel saddened by the way that mankind was treating its most important asset.

As they neared Scottsdale, both were stunned to see how little the old town had changed. The quaint area, through strict zoning laws, looked almost the same in 1968 as it did in 2022. If it wasn't for the rows of diagonally parked, 1960s cars, Craig wasn't sure he could have seen that much of a difference.

They reached the north end of Scottsdale and pulled up at the Dessert Inn. It was a classic, 1950s motel of the style that has, in modern times, almost completely vanished from the western roadside.

They dumped their few belongings in the room then immediately got back in the car and consulted one of the road maps. They took Cave Creek Road then turned onto 166th Street North. Connor slowed the car to a crawl as they passed through the characterless neighbourhood.

While the surrounding scenery was breath-taking, the run-down, 1940s, post-war houses were a depressing contrast. Having been built quickly to house returning vets from the war, they had never been intended to last that long. Couple that with the brutal heat of the summers and freezing winters, they had not fared well.

Some residents had tried to cheer them up with a little paint and an attempt at cultivating a front lawn, but most were left to slowly rot back into the unforgiving landscape.

They found number 237 just beyond a slow curve in the road. Connor pulled the car to the curb and switched off the engine. The house looked tired as if it had given it's all many years earlier and was now just waiting to die. Maggie's Chevy Nova was in the driveway. Never a particularly striking vehicle, hers looked to be on its last legs. Its hood was sun-bleached to the point where some of the paint had burned away entirely revealing rusting steel.

"Nice place," Craig said.

"Probably all they could afford," Connor shot back.

The two men watched the house in silence for a minute until a thought stuck Craig.

"Why did Beyath kill Maggie?"

"You know why," Connor replied, surprised at the question. "She did it to screw up your life."

"I know, but why Maggie? Why not Helena. It would have made far more sense for her to kill Jenny's mother while she was still carrying her. The result would be the same, but knowing that Jenny was actually alive, even if unborn, would have made it even more horrific."

"Yes and no. In the timeline Beyath created, you never knew Jenny or Helena so, you have never experienced the grief of their loss."

"Still," Craig insisted.

"We discussed that very question when the timeline shifted," Connor explained. "Obviously we can't be certain of Beyath's reasoning, but it's just possible that she, like us, has no idea of the actual consequences of trying to manipulate a timeline. What if she had tried to kill Helena before Jenny was born but failed?"

"That's a shit load of supposition," Crag said.

"Supposition is all we have to work with most of the time. We have no idea of the ramifications of a timeline being intentionally changed. I think Beyath decided to kill Maggie so that there would be no possible alternate outcome. She went back far enough on the family tree to ensure that Jenny could never exist."

"Do you really believe that Beyath is that calculating?" Craig asked.

"Obviously, her brain no longer functions on a normal sentient level. Her human sanity was probably destroyed way back when she first started playing with interdimensional transitioning. That said, she's had four hundred years to hone her cunning and instinctual reasoning. I doubt that the old witch is particularly cerebral, but her instincts for self-preservation are extraordinary."

Craig considered Connor's words.

"Are we going to be able to kill her?"

"Now there's the real question," Connor said, nodding.

"So, what's the real answer?"

Connor took a moment to find the right words.

"I think that as long as she has no idea that we have found a way to travel back to when we know she will enter our dimension, and thereby become vulnerable, we have a chance. When she steps through that portal, she becomes mortal. Powerful and deadly, but still mortal. As long as, between us, we can kill her before she has a chance to go back through, we should be able to finish this, once and for all."

"I hope you're right," Craig replied.

"Why don't we have a little walk around the neighbourhood and see how close we can get to the house."

"Why?" Craig asked. "We can't do anything until

tomorrow."

"There's something I want to see. I'd hate to go through all this only to find out that Beyath wasn't even here."

"Is that even possible?" Craig asked, alarmed.

"I would have thought that by now your opinion of what is and isn't possible would have become fluid enough to not ask that question."

"Good point," Craig conceded as he opened the car door. "Let's have a mooch around."

It felt as if someone had opened a blast furnace door. The sky was an impossible shade of cobalt blue as the sun beat down on the shimmering, cracked macadam. Craig had become used to the cooler temperature in Sedona and had forgotten that Scottsdale was smack dab in the middle of the Arizona desert.

They walked around the depressing subdivision, all too aware of how much they were standing out. Nobody in their right mind would go for a stroll on a 115-degree day. Everyone else was either at work, or safely within the more temperate interior of their homes, their swamp coolers set on high.

They made a point of checking out all the houses so that once they returned to the target house, it wouldn't seem strange that they were giving it any particular attention. That was of course if anyone was even bothering to watch them.

Connor led them to the street behind Maggie's house and was delighted to find a vacant square of land almost directly behind hers. They made their way to the back of the lot and pretended to have a conversation next to the dividing wall between it and Maggie's property.

Craig had no idea what Connor was looking for, but after a few moments, he saw the other man tense and followed his line of sight. The house was L shaped, and at the far-right end, a black rain-gutter downpipe was bracketed to the wall.

"What are we looking at?" Craig asked.

"Look between the gutter and the wall," Connor replied.

"All I see is shadow."

"Look harder."

Craig chose one spot close to where the pipe met the guttering and stared hard. For the longest time he saw nothing, then he did, and what he saw caused goosebumps to rise on his bare arms.

Spiders and snakes were using the darkness of the pipe's shadow to climb unseen up the side of the house. Craig focussed on one particular tarantula and watched as it reached the roof eaves and then skittered along upside down until it vanished. It took Craig a moment to realise that it had gone into the attic through a small rectangular vent hole. The screen that should have stopped any unwanted entry was bent open.

"What the fuck," Craig whispered as chills rocked his body. "What the hell is that about?"

Connor turned to face him. He was smiling.

"Good news. Beyath is here."

CHAPTER 39

Once back at the hotel, Craig insisted he take a shower before anything else. He was still feeling creeped out by the parade of creatures that had been cramming themselves into Maggie's attic.

On the drive back, he'd asked Connor if they should somehow tell her, but he replied that the creatures had no interest in Maggie whatsoever. They were there to feed on Beyath's dark energy.

Later in the day, they swung by the house one more time and were reassured to see that both Maggie and her husband's cars were parked in the driveway. Craig desperately wanted to tell them both to run out of the place as fast as they could and never look back, but he knew that he couldn't say a word to either of them. Maggie especially, could never know that she was basically, bait.

*

Craig woke early the next morning and still had the taste of barbeque in his mouth despite brushing his teeth twice before going to bed. He hadn't slept well, but this time it was because of Connor's snoring and talking in his sleep. Craig hadn't shared a room with anyone since his days in the Corp and felt very uncomfortable trying to go to sleep only a few feet from a man he hardly knew.

Craig understood the reason for the shared accommodation. After all, he was still a recovering alcoholic and under extreme stress over what the next day would bring. Nobody would have been surprised if, given a private room, he didn't try to sneak out during the night and find somewhere or someone who would give him a few shots of tequila.

After showering and brushing his teeth yet again, he walked back into the room and saw Connor glued to the small black and white TV screen.

"What's up?" Craig asked.

"A Greyhound bus crashed not far from here. Sounds like a bad one."

Craig gave him a puzzled look. He couldn't understand Connor's interest in something so unrelated to what lay ahead for them.

"Before Beyath fully transitions into our dimension, there is always a horrible accident somewhere close. Usually, it involves the death of at least one family," Connor explained.

"And you think that accident is related?" Craig said, pointing to the dour-faced reporter.

"Has to be. I'm not a big believer in coincidences and a crash like that, less than a couple of miles from here while she's in full transition mode, could only mean one thing. It's her or at least her energy."

"Maybe we should rethink this whole plan. Anyone who can cause a wreck, miles away just by her bad joojoo, doesn't sound like someone we can fight with a couple of pop guns."

"45s are hardly pop guns and if we manage to hit her with a few rounds while she's taken on human form, she'll die like anyone else," Connor said, trying to sound reassuring.

"That's a big if," Craig mumbled.

"That's why they assigned the task to us," Connor replied allowing his Irish accent to strengthen for emphasis.

Craig glanced in the mirror. Though he was only in his forties he looked at least a decade older. He didn't share Connor's belief in their capabilities. It also didn't help that Craig's addled mind was telling him to step outside and find the first ride that would put a couple hundred miles between him and that house.

"Everyone feels nervous before a mission," Connor reminded him.

"Maybe, but not everyone is about to fight it out with a four-hundred-year-old witch."

"I've encountered a few humans who make Beyath seem downright rational."

"I doubt that," Craig replied.

"Try going up against some of the Northern Irish Provos back in the '80s and '90s and you'd know what I mean. They used to kill just to remind others that they still could. And when I say kill, I mean dismember and distribute the parts via Royal Mail. Nasty bunch."

"Maybe, but they were at least in the same dimension as you."

"Maybe," Connor said as he finished putting on his black hi-tops. "I'm famished. Let's go find ourselves some breakfast."

"I don't think I could eat a thing."

"Doesn't matter what you think. Food is fuel and we need to top up while we still can."

Craig resignedly sat in the car while Connor drove them onto the main road. Within minutes they spotted a Denny's restaurant up ahead. Just the sight of its iconic, yellow, hexagonal sign brought unwanted memories flooding back.

When Craig had returned from his final tour in Iraq, he was already suffering from PTSD and quickly found that alcohol was by far the best short-term cure. Many a night he'd drank till he could hardly walk at one of Oceanside's many dive bars and would then usually get a craving for one of Denny's infamous Grand Slam breakfasts. There was something about pancakes, eggs and bacon at one o'clock in the morning that just seemed right.

As he looked at the approaching sign, he could taste not just the tequila and pancakes, but also the sour flavour of the vomit that always came soon after finishing the meal.

"Can we go somewhere else?" Craig asked, trying to swallow a little trickle of regurgitated dinner.

Connor was about to argue, but after taking a quick look at his passenger, he could see that no good would come from pushing Craig to eat somewhere he didn't want to.

They drove on for a half mile and came upon the Happy Highway Coffee Shop. Craig only ordered an English muffin and grape jelly, but when Connor's plate of waffles and extra crispy bacon arrived, his appetite suddenly returned with a vengeance. He ordered the same as Connor and not only devoured everything on his plate, but also used his remaining muffin slice to sop up the last of the syrup and butter.

"What time are we going to start?" Craig asked. "You seemed a little unsure, last night."

"I was. Until I saw the news about that crash this morning, I couldn't be a hundred percent sure that Beyath was there and was almost finished with the transition. I think that we should swing back to the hotel, grab our stuff, then get over to her house. I'd like to follow her to the market and see if there's any possibility of having a little chat with her."

"Why not talk to her in the house?

"You know the expression 'the walls have ears'? Well, in this case that may just be true. It'd be better to find a way to talk to her in a public place. That way she might just listen to us."

"She's not going to believe a word we say."

"I think she just might," Connor replied. "It would be much easier having her working with us while we're in her house than having to rush in to get her out of there at the last minute."

"Maybe we should just stop her from returning from the market," Craig suggested.

"We can't do that. Beyath needs to sense that she's in the house before she comes through the portal."

"If she refuses to listen to you at the market, she most definitely won't let us into her house. I wouldn't even be surprised if she called the police."

*

An hour later the two were parked in the same spot as the previous day. The only car outside number 237 was Maggie's Chevy Nova. It was almost eleven o'clock and neither had any idea of when exactly she would leave the house and head to the market. From police records, they knew when she was last seen at a Safeway supermarket, but no one bothered to note when she arrived there, and worse, which Safeway was being referenced. There were three in a five-mile radius and if Connor was to attempt to speak with her while she shopped, he had to know which one she was going to.

The only way to do that was to follow her. He was a little concerned about her spotting the Ford Bronco out on the open road, but Craig pointed out that every car in that area seemed to be some sort of a truck.

Just as Craig was about to ask for another run through of the purported plan, everything started to shimmer. Craig at first thought it was only happening to him but as he looked over and saw the expression on Connor's face, he realised they were both seeing it. At one point both men became momentarily opaque, then suddenly everything snapped back into solid focus.

"What the fuck was that?" Craig asked, terrified.

Connor took a moment to gather his thoughts.

"If I had to guess, I'd say that Hania has just had another bad turn."

"Are we safe, now?"

"I don't know," Connor replied.

For the longest time, the two simply stared at one another. There was no need for words.

*

By eleven forty-five they were both sweltering. Connor had insisted that they not have the engine running as that would almost certainly attract some unwanted attention. Instead, with no air-conditioning, even with the windows wound down, the temp inside the vehicle had to have been well over one hundred degrees.

Thankfully, at ten to twelve, the front door opened, and Maggie emerged from the house. It took an extra effort for her to swivel herself into the driver's seat because of her baby bump, and some additional minutes more to get herself comfortable and strapped in.

It was a good job that Connor hadn't assumed which market she'd go to, because he would have been wrong. Instead of going to one of the two closest stores, Maggie drove south to the 101 then down to the corner of Scottsdale Road and Thomas Road.

The store was a big one. It took up one entire corner of

the intersection. Maggie found a parking place close to the entrance, but Connor chose to park a good distance away. He was determined not to spook the woman before they had the pleasure of doin so.

CHAPTER 40

Connor and Craig gave Maggie a ten minute's head start in the market so she could get into her shopping zen. At the last minute, Connor decided that a change in strategy was needed. He felt that Craig should be the one to initially approach her, then he would join them when Craig signalled that she was amenable to continuing the conversation. When Craig asked him why the change in plan, Connor simply said, "Cause you and her are family."

The two entered the market together, but Connor hung back near the checkout counters leaving Craig to find Maggie. It didn't take long. She was in the dairy aisle looking for Safeway specials on milk, butter and cottage cheese.

Craig momentarily felt guilty about the change he was about to make in her perception of reality, then realised that, should things go well, in the corrected timeline he would never even have the conversation with her. Shaking his head at his own confusion, he took a deep breath and walked towards her.

"Maggie?" Craig asked, smiling. "Maggie Frost?"

"Why, yes," she replied, not the least bit perturbed.

"May I speak with you for a moment?"

Maggie paled as a thought struck her. "Is it Allen? Oh God, has something happened to him?"

"No," Craig replied emphatically. "He's fine. It's you that may be in some danger."

Maggie seemed to relax a little, but at the same time, her natural, social defences took over.

"Who exactly are you?" she asked. "If you're the police, I'm afraid that I'm gonna have to see some identification."

"I'm not the police," Craig said. "I'm an ex-Marine working on a special project that involves you."

Maggie shook her head. "I've heard about things like this. Strangers claiming to need money to protect you. Well, I think that's nothing but a load of hooey, and I'm gonna report you to the manager this very minute."

Maggie turned away and strode towards the front of the market.

"You had a mirror delivered to your house a few days ago," Craig called after her.

Maggie stopped but didn't turn around.

"You don't know who it came from, but since it arrived, there have been some unusual things happening in your home."

"Go on," she said, still not turning to face him.

"The mirror arrived looking old and worn but then suddenly looked as if it was brand new," Craig said.

"Allen fixed it up," she said turning halfway around.

"You know he didn't. Nobody could have made it look

that good that quickly."

"What else?" Maggie asked.

"Since the mirror arrived, you've found yourself looking at it more and more often."

"There's hardly anything strange about that," she said. "Vanity is vanity."

"You've also been hearing strange sounds coming from the attic."

That last one made Maggie shiver. They had been hearing critters above their bedroom, and now that the man mentioned it, the sounds only started after the mirror arrived.

"You may have even seen things like spiders or snakes trying to find ways of getting into the attic," Craig said.

Maggie turned fully around, facing him. She'd lost some of her colour and had to use a hand to steady herself against the dairy-chiller door.

"What are you trying to tell me?" she asked.

"I'm here with another man, and we'd both like to try and explain everything that's happening, but only if you're agreeable."

"I'm not leaving here with you, if that's what you think," she stated.

"I would never even suggest such a thing. I noticed a little pharmacy with a soda fountain and a couple of booths at the front of the store. My friend Connor and I will wait there for you."

Craig started to walk away.

"Wait," Maggie said. "What's your name?"

"Craig, ma'am. Craig Edmonds," he replied before walking down the aisle and joining Connor at the front of the market. As he approached, Connor looked over questioningly.

"Well?" he asked.

"We'll know in a minute. I said to meet us over there in the pharmacy."

"Are you sure she's going to come?" Connor asked. "Did you make it clear how important all of this is?"

"Sort of," Connor answered. "I didn't think it was a good idea to put too much pressure on her until we were in a position to explain everything."

"So, what did you tell her?"

"I told her that she had received a mirror and that her attic was full of critters."

"And that's all?" Connor asked, incredulous.

"I think it was enough," Craig insisted.

"If she doesn't come over, you realise that we're in serious shit?"

"Of course, I realise that. I just think that her curiosity will be enough for her to sit with us for a few minutes."

Connor was about to say something else when Maggie, who had approached the pair unseen, interrupted.

"I'll give you both five minutes to tell me what the heck is going on, and you'd better impress me, or I'll have the manager call the police."

Embarrassed at having been caught unawares, Connor and Craig walked Maggie to the pharmacy and let her choose which booth to sit in. The men sat side-by side while

Maggie sat perched on the end of the opposing bench seat, ready to make a hasty exit should that be called for.

As Connor started telling her the history of Beyath and the damage that the witch had already done, Craig could see Maggie's eyes glaze over. It was obvious that she wasn't buying any of it.

"Before you say anything else," Craig said, interrupting Connor, "why don't you show Maggie the newspaper articles?"

"What newspaper articles?" she asked, her curiosity peaked.

Connor reached into his back pocket and retrieved the two clippings that Hania had left for them in the cabin.

"I didn't want you to see these until I'd given you some background, but I think Craig is right. Perhaps you need to see the end of the story before you can understand the beginning."

Maggie looked unimpressed as Connor unfolded the two pages and passed them over to her. He slid them across the Formica table.

Maggie wondered what the heck she was doing even sitting with these two clowns as she looked down at the circled article. The first thing she saw was a photo of her taken at least two years earlier. She was grinning at the camera, and even in black and white, it was clear that her green eyes were sparkling with happiness."

"That picture was from my wedding," she stated.

"Read on," Craig said as gently as possible.

Maggie read the short article to herself. The colour that

had returned to her face after the initial encounter with Craig, vanished and her hands began to shake.

"This says that I disappear," she said in barely more than a whisper. "It says I disappear today."

"Now read the next one," Connor urged. "I'm sorry about this, but it's going to cause you some distress."

Maggie briefly looked at each man then read the next article.

Her hand flew to her mouth.

"What is this about? This says that Allen killed himself in his car," she stammered. "Who the heck are you people?"

"We're the people charged with making sure that none of that happens."

Maggie looked from one to the other trying to work out whether to listen to anything else they had to say. She knew that it was possible to have fake newspaper clipping created, but it was expensive, and she couldn't see the point. If she was an heiress worth millions, she could understand the allure of a complex con job, but she and Allen hardly had two dimes to rub together. The other thing that wouldn't let her mind reject what the men were saying was that the article about Allen's crash, which was dated six months in the future, had a picture accompanying it.

It was grainy but she should still make out the details. Though the car was totalled, the back of it was strangely intact. Maggie could see the license plate and it was indeed his. The worst part was that on the chrome bumper was the sticker she had given him only last week. It said: 'WORLD'S BEST FUTURE DAD'.

That alone sent shivers throughout her body.

"Can we please explain who we are and why we are here?" Connor asked.

Maggie glanced at the photo one last time.

"Yes," she said in barely a whisper. "I think maybe you should."

CHAPTER 41

Connor did most of the talking. He started over with the story of Beyath, then moved to Craig's involvement and the changes to his timeline. Connor finished with what was waiting for her back at the house.

Though looking even paler, Maggie managed to keep her emotions in check.

"Why me?" she asked.

"Unfortunately, that's my fault," Craig said. "Beyath is not just a viscous killer but is also highly vengeful and feeds on mental as well as physical pain. Because of my attempts to end her life, she decided to destroy mine. What Connor has yet to tell you is that, in my original timeline, you give birth to a beautiful baby girl who in turn, produces another beautiful child. That child grows up to be my wife."

Maggie gasped. "So, she wants to kill me just to make sure that your future family can never exist?"

"Pretty much," Craig replied.

"How do I know any of this is true?"

"Why would we lie?" Connor asked.

"I don't know, but people do. Look at politicians. They somehow get paid to do it."

Their waitress, a redhead with massive blue eyes, stopped by the table.

"What can I get you fine folks. We have a special on pie and cake today."

Before they could answer, a child could be heard in the background having a mega-tantrum.

Craig and Connor ordered black coffees, but Maggie asked for a butterscotch milkshake with whipped cream and chocolate syrup. The young girl looked down at her as if she'd misheard.

"You're lucky I didn't ask for anchovies in that," Maggie said as she leaned back, revealing her sizeable baby bump.

The waitress laughed and went off to get their order.

"So, what is it exactly that you want from me?" she asked, once the girl was out of earshot.

"We want you to go home after finishing your shopping, but leave the front door on the latch. You then need to go to your bedroom and make some noise. Maybe sing something, then briefly … and I mean briefly … look at the mirror, then leave the room and go to the far end of the house."

"That would be the second bedroom," she commented.

"Perfect. Go there and lock yourself in," Connor said.

"Maybe I should just stay away from the house? Wouldn't that be the safest thing?"

"It would, but Beyath would remain alive and I'm pretty sure that she will find another way to get to you. Maybe not today, but sometime in the future when you least expect it. Do you really want to live with that threat hanging over you and your family?"

Before Maggie could answer, both Craig and Connor felt and saw their surroundings shimmer, then almost immediately return to looking normal and solid.

"Transparent," Maggie said, her voice shaky.

"We're trying to be as transparent as we can," Craig insisted.

"No," Maggie said shaking her head. "I mean you both looked transparent for a second."

"Our time-walking guide is very elderly and not in particularly good health. He is obviously having trouble keeping focus."

"So, what happens if he can't continue? You both just disappear?"

"We're not sure, but that is a possibility," Connor replied.

"That must be a little nerve-wracking for you," she commented before taking a long, calming breath. "Back to your question as to whether I would want the threat of being taken, hanging over me for the rest of my life; the answer is no. Look, I understand everything you've told me, but ... maybe I'm just too dumb to get my head around it all, but I don't seem able to completely believe all of this. I mean, alternate dimensions, vengeful witches? Would you believe you if you were me?"

"Probably not," Connor replied.

"What if I could prove to you that this is real?" Craig asked.

"You don't know what you're saying," Connor said, realising what Craig had in mind. "You can't shift within a time-walk."

"I can't shift within the time-walk itself, but there is one little trick I can do."

"If there is anything you can do to make me believe, please do it," Maggie pleaded.

Craig closed his eyes and silently screamed within himself and felt the world turn bright white.

He opened his eyes and saw that the three were still at the table. Connor was anxiously looking around and Maggie was staring at Craig, waiting for something to happen.

The red headed waitress stopped at their booth and asked,

"What can I get you fine folks. We have a special on pie and cake today."

The sound of a child having a tantrum filled the air.

"Nothing for me," Maggie managed to say despite the sense of terror that she was suddenly feeling.

The men ordered coffee as before.

"Was that you?" Maggie asked, "Or did I just have the most realistic déjà vu ever?"

Craig nodded. "That was me. I found out I could do that back in Iraq."

Maggie wondered where Iraq was as she stared back at them.

"I'm going to need to think this over," she said.

"There isn't much time," Connor stressed.

"I get that, but you are asking me to let you into my home

and voluntarily lock myself in a bedroom. No matter how good a story or demonstration you may have given me, that just reeks of danger. Not from a witch, but from you two."

"How long do you need?" Craig asked.

"Why don't you both go back to your car and give me fifteen minutes alone."

"We can do that," Connor replied. "We're parked on the south side of the lot. We'll be in a muddy Ford Bronco."

"Is that the one that was parked outside my house yesterday?" she asked.

"That was us," Connor said, surprised that they'd been busted.

As Connor reached for the newspaper clippings, Maggie put her hand over his.

"Do you mind leaving those with me?" Maggie asked.

*

The Bronco was boiling hot and lowering the windows did nothing to cool down the interior as it was the same temperature outside. Craig checked his watch again and saw that it had been sixteen minutes since they left Maggie in the pharmacy."

"Doesn't look like she's coming," he commented.

"That's not our only problem," Connor said as he stared into the rear-view mirror.

Craig looked behind them and saw a Scottsdale City Police car approaching them.

"Shit," he said angrily. "With the guns and the cash in the

trunk, we're completely screwed."

"Yup, that about sums it up," Connor agreed. "Looks like Maggie chose not to trust us."

"I don't believe that," Craig replied.

"You'd better because we are seconds away from being arrested. Whatever you do, don't try to resist. Better we stay alive than get shot."

They could hear the patrol car's powerful V8 and knew it was only moments before it would stop alongside them.

They held their breath waiting to hear the engine being shut off. Instead, the revs picked up and the car passed them, veered to the left and pulled into an empty spot close to the Safeway entrance.

Craig and Connor watched in rapt fascination as two uniformed policemen got out of the car, grabbed a shopping cart, then laughing, walked into the store.

"I've decided," Maggie said through the open driver's window, causing both men to jump.

"I might be outa my little head, but I'm going to trust you boys. Please don't prove me wrong."

"We won't," Craig assured her. "Especially as you're going to be my grandmother-in-law."

Maggie studied him long and hard.

"I hope to hell you took better care of yourself in your original timeline," she said, shaking her head.

"Thanks to your granddaughter, I do … or so I'm told."

"Will I remember any of this?" she asked, gesturing to her surroundings.

"If all goes well, no," Craig stated.

"Shame. Knowing that my grandson-in-law was responsible for saving the whole family tree would have gained you some serious brownie points."

"I guess I'll just have to find some other way to earn them."

"I guess you will." Maggie smiled. "I'm parked over there," she pointed to the north end of the lot. "Do you want to follow me? I know you already know where I live, but what you don't know are all my short cuts. My way will save you ten minutes."

"In that case, thank you. We'll do just that," Connor said. "Maggie ... one thing; if you do get home before us, don't go inside. Please wait until we get there."

"I understand," she replied.

"Do you remember what you need to do?" Connor asked.

"Leave the door on the latch, make noise, go to my bedroom, look in the mirror then lock myself in the guest bedroom."

"Perfect," Connor said.

"Am I in a lot of danger?" Maggie asked.

"Yes," Craig answered. "But with us there, you stand a much better chance of surviving."

"Both of us?" she asked patting her belly.

"Yes. Both of you."

Maggie's way was much quicker. They didn't go near any main roads and at one point, even drove on a dirt track for a spell.

Maggie pulled into her driveway and hoisted a sizeable bag of groceries up out of the trunk. She managed to balance the shopping in one arm as she opened the front door with the other. She shot them a quick glance, offered up an encouraging smile then stepped into the house.

CHAPTER 42

Craig and Connor jumped out of the Bronco and ran across the road. After easing the front door open a crack, they stood listening to the sounds coming from within. They could hear Maggie noisily emptying out the shopping onto the kitchen table then heard her walk right by them on her way to the master bedroom.

The two silently slid inside. Craig was astonished at how drab the interior was. Though he could smell furniture polish and detergent, there was also an odour of old drains and mildew. What sent a wave of chills up his back was a background smell that seemed strangely familiar while at the same time, terrifying.

The scent was a mix of something old and earthy, yet it reminded him of an ancient crypt he and two other soldiers had been forced to check out on the outskirts of Bagdad. It had smelled of fetid dryness as if the corpses had long ago stopped rotting and instead had taken on the pungent reek of desiccated remains. Craig tried to ignore the odour, sensing that it carried with it a dark portent of something unspeakably evil.

Connor, sensing Craig's distraction, nudged him hard so that they could follow closely behind Maggie. As she approached the master bedroom, they crept silently behind her. The moment she reached the room, they stepped to the left into house's only bathroom.

Maggie whistled discordantly only a few feet away as the men marvelled at her bravery for being in the same room as the mirror knowing full well what was behind that reflective surface.

As Craig and Connor stood in complete silence listening to Maggie in the other room, they could also distinctly hear what sounded like movement and scratching above their heads.

Maggie suddenly stopped singing and they heard her walk past them along the hall. Connor eased the door open, and they positioned themselves at either side of the entrance to the master bedroom.

Both had a clear view of the mirror.

They stood silently, waiting for the first ripple to appear on the surface of the glass. As they stared at the mirror, both began to feel strangely sleepy. At one point Craig's eye's closed until Connor nudged him and signalled that he was going to check out the room.

Craig stayed in the hall as Connor did a quick sweep of the bedroom in case Beyath had already come through the portal. He checked under the bed, behind the curtains and even in the small walk-in closet.

Connor looked back at Craig and shrugged.

Craig was about to enter the room when they heard a scream come from the other end of the house. Connor was the first to react. He spun around and ran full tilt down the dark hallway. Craig started to follow him, but just as he took his first step, the hallway ceiling bowed downwards then split in two, sending plasterboard, spiders and snakes crashing to the floor. There was suddenly no way for the two of them to move without stepping on something living.

Craig felt as if liquid nitrogen had been injected into his veins. The threadbare carpet had turned into a thick layer of brown writhing forms.

Thousands of them.

Craig immediately froze in place, unable to move. His PTSD had returned with a vengeance.

"Don't look down," Connor shouted at him as he stomped his way across the sea of snakes and arachnids.

Craig did as he was told, but with each step he took, he could feel the spiders squelching underfoot leaving a slick spot of dark grey goo. He had to stop himself from retching as an almost feral odour began to fill the hallway. The snakes were somehow able to avoid the footfalls but began snapping at each other out of confusion.

Connor reached the guest bedroom door first and kicked it just below the plastic knob. It slammed open revealing Beyath standing in the middle of the room. Connor momentarily froze at the sight of her. Her body was emaciated to the point of fragility, or at least that's how she looked. Her skin, now turned to something akin to rough, tanned leather, was almost black. Her head was cadaveric and what little flesh there was, was pulled back so tightly that every bone was visible beneath.

Connor saw that Maggie was at the far end of the room and seemed to be floating about four inches above the floor. Her face was emotionless, but she at least looked alive.

Craig reached the doorway.

"What the fuck?" he shouted before he could stop himself.

Beyath turned and recognising him, began to grin. As they watched in horror her mouth widened revealing rows of razor-sharp, discoloured teeth. Her black, pointed tongue flicked back and forth as she emitted a raspy hiss.

Connor raised his gun, but before he could train it on her, his entire body went rigid, then he too rose above the ground as his eyes became unfocussed and glassy.

Craig somehow found some untapped inner strength and reacted, but not in the way Beyath expected. Instead of focussing on her, Craig dropped to the critter-infested floor and pointed his gun at a cheap, plastic-framed mirror that hung on the back of the open closet door.

He fired twice reducing it to silver slivers that cascaded to the floor.

Beyath let out a primordial scream that caused Craig to recoil away from the unbearable sound. He was about to aim at Beyath when, with horrific speed, she flew over him with Connor and Maggie floating behind her.

Craig wondered why Beyath hadn't put him into a trance, thereby leaving him able to move. It was almost as if she wanted him to feel helpless yet witness her destroying

Maggie and Connor. He watched the three drift through the hallway and into the main bedroom. Craig tried to get to his feet to follow them, when the spiders, as if on command, all rushed towards him and began climbing up his body, their sharp claws piercing his flesh even through his clothing.

Craig knew that if he let the attack occupy his attention, Beyath would be able to retreat back through her portal, at which point there would be no way to stop her.

Craig's training kicked in and despite the terror he was feeling, he rose to his feet while still covered in arachnids. He shook himself like a dog, sending dozens of the creatures flying off him. He used his hands to brush the ones from his head and face then ran down the hallway.

The spiders for some reason stopped chasing him, however the snakes all turned and raised their flat, arrowhead-shaped heads. In unison they began shaking the ends of their lithe bodies, causing the sound of their rattles to fill the confined space.

Craig saw no way through the reptilian blockade until he noticed that, hanging down from the destroyed ceiling, was rubber-coated, wiring conduit that had fallen through the collapsed ceiling

Without any forethought, Craig ran towards the line of snakes then at the last minute jumped into the air and managed to grab the cable. It was hardly graceful, but he managed to swing over the rattlers right up until the moment when the cable gave way. He fell hard less than two feet from the master bedroom door.

Craig somehow got to his feet hoping that he was out of

range of the rattlesnakes when two of them struck at the same time. One sunk its fangs in his right calf, the other in his left ankle.

The pain was excruciating. It felt as if both affected areas were on fire. Despite that, Craig kept moving.

As he reached the bedroom doorway, he saw that Connor was floating towards the mirror and that Maggie was following close behind as Beyath glared triumphantly back at him.

Craig rushed towards them hoping to stop their progress towards the portal, but suddenly froze in place as Beyath placed him in a trance. He could see and even feel but couldn't move any part of his body. He felt utterly helpless as the other two neared the portal, knowing full well that the moment they passed through, they would cease to exist.

Without warning, the room began to shimmer. For a millisecond, Craig thought he saw the inside of the Sedona cabin, but just as quickly, that image disappeared, and Craig fell to the ground. It took him a second to realise that Hania's failing ability to hold the time bubble intact had caused the witch's trance to fail.

Beyath was momentarily disoriented by the change in Craig's energy and wasn't immediately aware that her powerful hold on the three had been interrupted.

Connor and Maggie both dropped to the ground and in an amazing show of agility, Maggie managed to flip herself onto her back and roll under the bed.

Connor, despite feeing disoriented and with the wind knocked out of him, reacted out of pure instinct. Sensing that he was no longer in a trance state, he tackled Beyath to the ground and looped an arm around her throat, putting her into a strangle hold.

While Beyath was sufficiently distracted, Maggie crawled unseen into the closet and closed the door.

Much to Connor's shock and amazement, Beyath fought back with incredible, almost superhuman strength, violently contorting herself to get free of his grasp. Despite being substantially larger than her, there was nothing Connor could do to restrain her.

As Craig tried to crawl over to help, Beyath shot to her feet and immediately locked both Craig and Connor in a new trance. Both were again stuck floating just above the floor, unable to move a muscle. Beyath approached each of them and with feral-like curiosity ran her darting tongue over each of their faces.

Beyath opened her shrivelled mouth wide, revealing the rows of blackened teeth. She stepped towards Connor and just as she was about to rip into his flesh, she heard the sound of something metallic coming from beyond the closet door. Beyath let out a reptilian hiss as she spun around. She knew who had made that noise and that she was finally going to be able to end the young woman's life.

Beyath turned back to Craig and for a moment studied his face. She then leaned forward and whispered in his ear.

"This time, you can watch her die," she whispered.

Craig could do nothing but look on as the witch stepped over to the closed door. When she was only a foot away, she waved her gnarled right hand in the air.

The closet door slowly opened.

Beyath was about to step closer when a deafening blast filled the room. Connor and Craig collapsed to the floor as their trance was lifted. They saw Beyath as she was flung backwards by the force of the shotgun's discharge. Her right shoulder had been blown off and black blood was oozing onto the floor.

Even in that condition, she managed to drag herself with incredible speed towards the portal and looked as if she was going to make it, but as Craig and Connor rushed to try and grab her flailing legs, Maggie stepped between them and fired the second barrel of the 12-gauge shotgun.

Beyath had managed to get within inches of the portal frame when Maggie fired the shot that transformed Beyath's head into a fine black mist. The portal instantly slammed shut leaving in its place the normal reflective surface of the mirror. Without taking a breath, Maggie used the butt of the gun to smash it into a million pieces.

Craig started to say something when he felt a terrifying pulling sensation all around him. He tried to reach out to Connor and Maggie but had no control over the force that tore him away from that moment in time into total blackness.

*

Though he was unaware of what was happening, Craig's spiritual energy was dragged through his various timelines. Even though the entire resetting of his mortal existence was almost instantaneous, he was able to subconsciously see images flash through his dissipating memory like pictures being scrolled on an iPhone.

Though not conscious in any real sense, the essence of his mind recalled flitting memories. There was a cramped room in a French townhouse, a framed mirror rippling like a disturbed pond, a snow-covered hillside sloping down to a picturesque cottage and finally, the last image of all, a comfortable living room where two children sat catatonically on a sofa, their eyes staring vacantly forward.

As that last image faded to black, the alternate timelines that Beyath had created dissolved into nothingness as if they too had never existed.

CHAPTER 43
Present day

The bang shook the entire house. Craig had been prepared to ignore the early morning disturbance and go back to sleep. His wife Jenny, however, had no intention of letting that happen, neither did Steeler, their oversized yellow lab. He was barking up a storm somewhere downstairs.

"Aren't you going to see what that was?" Jenny mumbled.

"At this time of the morning, I don't care."

They heard Sally, their four-year-old, start crying in her bedroom just across the hall. Tim, their five-year-old, then came moping into the room and jumped on the bed.

"Mommy, what was that noise?" he asked.

"Daddy is going to go down right now and make it go away. Aren't you sweetheart?"

Craig begrudgingly got out of bed and put on his winter bathrobe and threadbare slippers. The house was cold, then again it was winter, and they turned the heat off at night to save money.

He walked downstairs, grabbed the emergency flashlight and opened the front door. An icy wind swirled around his lower legs.

Craig felt the strangest sensation that he had lived that moment once before.

He stared out into the night and at first couldn't see the cause of the crash.

"What the hell?" Craig said as he focussed the light towards the back of the property.

"What is it, honey?" Jenny shouted from the bedroom.

"You know that old, dead pine tree at the back of our property?" Craig asked.

"The one I've been asking you to cut down for two years?" she shouted back.

"Well, looks like I don't need to. It came down all by itself," Craig said as he shut the door and ran back upstairs.

"Why did the tree fall down, Daddy?" Sally asked as she stepped into their room. "Are all the trees going to fall down?"

"No, my little angel. That was an old gnarled-up tree that died many years ago, it just never knew it."

"Are we safe?" she asked.

"Completely. This is the safest house in the whole wide world."

EPILOGUE
9 months later

Craig was happy to be on the open road with his family. The sheriff's department in Kanab had been extremely busy for the past three months. A sudden urge among those able to work from home had caused an unexpected exodus from the cities across America as people tried to find the perfect small town where they could live a simpler, safer and healthier existence.

Kanab was one of many that was suddenly 'discovered'. The sleepy town had had a population that hovered around the 4500 hundred mark and an infrastructure that could handle that load.

Within a single year that number had almost doubled as every home on the market, even the ones deemed unsellable, were sold. Lots that had graced the MLS for decades were snapped up as the town experienced its biggest building boom ever.

What the newbies didn't expect to encounter was a town

council filled with third generation residents who didn't want their perfect little town to change. Heated arguments ensued. Threats were made. On too many occasions, fists were even raised.

These events took some of the lustre off Kanab, but the biggest problem by far was when the non-LDS city-folk arrived in town and managed to find sufficient alcohol to make themselves a danger on the narrow, unlit roads.

The result was that the sheriff's department had to, with very little notice, create a well-staffed night shift to get these inebriates off the road. As there was no current budget for the three additional deputies, everyone had to do double shifts and weekend work. This, in turn, soon began to burn out the serving officers and made it harder for them to focus on their primary responsibilities.

When Jenny suggested surprising her family by driving the three hours to Sedona and turning up at Grandma Maggie's birthday party, Craig jumped at the chance for a temporary change of scenery. Jenny had coordinated the surprise with her mother, but no other family members had any idea that their Kanab relatives would be showing up.

Jenny was delighted that, due to the number of family members wanting to celebrate Maggie's 77th birthday, the bash was moved from her family's house to a Mexican restaurant tucked at the back of the Tlaquepaque Arts and Shopping Village in the centre of Sedona. When Jenny had been growing up, it was her favourite place to go for special occasions.

As they passed Bell Rock, their two children, Tim and

Sally, both started making bell sounds.

"Ding Dong. Ding Dong," they said between giggles.

"I'm so glad you gave them the inspiration for that," Jenny whispered to Craig.

"I thought it was cute. I never for a second imagined it would become a thing."

"Oh, it's a thing," Jenny said as the ding-donging continued from the back seat.

Craig found a parking space close to the entrance to Tlaquepaque and managed to herd the kids towards the restaurant without too many diversions. They were shown to a large private dining room where at least thirty other guests were already seated.

After what seemed like endless hugs and greetings, especially from Maggie, Craig and his flock were seated at the far end of the larger banquet table. After only a few minutes, an attractive waitress appeared and deposited numerous drinks from a heavily ladened tray. Once she lowered it, Craig could see that she was pregnant. Six months was his guess.

"Hi," she said, turning to the Edmonds family. "My name's Danielle and I'll be your server at this end of the table."

For a brief moment Craig and Danielle's eyes met. Something stirred deep in his memory banks, though for the life of him, he couldn't think why. He was certain he didn't know her but, there was … something.

"Do I know you?" Craig asked.

Danielle, having been a waitress for many years, had

heard every line imaginable, but to get hit on in her condition, and with the guy's wife sitting right next to him … that was a new one.

"Maybe in another lifetime," she said with a smile. "What can I get you guys?"

As she started taking their order, the restaurant manager stopped by the table and asked if everyone was doing okay. After a unanimous round of yesses, he stopped next to their waitress and gave her a gentle kiss on her cheek.

Danielle noticed the concerned looks from some of the guests.

"Don't mind him. He's just my husband," Danielle said as she playfully punched him in the arm.

As Craig looked at the waitress and her husband, he wondered why he had felt so strangely about her when he first saw her. He looked closely at her as she laughed with members of his family and had no doubt whatsoever that he'd never seen her before at any point in his lifetime.

BV - #0162 - 111022 - C0 - 197/132/19 - PB - 9781803780771 - Matt Lamination